More from October 15th Publishing Co.

Cut From The Same Cloth 1&2
Money By Any Means
Cut From A Different Cloth
Friends Are Foes 1&2
InstaFamous 1&2
Legendary Love 1-3
You and I: A Murderous Love Story
...And So We Hustle 1-3
Unapologetically Yours
I Came Back For You
Money Making McCoys
The Life & Times of Butterfly Reid VOL. 1
Love Me Deeper

Contact Us

october15thpublishing.com
Instagram @ natalie_sade_edits
Facebook: Natalie Sade
Twitter: @ natalie_sade_edits

ISBN: 978-0-9911209-9-4

Cover image by Oasha Ellesè & Channing

THE LIFE & TIMES OF

Butterfly Reid

VOL. 2

DELL PALMER

CARTERSVILLE is an independent state in the United States. The state population is estimated at 620,000. The state has 10 major cities and 15 towns.

ALEXANDRIA is the largest city by population in Cartersville. Although space is limited, it has the most residents because of its commercial and financial centers. Approximately 200,000 residents are divided into four districts: Monroe, Georgetown, Morris and Henderson County.

Chapter 1

POUNDING, SORENESS, SENSITIVITY TO LIGHT. As Butterfly fought to peel her eyes open, she was greeted by an excruciating headache. She had cried herself to sleep and kept waking up periodically just to realize she wasn't with Raphael anymore, which led to more tears. She grabbed her phone and sent a message to her two clients for the day. She wasn't even going to attempt to put on a happy face to get her work done. She needed at least twenty-four hours to gather herself. In the email, she explained that she had to cancel their appointments for the day. She gave them the openings she had throughout the week and promised them ten percent off their services.

Next, she texted Phe; he was supposed to get Moon, but she couldn't see him so soon after their break-up. The thought of it still hurt too much and she needed Moon to love on her and smile at her and lift her spirits. *My client cancelled,* she texted, not wanting him to know the destruction he had caused. He had taken her off her square, paused her hustle, and made it impossible to function as if her world wasn't falling apart; a gift she had mastered over the years. *I'll keep Moon today*, she let him know. After sending the message, she dragged herself out of bed and into the bathroom.

Tears ran down her face, falling into the steaming water she was immersed in. She was trying to clear her mind, to meditate, but all she felt was abandonment, heartache, and loneliness. It kept creeping into her psyche reminding her of how she had loved and lost...again. She had tried so hard with him, had given him all she could and was fighting to have more to give, but he didn't see that. He didn't see her progress; only the long road she still had left and he had given up. Something he swore he would never do, and she had believed him.

"Fuck him!" she spat, hurling a glass candle at the wall. That felt good—well better—because anger resonated with her desire to move on. Sitting in sorrow would only leave her stagnant. She ran a business and had a daughter, so standing still wasn't an option. Anger hyped her up; she was bathing now instead of just soaking in her misery. Moon's wails prompted her to move quicker; she rinsed her body and got out of the tub. Butterfly dabbed her body dry and then covered herself in a robe. She caught a glimpse of her red, swollen eyes in the mirror; tears welled, but anger dried them up. He left her; he gave up; she didn't. She was fighting, trying, and changing all for him, them, their babies and the brownstone in Monroe Heights. Amid all of that and without caring about his promises, he abandoned her. Even as she cried for him, he walked away.

She took a moment to let Moon cry because her energy was too negative to touch Moon just yet. She needed the anger to get through the days without him; she wouldn't hold on to it for too long because she knew it could poison her from the inside out and create a person she didn't recognize and Moon didn't respond to. She would never transfer it to her baby though. She would use it when thoughts of him crept into her mind, when tears flooded her pupils, and when the pain was so much that it filled her chest, collapsed her lungs and forbid her another breath.

Lighting some sage, she slowly waved it around her body and took slow deep breaths, refocusing her attention and intentions. When she was calm, she smiled into the mirror, proud of being able to control her emotions and dashed to get her baby. "I'm sorry," Butterfly cooed as she bounced Moon. "Good morning, you're up early," she continued as she kissed her cheeks.

With Moon settled on her breast, Butterfly rested on the couch. Both clients had responded with rescheduled dates and Phe had also replied. She took a deep breath and dropped the phone into the pocket of her robe. Unable to stay seated as multiple emotions zoomed through her body, she got up and prepared herself some rice. While it cooked, she headed downstairs to make the corrections on her calendar. She didn't have to do it right then, but she needed to keep moving.

After she was done and still sitting at her desk, she was ready to read his reply. *I can still get her. If you need some alone time.* The anger she had decided to allow to live between them tried to subside. He was so thoughtful; even after the break-up, he was still trying to take care of her, but she wasn't ready for that. Her heart yearned for him, so although he had promised that they would still be family in the event of a break-up, she didn't want that; not yet. She couldn't take it. He had to give her more time. *No, I'm good*, she typed and prayed that he read it as nonchalantly as she meant it. She laid her head back and steadied her breathing until her phone dinged indicating that he had responded. *Can I FaceTime her later?*

"Ugh!" she pouted and flapped her free arm up and down. She wondered why he needed to see Moon. Shit, she was only five months. She couldn't talk, so what would FaceTiming do other than disrupt Butterfly's "moving on process"? *Yea sure,* she texted back before anger consumed her. She forced it away by breathing positivity in and then out into the world. She needed anger to deal with the break-up, but she didn't want it while she breastfed her baby.

AFTER RECEIVING HER TEXT, RAPHAEL DROPPED HIS PHONE ONTO THE BED. He had replayed the night's events in his head, *how did it escalate to a break-up?* That wasn't what he wanted; he only wanted her to completely reveal herself to him. Now, he was wondering how that was possible. Learning a person completely took years; shit, there were things about him that she didn't know. Nothing as big as the secrets she held, and that was why it was important to him that he knew everything. He had tried to be patient, but anticipating the next shoe dropping and feeling like she purposely withheld things, caused him to rush the process. Now, he was wishing he had handled things differently. Then, he began to think the break-up was necessary. He hoped it would show her how serious he was and make her consider him when she was keeping secrets.

A knock at the door pulled him from his thoughts. "Yea," he yelled out.

"Where is the baby?" Candy asked, entering his bedroom.

"Bug ain't working today," he answered.

"Oh, so you free today?" Kwame asked, walking into the bedroom. Kwame was on his way out the door with Quel when he overheard their conversation.

"Yea, for a few hours, then I have some clients," Raphael told him.

"Cool, we going to the arcade; come hang with your lil bros," Kwame said with a smile and his hands up. Raphael didn't feel like it, but he figured it would give him some time with them and help take his mind off Butterfly.

"Aight," he agreed. "Let me get dressed," he said, climbing out of bed.

"Bet," Kwame said as he and Candy left the room.

After spending two hours with his brothers at the arcade and then at a pizza spot, Raphael had come to the shop. He only had two clients set up, but he ended up taking three walk-in clients. When he was done for the day, he sat in his barber chair to make the FaceTime call that had been on his mind all day. After twenty-four hours without them, he was happy to see Moon; he had missed her, but he also wanted to see Butterfly. As the phone rang, he adjusted his shirt and made sure nothing was on his face. When Moon's beautiful round face graced the screen, he fell back against his chair with a smile on his face. Her radiant eyes popped out at him making his heart melt.

"Hey baby," he greeted. "What are you doing, ma?" he asked. Moon cheesed so hard that drool ran down her chin as she gripped the phone with both hands trying to take it from Butterfly. Moon was now touching the screen as if it were his face and cooing into the phone. Her little lips moved as if she was really forming sentences. The phone call was supposed to make him miss her less, but it had only increased his urge to hold her.

Raphael could see that Moon was sitting on Butterfly's lap as she held the phone in front of Moon's face. Butterfly's cleavage peeked out of the top of her tank top as Moon's head bounced back on Butterfly's breasts, the only portion of Butterfly that was in the video.

"What y'all been doing?" he asked, no longer using his baby voice. Butterfly didn't reply. "Butterfly?" he called.

"What?" she spat.

"Damn," he said, taken aback by her anger. "I was asking what y'all were doing."

"You said you wanted to talk to Moon. We wouldn't be on the phone for any other reason," she informed him.

"And I do want to talk to her," he replied.

"So, talk to her," she responded.

"She can't talk, Bug, so obviously I would need to talk to you to check on her." Butterfly didn't speak. "Prop the phone up and let me watch her play," he requested. That made her smack her lips.

"Do you want me to record her playing and send it to you?" she asked, turning up her nose and rolling her eyes although he couldn't see her.

"Nah," he said, matching her attitude. "I want you to do what I asked you to."

"I'm not about to—"

"You don't have shit else to do. You not working," he said, cutting her off. "Prop the phone up, put her in her play pen, and get yo' mad ass on," he demanded. Between the argument with his mother and his break-up with Butterfly, Raphael felt like he couldn't win for losing. He and his mother had never gone twenty-four hours without discussing any disagreements, but with her work schedule and his, in addition to his emotions being tied up in Butterfly, they hadn't spoken.

Butterfly wanted to go back and forth with him, but she had Moon in her arms and wasn't about to argue with him. She set everything up and then went to the bathroom. After pacing the floor for a few seconds, she yanked the lighter off the counter, snatched up a candle and lit it. Then she blew it out; her energy was too fucked up to even attempt to meditate, so she leaned against the wall and cried instead.

Chapter 2

TWO THOUSAND, EIGHT HUNDRED AND EIGHTY MINUTES. It had been two thousand, eight hundred and eighty long, hard minutes since she had seen Raphael. Since he said he didn't want to be with her anymore, since her heart shattered, since she had slept peacefully through the night, and since she had enjoyed food. Now, she had to force herself to eat, drink, and shower. No one's departure had ever sent her into this level of sadness. Maybe with everyone else she hadn't had time to miss them because she had been immediately thrust into another situation and had to fight or flight, but flight was never an option. When Beverly died, her whole life changed. Her living situation had gone from comfortable to crowded at Stacy's apartment. Then she was thrown into foster care where she literally had to focus and watch her back so she wouldn't get jumped and have her earrings snatched. Olivia's exit was one she couldn't remember; she only felt it and that only occurred as she got older. Or at least, she had recognized the absence of her mother as she got older. Maybe she had always felt it, but since it was a part of her norm, she hadn't named the emptiness.

However, Raphael's scent was permanently lodged in her nostrils; the bed was cold, even in the heat of the summer, without him. Food—her food—that had been praised by so many, was bland without him. She only had Moon to bring her love and joy, and Phe was on his way to take her away too. Butterfly was dressed in a pair of Nike leggings and a T-shirt; Moon was in a cute romper and sandals. Her bag was packed and at the door as Butterfly peeked out the window watching the street for him. She finally saw him; not him exactly, but his flawless black, white, and gray Air Max sneakers. She knew it was him because of the way his feet moved up the block. She took a deep breath, put on her game face and gathered Moon. Before he could knock, she snatched the door open and shoved the bag into his chest; caught off guard, he stumbled back. Before he had it on his back, she was trying to hand Moon to him as she blocked the entrance to the shop.

"Can I come in?" he asked.

"For what?" she questioned, leering into his eyes. She was mad; she had to be or she'd be a sad, weak, mess and she couldn't give him that.

"I want to talk," he admitted humbly. She was so hurt; he saw it and that hurt him.

"Why? You said all you had to say. No," she said, shaking her head. Her frustration was rising—quickly—at levels she couldn't control. "We can't talk; you can take Moon and go. Or you can leave her, but you gotta go," she let him know. He took Moon into his arms and she rested her head on his shoulder.

"Why are you being like this? We can't have a conversation? This ain't you," he said, looking down at her disappointedly.

"Yes, it is. You saw a glimpse of it the night I saw Melo," she informed him. "What? You thought you were immune to it? No, everybody that leaves me gets the same treatment," she said, glaring up at him. He lowered his head and ran his hand down his face. He had hurt her and he was aware of that, but he hated to be included in the category of people who had left her. He had taken a break, just to regroup. He should have just left that night instead of breaking up with her; he had realized that over the last two days. He wanted to come back, figure it out, and work through their issues, but she didn't seem open to that.

"I'm sorry," he mumbled.

"Don't be," she said, trying to close the door. He wouldn't move out of the doorway.

"I want to talk about what happened."

"I just want you to leave." She was holding the door and looking down. He was leaning against the doorframe.

"Bug, I can't use the bathroom?"

"No," she said, looking up at him. "You may not step foot in my shop, apartment, nothing. You can only be around me when we swap Moon. You *may* take her because I'm a woman of my word—even when it's hard—but that's all I have for you."

"I'm in love with you, Bug," he replied.

"You're in love with the idea of me. The real me is too much for you. Step back, please. I don't want to close the door on my baby." He stepped back, and with her head down, she closed the door and locked it.

Her heart raged against her chest; she was finally able to exhale. She had been holding her breath hoping that doing so meant holding on to the anger she needed to block his love. It was hard to be mean face-to-face, harder than she imagined, but it was the only defense she had against the love she had for him. He said he was sorry—he wanted to talk—she wanted that too, but that was no longer an option. Even knowing what she had gone through and the issues she had with people leaving, he had still left. She didn't go backwards; life had taught her to keep moving because *it always gets better*. So, regardless of how hard it was, she always moved forward. It was what had saved and comforted her.

"WHAT THE FUCK?" KWAME SAID, BURSTING INTO RAPHAEL'S BEDROOM. "This is the third day I have come home and there's no food in the fridge, the house don't smell like food and Bug ain't here. Did you really take her away from us?" he questioned, only half-joking.

"She ain't yo' chef, nigga," Raphael replied, looking over at Moon to make sure Kwame's outburst didn't wake her.

"I know, I know, that's your shorty and we gotta respect it. But for real, where she at?"

"We not together," Raphael revealed.

"What?" Kwame gasped.

"We're taking a break." Raphael said that for two reasons: one, he didn't want to talk about it and hoped that would make Kwame move on. Two, he prayed that was all it was.

"Damn, so that's why you been in your feelings. Shit, bro, you gotta fix that," Kwame said. In his opinion, Butterfly and Raphael were made for each other, so he wasn't really taking the break-up seriously. He figured that they had gotten into a fight and would be back together in a few days.

"It ain't that simple," Raphael said.

"Yea, it is," Kwame said, turning to walk out of the bedroom. "Just go kiss all over her," he suggested, then looked back at Raphael with a smirk. "They like that," he added with a wink before he exited the bedroom. Raphael leaned against the headboard and thoughts of Butterfly flooded his mind. He missed her, wanted her; shit, he needed her, but she wasn't trying to hear anything he had to say. She was mean—worse than mean—she was bitter. A trait he didn't think was possible for her to possess. He was happy that she had kept her word when it came to Moon, but he needed her too.

That thought led to what she had said to him. The shot she threw about being a woman of her word even when shit got hard. When she said it, it pierced his heart like a spear being lodged in his chest. He saw the distress in her eyes and on her face; she was masking it with anger and doing a great job, but he knew her— deeper than she could ever imagine, so he knew it was a front. Still, that didn't stop her rejection and hurtful words from wounding him.

"Bug!" Candy called, walking into his bedroom and looking around. "Where is she?"

"Not here. What is it?" he asked; he could see the agony on her face.

"Nothing, I need to talk to her; when will she be here?"

"Talk to her about what?"

"Girl stuff," she huffed, irritated by his line of questioning.

"Girl stuff?" he repeated, looking her up and down.

"Ugh!" she fussed. "Not that. All boys think about is sex. Me and Arian got into a fight and I need her advice," she finally told him.

"Shiiitttt," he said, dragging the word out as he thought about their problems. "She can't help you with that."

"I'll just call her," she said, smacking her lips and leaving the bedroom.

Thirty minutes later, she reentered the room. "I've called her twice; she's not answering, and she hasn't called me back. Even when she's working, she normally at least texts back."

"We broke up," he finally admitted.

"Broke up? For what?"

"We got into an argument; it just escalated."

"But you have Moon," she pointed out.

"That's my baby," he said matter-of-factly.

"I know...but...so, it's not serious? The break-up."

"I don't know."

"When did it happen, Phe?"

"Few days ago."

"And you haven't gotten back with her?"

"I tried, but...," he answered.

"But what?" she probed. "What happened? Did you cheat?"

"Hell nah. We just had an argument."

"Well, what did you do to try to get her back?"

"I can't do shit if she won't talk to me," he replied.

"Shit! Niggas all over Monroe just fucking up I see," she spat and left the room.

BUTTERFLY LOOKED DOWN AT HER PHONE AND SAW CANDY CALLING FOR THE THIRD TIME. She silenced the call and went back to peeking out of the window. A black Maybach had been parked across the street for over two hours. It was the same one that was there yesterday; the one she had seen Darius climb into momentarily, and then climb back out and leave. That led her to believe that D'Angelo sat in the backseat. She was missing Moon and devastated over Raphael; she didn't feel

16

like being stalked by the man responsible for her mother's death, even if his wife didn't do it. She still hadn't done any research on Edee, but the mention of her involvement confirmed a thought Butterfly low-key always felt, which was that his wife wasn't the killer. Over the years, she had silenced that thought by telling herself it was a crime of passion and that anyone could be pushed to the edge, especially when emotions were high.

She didn't understand why seeing her now was so important to him. He had never reached out when she was being bounced between juvenile centers and foster homes, nor when she was living in Sienna's room. Now, all of a sudden, he had to see her. So much so that thirty minutes ago, he had briefly gotten out of the car and sat on a bench staring in the direction of her shop.

Anger rose up in her; for him, for Raphael and for the life she had led due to her mother's death and her aunties' rejections. She raced to the nightstand and pulled out the chrome nine she had bought. Another secret she had kept from Raphael, but only because they had broken up before she could show it to him. She charged down the stairs and out her front door before practical thinking could deter her from releasing some of the anger that consumed her.

She beat on the back window with the butt of the gun. The driver hopped out with his hands up and was about to speak.

"Get back in," she instructed before he could utter a word. "Tell him to get out." The back window rolled down.

"Put dat ting away and get in," D'Angelo commanded calmly.

"No, you get out," she replied. Finally, he climbed out. He was ready to tell her everything he had wanted to say since the day he left her. "Look, you can't force me to see you. I'm going through a lot of shit and this," she said, waving the gun from the car to her apartment, "is only going to fuck shit up worse. What, you need a kidney? I'm not giving you one. Ain't shit I can or will do for you," she told him.

"You're as crazy as your mother," he laughed, "so much spunk and sass." He smiled. "Meh don't want a ting from you."

"But you're here all the time. You can't bully me into talking to you and trying to will only piss me off more."

"I know you tink—"

"I don't care what you know or think you know. I have my own shit that I'm dealing with, okay?" she said, infuriated that her eyes were filling with tears as the thought of never having Raphael again raced through her mind. When they fell, she wiped them with the back of the hand that held the gun. "I don't have time for your shit. I'm tryna—" her sentence trailed off. He walked toward her; he wanted to hold her and fix whatever was going wrong in her life.

"No!" she yelled and pointed the gun at him. "I can handle this. I've been through so much worse. Shit you couldn't even imagine. But I don't want to deal with you and your sudden change of heart. I don't care why you're here now or why you want to speak your piece. I waited for you," she admitted for the first time to anyone. "You can wait for me or you don't have to, I don't care. If I ever want to reach you, I'll go through EJ. Until then, do what you do best and leave me the fuck alone," she said and stormed back to her shop.

D'Angelo was heartbroken as he watched her walk away. She didn't know him, didn't know that he would do anything to take away any pain she was feeling, even if it caused him pain to do so. He wanted to build a relationship with her, but he knew it had to be on her terms. He sat in the car for thirty more minutes before he told Petey to drive off. He had to give her time and trust that they would connect again. In the meantime, he prayed that God would get her through whatever she was facing.

"HELLO?" Butterfly said, answering the phone for Raphael a couple of hours later.

"I'm on my way with Moon," he let her know.

"Okay," she said and hung up before he could say anything else.

When he arrived, she stood behind the door with enough space for him to hand Moon and Moon's bag to her.

"Man, move so I can come in," he fussed.

18

"Come in for what?" she inquired.

"We need to talk; this shit is stupid," he replied.

"What shit?"

"Being broke up."

"Phe, gon' with that shit. Hand me her bag," she hissed. He did, and she tossed it to the side and then reached for Moon. He pushed the door in and backed her into the wall. "Stop, Phe," she fussed.

"Stop being mean, you look stupid; that ain't you," he told her as he stood over her and she looked down at the floor. "I miss you. I'm sorry," he told her.

"You shouldn't have done it," she replied.

He huffed. "It wasn't for nothing, Bug. You can't keep lying." That pissed her off; her whole body heated up and her face scrunched up, but no words would come out.

"Ugh!" she yelled and pushed him. She was beyond frustrated by his one-dimensional view on what she should reveal and when.

"I have to be more patient; I understand that now," he said.

"It doesn't matter," she said.

"What?" he questioned, shocked by her unwillingness to compromise.

"You want me to tell you everything because you're ready to hear it. It's hard, but I'm trying! You can't just snap your fingers and expect me to pour my heart out. This..." she said, waving her finger between them, "being with you...open like this, trusting you, is the hardest thing I ever had to do, but I gave it my best shot." She was filled with rage. *Calm down; think about the baby.* She caught herself and tried to calm down. Moon was asleep with her head resting on Phe's shoulder and she didn't want to frighten her. He tried to hug her, but she pushed his arm back. He placed his hand on her hip, she moved.

"You left; you gave up. I'm so tired of y'all doing that to me. Loving me then leaving me. I can't take it. It hurts," she voiced.

"Baby, I'm sorry. I'm sorry I left you; that shit was a mistake. We both have shit we need to work on. You saw your brother and instead of telling me who he was, you pretended not to know him. You lied," he said with emphasis. "That wasn't you forgetting, that

19

was you lying," he told her. Although his voice was calm, his tone made her feel his anger. Butterfly stood there with her arms folded, pretending to be unmoved. "Get her," he said, leaning his shoulder down so she could take Moon.

"You mad now?" She smirked with her eyebrow lifted.

"Don't antagonize me," he warned.

"Well, I've been pissed," she said, ignoring his warning. "So, join the club," she said with Moon now in her arms. He glared at her with so much fury she assumed it was hate.

"Good," she said with a forced smile. "Now that you hate me as much as I hate you, we can just move like that." He didn't reply; just walked out of the shop. She thought maybe that hurt more than any words he could have said.

Butterfly knew in that moment that she was done being mean. Not because she couldn't hold a grudge or say 'fuck you' to someone and completely mean it, but because being mean to him wasn't genuine. It wasn't what she truly felt. It was forced and anyone could tell that she was making herself do it, which was lame.

He hurt her, but she loved him. She couldn't have him, but that didn't mean she had to be a bitch to the man that helped to deliver and care for her greatest gift. Raphael loved her and protected her, and only wanted what was best for her. He didn't try to isolate her or have her love only for himself; he encouraged her to reconnect with her loved ones because he wanted her to be whole and fulfilled. He wasn't arrogant enough to believe that he was all she needed. He knew, even though she didn't, that she needed friends and family.

He was selfless, and he was good. She completely understood how he had come to his wits end and probably figured that breaking up was the only way. Then their love, which was always working for them even when they weren't, reminded him that he had to be patient. He tried to fix it, but she refused. Her bitterness and fake anger were the reasons she was still without him. The reason he now looked at her as a bitter bitch, and she had to deal with that. With Moon and her bag, she headed up the steps to her apartment. She felt weighed down, not by Moon and her bag, but by her own baggage. Her feet felt heavy; each time she had to lift one, it felt like it would be the last time she had the power to do so.

IN THE BED WITH MOON AS LAURYN HILL'S SONG "TELL HIM" PLAYED, BUTTERFLY CUDDLED UP NEXT TO HER AND LET DOWN EVERY GUARD SHE HAD PUT UP. She allowed the love of her child and the love she had for her child to comfort her, chastise her, and make her better.

DECIDING HE NEEDED TO CLEAR HIS HEAD BEFORE HE WENT HOME, RAPHAEL STOPPED AT BROWER PARK. Taking a seat on the bench, he lowered his head. The descending sun cooked his neck with fury as if it wanted to shine bright one last time before the end of the day. Or maybe it had just gotten into an argument with the moon, who it loved so much, and was torturing anyone in its sight.

From outside the gate of the park, Ebony saw him. It had been a while since they had spoken. Because of the way he stopped contact, she wanted to keep walking, but she missed him and decided to put her pride to the side and say hello.

"What's up?" she greeted when she was standing in front of him. His head popped up and he took in her short shorts, crop top and white Converse sneakers.

"What's up?" he replied as she took a seat.

"Long time, no see," she commented with a smile.

"I know," he stated. "I been busy; work and shit."

"And a girlfriend and a baby," she added.

"That too," he said with a head nod. The memory that he was no longer with Butterfly and that she had handled him disrespectfully caused him to grit his teeth. He understood that she was suffering, but so was he. Even in breaking up with her, he had handled her carefully with love and respect. He sighed and ran his hand down his face trying to wipe the grimace off his mug.

"We was friends first," Ebony said, reminding him that he wasn't alone. "We was cool, ya know? Talking all the time, hanging out. I miss that. I'm cool on us being together," she said, looking into his eyes. "You know I never forced that."

"Nah, you never did," he agreed. When he fell back from their relationship, she automatically did too.

"Cool," she said in an upbeat tone. "So, let's be cool. Kalia is my best friend and she's with Quincy, so we're bound to run into each other. I don't want it to be awkward."

"Yea, you're right," he said, his mind on Butterfly.

"I'll even talk to your girl," she offered. Raphael looked at her. "Just to let her know it's all love," she explained.

"You don't have to do that but thank you."

"For real, I don't mind. I know how girls can be and..." Now his mind was back solely on Butterfly and the glare she had on her face as she stared at him, and the smirk she possessed once she knew she had gotten under his skin. He was irritated by her and Ebony's need to keep bringing her up when he was trying to get her out of his head.

"Nah," he blurted out, causing her to abruptly stop talking and look over at him. "We're not together," he revealed. He hated the way that sentence tasted coming off his tongue.

"Oh damn, I'm sorry to hear that. I mean, I know y'all have a baby," she said, looking at him sideways. She and Kalia couldn't figure that part out, and Quincy wouldn't give up any information no matter how many times they rephrased the question. If the baby was his, that would mean that he was with them both at the same time. That would hurt Ebony because while Raphael was popular with the ladies, he normally only had one at a time. That was something a girl could count on; if Raphael was rocking with you, it was only you.

"Yea, but it's cool," was all he said.

"I know you'll be a great father," she said, looking out at the kids on the swings. "I always thought that," she added with a head nod.

22

"Yea," he said, standing up. "I'm about to head home; you need me to walk you?" It was after seven and getting dark, so he wouldn't feel right leaving her alone.

"Yea, that's cool," she said, standing up. "Always a gentleman," she complimented as they trekked up the block. They made small talk and caught up on some things Raphael had missed as they made the five-minute walk to her apartment.

"You wanna come up?" she asked when they got to her building. "My mama would love to see you," she said.

"Nah, I really gotta get home," he let her know. "Later though," he said and continued the journey to his house.

THE NEXT DAY AFTER WORK, BUTTERFLY TOOK MOON TO THE PROMENADE FOR THE FIRST TIME. She woke up missing Raphael and knew that was a place she could go where she'd feel close to him. After that, she stopped in a market on the way home to get some fruit and vegetables. She was in the aisle with barrels of fresh fruit picking through what she needed. When she came to a carton of strawberries, she opened it to examine them closer. They were deep red and bursting with juice. She picked one out, wiped it against her shirt and then took a big bite. The sweetness made her close her eyes as she savored the taste.

"You love strawberries, huh?" Looking to her left, she saw Kwame with a wide smile on his face. She smiled bashfully and closed the carton, placing it in her bag. Kwame reached over her shoulder and gently pinched Moon's cheek careful not to wake her. "What's been up, shorty?"

"Nothing, working," she answered.

"You haven't talked to Phe?" he asked. She shook her head and tried to look away. The hard shell her anger had provided was gone, so the mention of his name caused her stomach to churn. It felt like her organs were being wrung out like a wet rag. "He can be an asshole sometimes," he joked. "Thinks it's his way or the highway," he continued. Tears spilled from her eyes. Frantically, she wiped her face, shocked by how quickly her true emotions shone through when she was fighting so hard to keep them hidden.

"I'm sorry," Kwame said, placing his hand on her shoulder. He still wasn't taking the break-up seriously; he was joking about Raphael expecting her to agree, then call, curse him out, and get back together. He never meant to make her cry.

"It's fine," she said, trying to smile through her tears. He pulled her to him and hugged her. He hated to see women cry. Hated for men who claimed to love them to make them sad and then leave them to deal with the emotions. Kwame had an affinity for beautiful women with unique styles, stories and bodies. He wasn't perfect, but he didn't make them cry or mad, he only ever made them feel good. Women were so different to him, different from men and different from one another. No two women were alike, and he liked to experience them on many levels.

"Thank you," she said, pulling back. "I'm fine. The break-up is fresh, but it's okay," she said, walking backwards to get away from him. She turned on her heels hurrying to the checkout line even as he called her name. He was mad at himself for not paying attention to her, for not seeing that he was causing her anguish, and he was mad at Raphael for letting it get that far. He had only come in the store because he saw her enter, so after he finished his conversation with a brown skinned, long legged goddess, he had come in to say hello. Now with fury moving through his body, he headed home.

"WHAT THE FUCK IS WRONG WITH YOU?" Kwame raged, charging into Raphael's bedroom.

"Fuck you talkin' 'bout?" Raphael fumed, hopping off his bed with a scowl on his face.

"You got that damn girl all in public crying," he accused.

"What the fuck are you talking about?" Raphael asked, confused.

"Butterfly! You still ain't fixed that shit?"

"She 'ont wanna fix it," Raphael said. He was calmer now that he knew what was going on, but he still stood face-to-face, chest-to-chest with his little brother in case he forgot who was boss. *Shit, I tried*, he thought to himself. Kwame scrunched up his face; his brother couldn't be that dumb.

"That fuckin' girl loves you. How you don't see that?" he questioned. "The mention of your name made her cry. You always talkin' 'bout, 'be a man'. Men don't let their women be sad," Kwame schooled him.

"I tried!" Raphael admitted.

"Try harder. That girl bends over backwards for you."

"And I bend over backwards for her." Raphael was seething. "You don't know what the fuck you talkin' about. Worry about your shit, nigga. Keep ya dick in ya pants and don't bring home no babies or diseases. As far as me, nigga," he said, stepping closer into Kwame's space, "I'ma always handle my motherfuckin' business," he hissed.

Serena burst into the bedroom after hearing them yelling. It had been years since she had to break up a fight between them, so she was alarmed when she heard the commotion. She pulled them apart as Kwame continued to talk shit. "Handle yo business then." He chuckled and walked out of the bedroom and then out the front door.

"What was that about?" Serena asked.

"Me and Bug broke up," he said, taking a deep breath and flopping down on the bed. After the things she had said about their relationship, he hated that he had to admit that to her.

"What? When?" she asked. "You just had Moon," she pointed out as her mind tried to make sense of what he was saying.

"You want me to break-up with her too?" he quipped through tight lips.

"Don't take your anger out on me. You want her back, go get her, but don't start shit with me," Serena fussed. They hadn't really talked since she expressed her feelings about Butterfly. She wasn't trying to hurt him, but as his mother, she felt like it was her job to point things out. She walked out of his bedroom and slammed the door behind her. He laid back on his bed, frustrated, mad, hurt and missing his girl.

WHEN BUTTERFLY HEARD THE DOORBELL FOR THE SHOP, SHE PICKED UP HER PHONE TO CHECK THE CAMERA. The shop had been closed for hours and since Raphael was no longer in her life, no one should be at the door. It was Kwame. She didn't feel like company and didn't want to talk about Raphael, but she also didn't want to be mean to him. She figured she could run down, see what he wanted and then rush him off by saying she needed to get back to Moon.

Opening the door, she saw that he was gone, but a Brother's sack was on her front step along with a cup holder that held a strawberry shake. She walked onto the sidewalk in search of him. Up the block, she saw him about to cross the street. He looked to his left and saw her; he smiled and nodded before turning back around and continuing his path up the next block.

She made her way back up to her apartment, and although she was smiling, tears flowed freely; she was so emotional that even that nice gesture made her cry. At her kitchen counter, she pulled a fork from the drawer and sat down. *I'm sorry I made you cry* was written on the back of the receipt. Smiling, she pulled out her treat; it was a slice of cheesecake covered in huge strawberries. She put her straw in the shake and slurped. It was delicious. She removed a strawberry from the cheesecake and took a bite; it was fresh and juicy. She forked the cake and put it in her mouth, her eyes closed in delight; it was so good.

Chapter 3

IT WAS FRIDAY, BUTTERFLY'S CREATIVE DAY WHERE SHE GOT TO DO STILETTO NAILS, COFFIN SHAPED NAILS WITH JEWELS AND CRYSTALS ADDED, AND CREATE THINGS LIKE ROSES, BASKETBALLS, AND LETTERS WITH THE ACRYLIC. But it was also her busiest day of the week. The door chimed alerting her that someone had entered, she spun around to greet the customer and saw Candy. She froze.

"Hey," Candy said; Butterfly, caught off guard, just stared at her. She had been avoiding her by not answering her calls or texts and she hadn't returned any of them. Candy had stopped calling and Butterfly figured they had an understanding. Butterfly was sure Raphael had told her about the break-up. She knew for a fact that Candy would side with him, so what was she doing at the shop?

"Hi," Butterfly finally said. "Did you have an appointment today?" she asked, knowing she didn't but not knowing what else to say.

"No," Candy answered. "But you're not answering my calls, so I had to pull up." The sentence sounded like a joke, but Candy didn't laugh or smile. She stood before her in black midi shorts, a burgundy Lebron James Cavalier jersey and matching Huaraches.

"Sorry, I...just," she said, unable to come up with an excuse.

"Think that because you and Phe broke up you can get rid of us all," she said, removing her backpack purse and taking a seat.

"I'm going through...a lot," Butterfly said, shaking her head.

"I can help," Candy stated.

She chuckled. "You're his sister."

"So? Pussy power," she said with her fist in the air. "Fuck that nigga," she added, making Butterfly double over in laughter. "Where's the baby?" Candy asked, still laughing a little.

"Upstairs; still asleep."

"I want to see your apartment," Candy said, standing up. Butterfly locked the shop door so she could quickly show her around. She led Candy upstairs and into the apartment.

"Oooh, I like this," Candy gushed. "It's like a love nest for you and Phe." The curtains were drawn, darkening the room and allowing the glitter-painted walls to decorate the room. "This is why he never wanted to come home, hell." They laughed as Butterfly turned on the lights. "It's so cozy," Candy mentioned while walking around the space. She made it to Moon's crib and scooped her up. "There's my baby," she cooed.

"Man, you're going to wake her." Butterfly laughed. "I need her to sleep as long as possible," she said, thinking about the busy day ahead of her.

"I came to talk to you and to keep her," Candy said, walking into the living room and taking a seat on a big pillow.

"Oh okay. Thank you. You don't have anything else to do?"

"Nope and there's nothing else I want to do," Candy answered. Butterfly nodded. "Look, Bug, I was your friend first. Phe took over, but we met first and I liked you, so eventually you would have come to my house, met my family and cooked for us. We would have fell in love with you either way. You can't dump us because of whatever is happening with y'all. We each have our own connection and bond with you."

"Y'all are his family and with us breaking up..." she paused and shrugged.

"We don't care about that; we fuck with you outside of Phe, okay? I don't care what happens with y'all, you're my best friend," she expressed. Butterfly knew everything she was saying was true and that it came not only from her, but also from Quel and Kwame. She was the family's spokesperson; she always reported back to Phe and now she was reporting back to Butterfly.

"Best friend?" Butterfly questioned.

"Yea, I tell you more than I tell anybody else. Kwame feels a way about your disappearing act too, so does Quel; he's quiet, but he's pissed. You can't take your anger at Phe out on us. If you only wanted to be cool with us through him, you should have kept it cordial...just hi and bye," Candy explained.

"Understood," Butterfly said, filled with emotion as she realized his family was choosing her and loving her, even though it no longer benefited them.

"Good," she said and then switched topics. "Me and Arian been beefing," she let her know.

"Why?"

"I feel like he wants sex. Like, I can't even kiss him how I want to without him trying to climb on top of me."

"So what? He's pressuring you?" Butterfly fumed.

"No, well...not with words. I didn't say nothing, but I stopped being alone with him. He picked up on that and got an attitude, like he didn't want to chill with me at all, so we got into a big fight...in front of everybody."

"Did he disrespect you?"

"No, just said I was acting like a kid."

"'Cause you don't want to have sex? You need to explain to him that you're not ready and he's making you uncomfortable," she advised.

"See," Candy fussed. "That's why I was calling you; I didn't know what to do and I couldn't ask Kwame or Phe."

"Soo...you did it?"

"Hell no! I ain't that dumb. I really care for him, but I like being a virgin. I don't have any of the problems my friends have. Plus, my mama got pregnant with Phe and fucked her shit up. I ain't doing that," she said, shaking her head.

"Good for you. Wise people learn from the mistakes of others."

"How long you make Phe wait?" Candy asked.

"Til I was ready," she sassed.

"Period, huh?" Candy giggled.

"Yea. Ain't no timeframe. It's when you want to; not to please him. Listen to your body, it'll let you know."

"Well as of right now, we just been arguing; then his phone went off and he hid it, so I just left, and we haven't talked."

"When was this?"

"Yesterday at the park," Candy answered.

"Well, are you going to talk to him about it?"

"I don't know, but if he doesn't reach out by Sunday, he's single and free to do what he chooses." They were quiet for a moment. "What you gon' do about Phe?" she asked.

Butterfly shrugged and then thought for a minute. "I was mean as hell to him. He probably don't even—"

"Yes, he do," Candy said, cutting her off. "He loves you. Apologize to him; he'll do the rest," Candy said.

"How do you know?"

"I know my brother." They were quiet again. "You better hurry, Ebony might come through and snatch him up," she teased.

"I'll beat her ass," Butterfly replied, laughing. She looked up at the clock and stood up. "I gotta get to work. Come down if you need me or if you get tired of being up here."

AFTER SPENDING TWO HOURS UPSTAIRS, CANDY AND MOON WALKED DOWNSTAIRS TO SEE WHAT BUTTERFLY WAS WORKING ON. She was finishing up a full-set that was amazing. They were square shaped with black and white polish and a different design on each nail. Candy admired the level of talent Butterfly had. She was in her own world working her 3D brush as she crafted three hearts going down her client's index finger. Candy then looked at a customer who appeared to be waiting for the current customer. She rocked coffin-shaped ombre nails starting with a light pink acrylic and ending in baby blue. Swarovski crystals adorned her middle finger.

"You do your thing," Candy nodded. "We're gonna walk around the block," she let her know and then exited the shop.

LATER THAT NIGHT, RAPHAEL WAS IN A DEEP SLUMBER. In his dream, he was in bed with Butterfly; she was lying on her stomach and he was on his side with his hand on her ass. The dream was so real, he felt the rising and falling of his chest. Peace filled the room as they lie together in a different world, but both dreaming about each other; their love bouncing from reality to subconsciousness. In the blink of an eye, it was snatched from him as his eyes shot open. He was alone and the bed was cold and empty. The room was lifeless, and he was lying on his back. He rolled over on his side and placed his hand in the center of the bed where Butterfly was supposed to be. "I miss you," he said before sliding back into the dormant state where he could be with her.

BUTTERFLY WAS RIPPED FROM HER SLEEP BY WHAT SHE SWORE WAS RAPHAEL'S VOICE. Sitting up in the bed, she looked around the room still half-asleep and hopeful that he was there. The realization that he wasn't caused her heart to stop and drop into the pit of her stomach. She sank back down in bed and wrapped her arms around her lonely body.

"I miss him, Mama. I need him; I want him so bad. It hurts more than anything I've ever felt. Why can't I put him in the back of my mind? Why can't I move on like I have so many times before?" She began to rock herself trying to ease the pain that crippled her body as she lay in bed. "Send him back to me, please. I'll do better, I promise. I need him," she prayed.

THE NEXT DAY AS BUTTERFLY LAY IN BED, SHE RECEIVED A TEXT MESSAGE FROM RAPHAEL. *I'm on my way to get her.* She hopped out of bed and quickly refreshed her hygiene. It was Saturday evening and she had been lounging around the apartment with Moon. Her hair, fresh out of corn rolls, was in a cute curl pattern all over her head. She wore spandex shorts and a loose-fitting shirt that hung off her right shoulder.

Calm down.

"I want to be with him and he wants me; even Candy said it," Butterfly said as she dressed Moon.

He wants the idea of you.

"Then, I'll tell him everything," Butterfly said.

No! Not yet.

"I'm not lying to him about anything else," she replied.

We need to discuss it with Reid first.

At the mention of Reid's name, Butterfly rolled her eyes. She looked up into the mirror, shook her head and focused her attention back on Moon. Moon laughed and kicked her legs as Butterfly moisturized her body.

"I don't...we don't." She huffed and paused to gather her thoughts. "She's doesn't decide; I'm in control. I decide," Butterfly said. She was trying to steady the tremble in her voice.

I know; but making this decision without consulting her could create big problems.

"I let y'all have him. I-I shared him with y'all and y'all lost him," she said. "What do you suggest? I don't have it in me to be mean to him," she said, looking back in the mirror.

Me either. She had tried and it was hard; that was why they needed Reid. *Time. Just make up with him and give the rest time. We'll talk and go from there.*

Butterfly dressed Moon, packed her bag, then headed downstairs. She hadn't talked to Raphael since their argument on Wednesday, but she had promised her mother that she would humble herself and apologize. Not only because she wanted another chance with him, but also because she owed it to him.

When she heard him knock, she opened the door. He stood on the stoop instead of trying to enter, but he did notice the smile on her welcoming face. "She ready?" he asked.

"Yea, you can come in," she said, stepping back. Her shapely legs led up to her round bottom that spilled from the tiny shorts she wore. He put on Moon's backpack that sat on the counter. "You think you'll need the stroller?" she asked, after handing Moon to him.

"Nah, we good," he said and walked to the door. Desperately, she grabbed his hand before she lost her nerve. He turned around and she dropped his hand and tucked hers behind her back. They stared at each other; he lifted his eyebrow and turned up his hand as if to ask what she had to say. She bit the inside of her mouth. He took a seat, giving her time to get her thoughts together.

"I'm sorry. I was mean to you and you didn't deserve that. I was...I was just hurt. My heart was broken, and I had never experienced that. I couldn't take it." She shrugged. "I couldn't cope, so I was mean and angry because when I allowed my true feelings to show, I couldn't eat, sleep, or work," she explained. "You've been so good to me; you've done so much for me and my behavior was selfish and ungrateful; everything I'm not. But, I...all I know to do when someone leaves me is to move forward. But I couldn't...I can't," she cried. "You're in my dreams, my thoughts, my work. With the way I acted, I know you probably don't—"

"I want you," he interjected, stopping her mid-sentence as he stood up. "I always wanted you." Pulling her to him, he gripped her wild hair, tilted her head and kissed her. "Go get dressed and come with us," he said after the kiss.

He was a little apprehensive about inviting her over because of the conversation he'd had with Serena. It had actually been an argument, but he didn't want to call it that. He had said things he regretted, but he wasn't sure if Serena felt the same. She accused Butterfly of purposely monopolizing his time and trying to trap him. He had insinuated that Serena had done the same thing to him and he vowed not to ask her for help with Moon anymore. He also wanted to limit the time he and Butterfly spent there, but his siblings were expecting him to bring some food back, so he had to go home.

"Come upstairs with me first," she said, kissing him again. Leaning over, she locked the door to the shop.

"She ain't even sleep." He laughed as they talked between kisses and Moon pulling their faces apart.

"She can be put to sleep."

"We can do it later," he said, taunting her.

"I—" she fussed, looking up at him. "I need it now," she told him humbly. "You don't?" she asked, stepping back.

"Spoiled ass girl," he chuckled as he shook his head and pulled her back to him. He knew what she was accusing him of, but instead of getting mad, he laughed.

"I bought a gun," she blurted out in the middle of their kiss.

"Why?"

"I like having one. It's clean. When I'm eighteen, I'll get rid of it and get one registered to me," she told him. She really didn't want to get one legally but figured it would make him feel better. He smirked, pulled her to him and kissed her again.

"D'Angelo was here—parked outside for two days. Not straight; he'd leave and come back. But he hasn't been here all day. I guess he got the hint. If I ever want to get in contact with him, I'll reach out through EJ. Right now, I just want to be with you, get our shit tight and take care of Moon. Emotionally, I don't want to deal with shit else. I'm getting to the point where I feel like I can breathe and reflect on my past and deal with my mother's death and my abandonment issues. I want to do that without adding my dad's shit or Melo's shit to my plate; it's full enough. I just need time to love myself, Moon and you, to build and plan and execute with you." She spoke from the heart. He smiled down at her.

"Come on so we can put her to sleep and I can bless you," he said, grabbing her hand and leading her upstairs.

"WHAT'S THIS?" HE ASKED. When they got upstairs, he handed Moon to her and rummaged through the refrigerator. She was now on the bed holding Moon and he was entering the bedroom with a plate of

34

pasta in one hand and a Brother's receipt in the other. He placed it on the bed and she picked it up.

"Oh, Kwame brought me a piece of cheesecake and a shake the other day. The one from Brother's that we shared that time."

"And you kept the note?"

"It was considerate, and I felt weird just throwing it in the trash after he went out of his way," she answered, taking in his body language. He sat at the foot of the bed with his back to her. "You don't want to know how he made me cry?"

"I figured if you wanted me to know, you'd tell me."

"I saw him at the market; I was getting strawberries," she said, then paused. "That's probably why he got me the strawberry cheesecake and shake," she realized.

"Yea, he pays attention."

"Anyway, he asked about you and I started bawling." She chuckled in embarrassment.

"He told me," Raphael admitted. She picked up a pillow and hit him with it.

"Then why'd you make me say it?"

"I wanted to hear it from you," he said, staring into her eyes. They were silent as Moon cooed and he ate. Butterfly was resting against the pillows feeling so at peace that she smiled.

TWO HOURS LATER, MOON WAS ASLEEP AND BUTTERFLY WAS BENT OVER THE KITCHEN COUNTER WITH RAPHAEL PLOWING INSIDE OF HER SHOWING HER JUST HOW MUCH HE MISSED HER. Their lovemaking had started with her kissing the length of his body, mesmerizing him and using her tongue to bring him to sexual heights he had never reached. Afterwards, they showered, and he began to get dressed.

"No," she pouted. In her mind, they had just started, and she wanted to at least get a round two.

"We gotta get to my house, Bug," he laughed, hugging her.

"After," she begged.

"Nah, 'cause I was supposed to bring food back." Her shoulders deflated as she let him go so he could finish getting dressed. He watched her fall onto the bed. "Bug, get dressed."

"Oh, I'm going too?" she asked, sitting up on the bed.

"Don't play," he laughed. She smiled, but he still saw the sadness on her face. "Candy will keep Moon tomorrow and I will fuck you all day, then you'll be sore at work on Monday," he told her.

"Good," she said with a wicked grin as she got up and went to her drawers to get clothes. "And can we go to the promenade too?" she asked over her shoulder.

"Yea, I'll take you."

"You went home and bathed before you came to get Moon?" she asked randomly. Well it was random to him, but it had been on her mind since she hugged him downstairs. He should have smelled like shaving cream or hair wax and had specks of hair on him. He also should have had his equipment bag if he was coming straight from work.

"Why?" he asked, knowing she was putting two and two together.

"Why'd you do that?"

"Why'd you answer the door in those short ass shorts? Why was you looking so nice and innocent?" he questioned. She didn't answer. "I wanted what you wanted," he said.

"We always want the same things. I just have to get better at communicating that," she said, pulling a cotton, sleeveless dress over her head. They smiled at each other and then he gently picked up Moon, careful not to wake her.

WHEN THEY GOT TO RAPHAEL'S APARTMENT, HE UNLOCKED THE DOOR AND LED THE WAY INSIDE. As they entered the house, Quel was walking from the living room to his bedroom with his phone against his ear.

"Mama got off early and brought food," Quel announced. Raphael stepped to the side and Quel saw Butterfly. A smile covered his face as he dropped his hand to the side, completely forgetting about his phone conversation. "Yooo," he said, throwing his head back. Raphael smiled back at them and went to the kitchen to put the food in the refrigerator; they could eat it for breakfast.

"Where you been? I was looking for you," Quel said, hugging Butterfly tight. "Don't do that shit again," Quel told Butterfly as he let her go.

"I won't," she promised before they parted ways. When she entered the bedroom, Raphael had laid Moon in the bassinet and was taking off his shoes and socks.

"I told you they love you more than they love me," he said. He was happy his siblings had been showing her so much love.

"I don't know about that," she cheesed.

"You see how they are about you." He was now shirtless. "My mama is probably sleep, but you can speak to her in the morning," he told her, pulling the covers back.

"Okay," she said, happy to be getting a pass. "Let's go wash our face and hands," she said before he could get in bed. He smiled at her and followed. In the bathroom, they washed up and brushed their teeth before going back into his bedroom, closing the door, turning off the light, and getting into bed.

Within thirty minutes of being in bed, Butterfly was all over Raphael. Lip to lip, tongue to tongue, center to center; she was insatiable. What started as a goodnight peck led to tongues twirling, slow grinding, gripping and groping. Slipping her hand in his pants, she took hold of his manhood and began to stroke it fervently. She wanted to taste it...again. She began to move below the covers. He tried to stir out of her grasp but was powerless. She was at his pelvic bone now, kissing, sucking, going farther south.

"Butterfly, stop," he begged, finally able to speak. She knew they couldn't do it there and yet she refused to behave. She wanted to ignore his plea, but knew she had to be respectful on her first night back. Climbing out of the bed, she grabbed her pillow.

"What you doing?" he asked.

"Going to sleep with Candy," she told him.

"Why?"

"'Cause I can't keep my hands to myself," she admitted.

"Man, get back in the bed," he said.

"If I get back in that bed, we're having sex; I have no control over myself." She laughed. "Your mom already don't like me and I don't want to give her more reasons," she explained, grabbing Moon's bassinet and pulling it with her.

"Why you taking her?"

"She went to sleep too early. I know she'll wake back up," she said and exited the room. When she opened the door to Candy's bedroom, she was sitting up in the bed texting like a madwoman. She looked up at the door with a scowl on her face; Butterfly threw her hands up in surrender. Realizing what she had done, Candy smiled.

"Y'all fighting already?" Candy asked.

"No," Butterfly answered, climbing in bed after she had Moon's bassinet situated. "It's the opposite."

"Ew!" Candy said, scrunching up her face. "Well, at least y'all learned from last time."

"So, Arian called?" Butterfly asked.

"Yea, talking about 'what you doing'," she said, rolling her eyes and neck. "I'm thinking, 'about to be single, nigga'. He had twelve more hours," Candy said, thinking back to when he called the first time that day.

"You were serious?" Butterfly asked.

"Yea. You can't be in a relationship and not talk for two days. He called and could tell I had an attitude, so we argued, hung up, and we've been texting since then," she explained.

"Did he apologize?" Butterfly wanted to know as she adjusted the pillow and laid on her side.

"We haven't really discussed the problem. I'm too irritated with him."

"Then talk to him tomorrow."

"No, I want to talk now."

"Then tell him what's wrong and be nice," Butterfly advised.

"Oh, that's easy for you to say now," Candy teased.

"And you know I'm speaking from experience. Trust me, you don't want it to spiral."

"What can I say?"

"I'm really mad at you, but I don't want to argue. I miss you; I love you; can we meet up tomorrow?"

"I don't know about, 'I love you'," Candy replied.

"You don't love him?"

"Not yet. I really, really like him and I care for him. I feel like if I loved him…" She paused and looked at the door as if to make sure no one could hear her. "I'd want to," she whispered even though the door was closed.

"Not necessarily. You can love him and still not be ready. You can also not love him and want it, I guess."

"Has that happened to you?"

"No," she answered, praying that didn't lead to a conversation about Moon's father.

"I know you love Phe. I didn't at first; I was pressed because I thought he was playing his self."

"How?"

"By chasing you. You didn't seem interested," she said. "But he always knew you were," she added. That made Butterfly smile.

"I have a hard time showing my true feelings sometimes. But yea, he always knew and I'm happy about that. He kept pushing me." She chuckled. "That's part of the reason we broke up."

"I'm glad y'all worked it out. It was lonely without you. We missed you."

Butterfly giggled. "Not Ms. Serena."

"Her too. In her own way," Candy said as she finished her goodnight text to Arian. She got comfortable in bed, put the pillow over her face and they both drifted off to sleep.

RAPHAEL AND BUTTERFLY HAD GONE TO HER APARTMENT AROUND NOON, FUCKED OFF AND ON UNTIL 7PM AND THEN ATE, SHOWERED AND CAME TO THE PROMENADE. She was looking out at the water and he was standing behind her. His body was pressed against hers with his hands gripping the rails. When he woke up that morning, she had braided her hair into individual braids, and it was pulled up into a bun allowing him to plant kisses on her neck.

"My name is Reid," she announced.

He chuckled. "What?"

She turned to face him. Her vibe seemed to change in a matter of moments causing him to step back and observe her.

"You and I having this conversation is long overdue, but I let her have her time with you today because if this is her last day with you, I want it to be filled with great memories," she informed him. She wore a natural mug on her face while Butterfly's face was more relaxed. And she was more rigid. It made him tense up.

"Butterfly, what the fuck are you—"

"My name," she said, tapping on her chest, "is Reid." They stood silently staring at each other for what felt like an eternity, but in reality it had been less than three minutes. He didn't understand what was happening, but he knew something was happening and he knew he wasn't talking to Butterfly.

"This is the thing you need to accept if you want to be with her. Me; I'm the thing. The rest of that shit was minute," she said with her index finger hovering over her thumb.

"Who, who?" His eyes were squinted, and his nose wrinkled as he tried to process the information. Not just what she was saying, but also how she was acting. "What?"

"Dissociative identity disorder is what the therapist called it. You may know it as multiple person's disorder," she said nonchalantly. Meanwhile he was losing his mind. Raphael looked around the pier at the other people seemingly enjoying their day. "If you can't accept it—"

"Why are you here?"

"To protect her."

"From me?"

"From who and whatever...sometimes herself. You like to fix things, I get that; we have that in common, but she doesn't need to

40

be fixed," Reid informed him. She spoke slower with more emphasis on her words. She had no plans to repeat them, so she wanted to make sure the listener heard every word.

"Of course you would say that. You don't want her to get better 'cause then she won't need you," he replied. He realized he was talking to her as if she wasn't Butterfly and he felt stupid. She was Butterfly; she looked just like her. She still wore the light blue jeans and the white tank top that stopped at the waistband on her jeans. She wore the same high top, white, black and red Nike sneakers, but she was different. Their vibe was different.

"Who says she's the dominant personality? I run shit around here, Raphael, and I've been doing that long before you. I got her through a lot of shit, okay? We don't need fixing; do you understand? We figured out how to make this shit work; trying to come between what we've built won't end well for you. I'm only telling you this because she loves you," she said, leaning against the rail.

"I love her."

"Can you accept her? All of her...as is? If not, just walk away. We'll get her through this—"

"We? How many are there?"

"That's irrelevant," she replied, rolling her eyes to the top of her head.

"How is that irrelevant?" he yelled, throwing his hands up. A few onlookers noticed their argument and began to whisper.

"You should know, I don't like being yelled at and I don't like a lot of hand motions," Reid said. Standing straight up, she glared at him as if she were 8 feet tall. As he took in her words and mannerisms, he realized just how well he knew her. His mind zoomed through the relationship and pinpointed moments where she was the one interacting with him.

"How do you expect me to take this shit?"

"I don't know. I don't have much concern for people's emotions. I'm very logical. I plan and I execute," she told him.

"You—we've talked before, huh?" That execute phrase stuck out to him.

"I can mimic her. We've talked multiple times."

"And I've talked to the others?"

"I'm sure."

"You always deliver the bad news?"

"Yea, and I go with you to Pappy's; she don't like to dance, and she don't like your friends."

"Yes, she does."

"No. She likes you and Moon."

"And Candy," he said.

"Nope," Reid said with a nonchalant head shake.

"You're with Candy?" he questioned; he didn't think so because Candy wouldn't have been receptive to her cold demeanor.

"I don't like you or Candy. I just protect her. This other shit is quite lame to me."

"Who paints Candy's nails, helps her cook; who cooks for us?"

Reid shrugged. "I don't know."

"Y'all don't know each other?"

"I know everything. I have to; I'm the protector," she said.

"But she doesn't know everything?"

"She needs to believe in miracles and shit. Keeps her sane. I remind her of reality."

"And so I'm supposed to..." His sentence trailed off as he tried to find the words. He didn't know what he was getting himself into, but he knew he loved Butterfly; he knew he could love her through anything.

"Let her tell you her story. She wants to confess it all to you, and I know you've been waiting for that. Then, you just love her still. But if that's not something you can do, then you just walk away. Here, I'll make it easy on you. I'll turn around and watch the water," she said, turning around. "And if you need to go, you go." Reid faced the water for a few moments before she felt his presence hovering over her. She wanted to relax in his embrace; he smelled so good. But this moment didn't belong to her.

"I came here when we were beefing," Butterfly revealed after five minutes of silence. Raphael had been waiting for something to happen. He didn't want to say anything for fear of saying the wrong thing. He wanted her to smile up at him, break into laughter and say it was all a joke. But he knew she wouldn't. Reid was too real; plus, this made certain things make sense.

"Why?" he asked.

"Because I missed you," she confessed. She turned to face him and wrapped her arms around his neck. He lowered his head and kissed her.

"I missed you too," he said against her lips.

"I'm so sorry, baby," she said. "If you ever break up with me again, I'ma be nice."

"You scared the shit out of me. I'll never do that shit again." He laughed.

"Whatever," she said and kissed him again. She turned around and was now facing the water with her back to his chest. "My mom died, well was killed, under the Freedom Bridge," she told him with the view of the Freedom Bridge in her peripheral vision. He wrapped his arms around her waist.

"Really baby? I—"

"It's fine. I like coming here," she said, knowing he was feeling bad for bringing her there. "I'm just telling you. I pray to her; I talked to her about you," she let him know. "You think that's weird? Like maybe I should be talking to my grandma since she raised me?"

"No, you know your grandma better, so you know what she'd say or think. Talking to your mom and connecting with her spirit allows you to get to know her. I think it's dope," he let her know.

"We gotta go get Moon," she told him after a few minutes of silence.

"Gimme a few more minutes to vibe with you," he said and kissed the back of her neck.

"When we get home...I need to talk to you," she said nervously. She looked over her shoulder at him. He kissed her cheek.

"Okay, baby."

Later that night after Moon was fast asleep, Raphael held Butterfly as she told him her deepest secret. She told him how her therapist in foster care diagnosed her with Dissociative identity disorder. The therapist thought the break came around the time of

Beverly's death. She put Butterfly on medication, but it caused her to sleep a lot and took away her passion for art. She then told him how she had a conversation with her "sisters", as she called them, and how they had vowed to work together to create harmony in their body and soon they were able to effortlessly coexist. He wanted to ask questions like how many were there and what she thought about Reid, but he didn't. He just listened. He felt bad for not telling her that he'd met Reid, but he believed that until he had come along, she had been Butterfly's protector and he respected that.

Chapter 4

"NOW THAT HE KNOWS, WE NEED TO REWORK SOME THINGS," BUTTERFLY SAID. After a grueling day at the shop, her body was yearning for the relaxation a soak in the tub would provide and the joy spending time with Moon would give her. Instead, she had to have this conversation to make sure that things ran smoothly.

"What things?" Reid asked. "You went MIA; me and Jada have been holding things down."

"You and Jada fucked things up," Butterfly replied.

"You said to give him the information slowly," Jada said, regarding all that they had been through. Butterfly knew he needed to know those things in order to truly love them, but she didn't want to scare him off.

"Slowly yes, but I didn't say keep so much from him that he leaves," Butterfly replied. After she met Raphael the first time, she knew he was for them. Something in her spirit told her that he could love them and accept them. After all she had gone through in her life, she craved peace. And she had found it in the depths of meditation, but she could never truly get lost in her thoughts for fear of what her sisters were up to. She felt that Raphael could not only love them but guide them too. In exchange, Butterfly made sure Raphael's family was taken care of; she knew they were important to him. If their relationship was going to work, he would have to accept her sisters, and she would have to take care of his family.

She understood that for a relationship to work with him, he had to love every part of her, so she and the girls had been spending time with him throughout the relationship. Over time, Jada and Reid took over the relationship while she focused on her peace. While Butterfly took care of Moon primarily, Jada also stepped in to help with her as well.

"He won't do that again," Reid said.

"I don't need you to tell me what he'll do," Butterfly said.

"Can you two get over whatever issues you have once and for all?" Jada asked.

"I'm not even allowed to talk to her. I have to go through you, remember?" Reid said to Jada.

"Not anymore, right Butterfly?" Jada said.

"Right. As long as we have order."

"We all have our areas of expertise. Let's just keep playing our positions," Reid said.

"But we discuss all major decisions, and I'll make the final call," Butterfly told them. Before they could reply, she turned off the light and headed upstairs.

RAPHAEL LAID IN HIS BED WITH HIS MIND RACING. *What the fuck did I get myself into*, he thought. The conversations he'd had with Reid and Butterfly yesterday were heavy on his mind. He tried to play it cool because he didn't want her to panic, but on the inside he was in full panic mode.

"What the fuck," he said, sitting up in the bed. "I can barely handle Butterfly how the fuck I'ma handle..." He dropped his head in his hands instead of finishing his sentence. After a few moments, he lifted his head as he thought on the matter a little more in depth.

Reid's words replayed in his head. "The fuck am I talking about, I've been handling all of them," he said. At the promenade, Reid said he had been in contact with her, unbeknownst to him, and he could tell that he had been in contact with the others too because of how she avoided the question.

Raphael got up, grabbed a pen and pad out of his backpack and sat back on the bed.

He wrote down the different characteristics he had experienced with her, then assigned a name to the group of traits. Butterfly was soft, clingy and very private. Reid had a hard exterior; where Butterfly seemed to want to avoid confrontation, Reid initiated it. She had started the conversation on the pier about having multiple person's disorder. He would have had to pull that information out of Butterfly piece by piece. Then he thought about Henson and Butterfly's attitude shift when he had confronted her about it. She always started off not wanting to talk about it; that was Butterfly. Then something clicked, and she told him everything unapologetically; that was Reid. Reid wasn't to be fucked with that was for sure; and although she wanted to come off as a heartless murderer, everything she did was out of love. Love for Butterfly.

Plus, she likes to dance, he thought. Thinking about them on the dancefloor made him blush. Their bodies were so in sync. He had experienced her rhythm, the sway of her hips, her body glued to his, grinding into him even before he had made love to Butterfly. Although he was alone in the room, he covered his smile with his hand as if he needed to hide it from someone. He knew Reid and she knew him.

He chastised himself. He was supposed to be figuring out how to love all of Butterfly and he was fantasizing about Reid. *Is she off limits?* he wondered. He cleared his throat and straightened his posture, preparing to get back to work.

For as clingy as Butterfly was, there was also an independent side to her. Not the 'I don't need you' energy that Reid gave off. It was more nurturing almost like 'I did it so you wouldn't have to'. He tapped the paper with his pen as he thought for a minute. He figured that was the third personality. She cooked for his family and loved his sister.

"There has to be three," he reasoned. His mind wouldn't allow him to consider that there could be more.

Once he had the characteristics in three separate groups, he came up with a strategy for approaching them. When he got to Reid he simply wrote: Let her run shit and dropped the pen.

Chapter 5

A WEEK AFTER BUTTERFLY REVEALED HER DIAGNOSIS TO RAPHAEL, EVERYTHING SEEMED TO BE BACK TO NORMAL. They were now at Raphael's house preparing to go to Pappy's while Candy watched Moon. Raphael wore blue jean shorts with fashionable holes in them and a white Gucci shirt with matching sneakers, both a gift from Butterfly. She rocked a blue jean wraparound-skort set that exposed her thighs. Her oiled legs led to her blue velvet Gucci pumps with a Sylvie bow; she also wore a matching mini bag. Butterfly always liked Gucci; she thought the clothes and shoes were creative. But, when she saw a pair of patent leather sneakers with a detachable, metal butterfly in the window, she finally went inside the store. She had learned that it was a moth and not a butterfly, but she was still in love and bought a pair. After seeing Raphael's reaction to her shoes, she decided to get him a pair of Gucci sneakers too.

"What?" she asked. She felt his eyes penetrating her frame; not lustfully, more like he had something on his mind.

"Nothing," he answered. She knew that he knew he was going to Pappy's with Reid, but neither of them spoke on it.

AT PAPPY'S, THEY WERE DOING THEIR FAVORITE THING, SLOW DANCING UNDER THE DIM LIGHTS. She was winding her body into his; her clit bumping his dick making her bite her lip.

"Chill," he said, holding her hips still. She slowly looked up at him.

"What?" she questioned with a smirk.

"I don't know," he said bashfully.

"We always dance; it's not that serious. Is it because you know I'm not Butterfly?"

"Kinda feel like..." He paused, shrugged then shook his head.

"Like?" she questioned. Irritation moved up her body and rested on her face.

"Cheating. I'm with Butterfly, Reid," he informed her.

"You're with Butterfly Reid. She's Butterfly; I'm Reid," she said, wrapping her arms around his neck and pulling him closer. They kissed with his hands on her ass as they grinded into each other. He pulled back. She huffed and rolled her eyes. "I'm ready to go," she told him.

"Nah, I told Quincy we'd go eat with them after."

"Then go," she said, walking away. She slithered through the crowd headed for the bathroom. Before she could make it to the door, he grabbed her and turned her around. She jerked away from him, pushed him and tried to walk off, but he grabbed her around the waist and backed her into a wall towering over her.

"Move," she gritted, trying to control her anger. Butterfly loved him; therefore, using her Jiu jitsu techniques on him would cause major disruption in the space they shared. However, Reid felt that showing him that she was more powerful would help to get things in alignment between her and Raphael.

"I'm not trying to hurt you," he said.

"You're not. You want Butterfly; that's fine. But this space," she said, circling her hand around her body, "isn't always going to belong to that spirit," she explained.

"Is that how y'all describe it? That's dope," he said, smiling down at her.

"Move; I need to use the bathroom then I'm going home. You can bring Moon to Butterfly in the morning," she said and shoved him. Her grabbed her again and pulled her down onto a circular couch.

"Oh my god! Let me turn into Butterfly for you so you can leave me alone," she said. Reid stretched her arms out and started shaking as if she was possessed. He froze for a moment, then burst into laughter. She laughed too.

"I'm not trying to beef with you," he told her.

"Good, because I can kick your ass," Reid said, standing up. He was still seated; her pussy was in his face. He looked at it, then smiled up at her. She bore a coy smirk.

"You're crazy," he said, running his hand up her thigh before he stood up. She looked up at him and he kissed her.

"Don't call them crazy; they don't like it. I don't care, but they do," she warned him.

"Why?" he asked.

She shrugged. "I don't know; ask them. You mind if I dance with someone else? I came here to dance, Raphael."

"It's not that I don't want to dance with you, Reid."

"I know; you just think it's cheating," she replied. She said it as if it were the stupidest thing in the world; he chuckled at her sarcasm.

"The way we dance... If she danced like that with somebody—"

"If you think the way we dance is cheating, you'd lose your shit if I told you the other things we've done," she replied and stormed off. He waited a moment, took a deep breath and went after her. He pulled her back to his chest and rocked to the beat. Soon the stiffness left her body and she moved with him.

The song changed and they adjusted their dance to fit the beat. With her butt to his dick, she threw her ass up and down; he held her hips and rubbed her butt as he danced behind her.

"I'ma tell Quincy we'll meet up another time. We need to go home and talk," he whispered in her ear. Reid nodded and continued to dance. After another hour of dancing they agreed that it was time to leave.

51

"We'll go to your place; you feel like cooking?" he asked as they exited Pappy's.

"I don't really cook, Raphael. We should stop and get something," she said leading him through the crowd. He tapped her waist and she slowed down to look back at him. He stuck out his hand and she grabbed it. He wasn't even going to waste his energy trying to lead.

"Wait, you don't cook?" he questioned. He looked at her like she had two heads.

She smiled. "I'm Reid," she reminded him.

"I see," he said. He would need to add that to his mental list of personality traits. He had ripped up the one in his notepad figuring it would be better to memorize the information. They came to a stop at the crosswalk and when it was their turn to walk, she wrapped his arm around her waist and led the way.

BACK AT HER APARTMENT, THEY BEGAN TO TAKE THEIR FOOD OUT OF THE BAG. "Y'all all vegetarian though?" he asked as they took their seat.

"Yea. We understand that because we share this space, there are certain things we all have to agree to do," Reid answered.

"Like what?"

"You're supposed to be ours," she said, taking a bite of her breakfast burrito. She shrugged. "That's how she pitched it," she said.

"Have y'all ever dated anyone else?" he asked as he poured syrup on his pancakes.

"No. That was the furthest thing from our minds, then Butterfly saw you," she informed him. He liked talking to her because she was unafraid of him; shit of anything, so she didn't hold back.

He laughed. "And she hit y'all with a sales pitch." She laughed too.

"I know you don't want me," she said and glanced up at him.

"I never said I didn't want you," he said. His eyes were focused on his food. The conversation wasn't hard for him, but she

52

intimidated him. Her hair was pulled back the way he loved, her face was perfect, she was open and honest and unafraid, and it made him feel...small.

"Your expression did. At the promenade, even tonight. You only danced with me because to you, me dancing with someone else means Butterfly is," she told him. Reid spoke as if what she was saying was no big deal, as if she wasn't sharing her heart with him the way he'd had to beg Butterfly to.

"I just don't really know how to handle all this, Reid. I want to be here with y'all; I just want to have an understanding and be respectful. I don't want to hurt her."

"You love her. I love that about you. We have that in common; we want to protect her first and foremost."

"I love you too, Reid," he confessed.

She laughed; that made him look into her eyes. "No, you don't," she replied.

"I love everything about this," he said, waving his hand up and down the length of her body. "Every spirit that lives inside of this temple, I love. But you act like you don't want me."

"Why; because I'm independent?" she asked.

"Butterfly is independent," he stated.

"Be—because I don't cower to you...beg you to love me?"

"I don't like you or Candy." He mimicked what she said at the promenade. She laughed. "When I think back over our relationship, I can point out when it was you...you act like you don't need me."

"I don't. I can take care of myself and them. Why can't it be enough that I want you?"

Her vulnerability invaded his heart and softened his resolve. "That is enough." He pulled her face to his and kissed her. "What all have we done?"

"I thought you could look back and see when it was me," she teased.

"For certain stuff."

"Like?"

"The time when you came back from the laundry mat with the weapons. You always want to move around solo too, and you like for your hands to be free. Like tonight how you wrapped my hand around your waist instead of holding my hand."

"Yea and I didn't tell you about Darius. I saw him; I avoided him. You should apologize to her. I had to take over the argument because she had no idea what you were talking about. She was inside me going crazy; she knew you were about to leave her. I never thought you would. When she took back over; it was too late."

"I regret that shit. I'll apologize to her."

"I'm physical," she told him. She placed a cubed pineapple halfway in her mouth and sucked the juice from it. "I like to fight and dance...and fuck," she said and looked deep into his eyes. "I like to kiss you...everywhere. She likes when you're on top—"

"And you like to be on top," he said; his dick was brick hard. He wanted her so bad; the food was boring and tasteless he wanted her in his mouth.

"I like to watch you cower." She smirked knowing she had him in a trance.

"And you don't respect my mama's house, huh," he said, trying to lighten the mood.

"Nope! She don't like us anyway," she said unapologetically.

"I know Butterfly don't care," he said.

"She cares," Reid said matter-of-factly.

"I thought she only cared about me and Moon," he pointed out. Reid froze momentarily and then smiled. He was confused about a few things, but he would have to figure that out himself.

"Talk to her about that; talk to me about me."

"I feel like we shouldn't have secrets," he told her.

"I like secrets."

"Why?"

"They keep things spicy!"

"You who has caused problems in my relationship," he leaned back, shaking his finger and her and laughed genuinely.

"I got your relationship started, sir," she sassed, working her neck.

"How?"

"I kissed you back. She was too scared," she told him.

"When?"

"At Sienna's."

"Wait; we had our first kiss?"

"You kissed her, and it scared the shit outta her, so she ran away. I kissed you back."

"Why?"

"'Cause she wanted you. I was trying to keep you entertained," she replied.

"You massaged my feet?" he asked.

"No, I'm not good with that sensual shit. That's Butterfly's thing. I just told her she needed to stop being a stick in the mud and give you something."

"Kissing me from head to toe...that's not sensual?"

"No."

"Why not? How slowly you kissed me...how you stroked me. You were so in tune with me," he said. "You sure you haven't wanted me all along?" he asked, raising his brow.

"I've had you all along, Raphael."

"So, it's been you, me, Butterfly and..." he asked her. He was hoping in all her honesty she would reveal the other spirit that lived in Butterfly's space.

"Chase her like you did when you thought it was just Butterfly," she said, getting up from the table. She walked to the trashcan and threw away her burrito wrapper. "I know we're not fucking tonight," she said and downed her orange juice before throwing away the container. "I know you need to check in with your warden to make sure it's cool to fuck with me, so you can get in bed...I'm gonna exercise," she told him.

He didn't argue with her because she was right, he did want to discuss things with Butterfly.

RAPHAEL WOKE UP THE NEXT DAY TO THE SMELL OF FOOD COOKING AND SMILED AS HE STRETCHED. He rolled out of bed and checked his phone. It was after twelve; he hardly ever slept that late. Raphael went to the bathroom to handle his hygiene before joining her in the kitchen.

"Good morning, baby," he said, walking up to her. She hugged him tight and the fresh smell of her hair caressed his nostrils. She had braided her hair in medium sized box braids and decorated them in hair jewelry.

"Good morning," she said before they kissed. "I missed you," she said between kisses. He thought about the times when she had said that before and he thought she was being dramatic, because in his mind they hadn't been apart outside of work. Even that made sense now.

"I missed you too, baby," he said, kissing her neck. He ran his hands up her silk nightie and cuffed her ass. She moaned and kissed his lips. Raphael hoisted her on the counter as she pulled his dick out. He let out a deep sigh when he entered his woman. She was so warm and the more he stroked, the wetter she became until he slid in and out of her with ease. She widened her legs begging for more and he filled her to capacity. She groaned so he gave her a moment to adjust to his size. She started back moving and so did he.

"The-the food, ba-ba-by," she stuttered as he rammed inside of her.

"I'll take you to eat," he said. His powerful thrusts sent shockwaves through her as her ass hit the counter and her pussy swallowed him whole. She wrapped her arms around his neck, squeezed her legs tighter around his waist and slung her body into him. She was on the brink of climaxing and the anticipation of it caused her to get wild. Raphael was losing his mind as his dick dug deeper into her treasure.

"I'm 'bout to come," he warned her. She stopped fighting to hold on and allowed the orgasm to rip through her body. Her pussy contracting around his dick prompted his release and they came together. He held her, softly kissing her neck as the aftereffects of their orgasms caused them to float.

"I'm so in love with you, baby," he said.

AN HOUR LATER, THEY WERE SEATED AT A BREAKFAST SPOT WAITING FOR THEIR FOOD TO BE DELIVERED. Her braids were pulled into a high ponytail and fell just above her shoulders.

"What?" she asked because he was staring at her.

"Nothing," he said and looked away. He hadn't even realized he was doing it. He was in deep thought trying to figure things out. It all made perfect sense in his heart but then his mind started to try to process it and he realized how hard this would be. He would essentially have to love, please and take care of three women.

"You're trying to figure out how to tell us apart?" she asked. The waiter walked up and delivered their food, so the couple sat quietly until he walked off. She used her fork to stir her red beans and rice.

"Tell me what you're thinking about. I wanna help you through this," she said.

"I think I know how to tell y'all apart. I'm not thinking about that."

"Then what?"

"How does it happen. Like the transition from one to the other. How does that happen?" He picked up his knife and fork and began to cut into his chicken fried steak.

"Triggers; I guess. Certain things pull out certain parts of me; same as you," she said using a playful, sassy tone. "How?" she asked.

"How what?" he asked.

"How can you tell us apart?"

"Oh." Raphael smiled and sat back in his seat. "Reid is the fighter; she likes her hair pulled back either in two braids or gelled back—"

"How you like it," she interjected. He didn't respond. "She's your favorite."

"Who told you that?" he joked.

"You like her style; the way she dances," she said.

"I like the way you danced for me earlier," he said, staring into her eyes. She blushed.

"Anyway, you like the individual braids or twists with the jewelry on them. You like me," he added. She smiled. "Who likes the 'fro?" he asked, putting down his fork and knife and staring at her. He was studying her every move. She liked when he did that; it made her feel important, but it also made her feel shy.

"I don't know," she lied.

"Why she don't wanna meet me?"

"She has."

"Why won't she let me chill with her, get to know her?" he asked.

She chuckled. "You have!"

"It don't count if I don't know I'm with her."

"So that's what you want?"

"I want to know all of y'all. Is that cool with you?"

"It's not up to me," she said.

He looked confused. "Who is it up to?" he questioned. She sucked her bottom lip into her mouth and reminded herself to watch her words.

"I just mean that's how it has to be."

"Nothing has to be, Butterfly; I'm asking what you want. What you expect."

"I want you to love me, every piece of me, and accept me. So, I have to allow you to get to know them and have whatever relationship y'all are going to have."

"Allow?" he said, picking up his knife and fork.

"You know I run you. Everybody knows that," she joked.

"Reid won't tell me her name either. Why do y'all hide her from me?"

"We don't. Reid is bold, that's why she introduced herself. I didn't introduce myself to you."

Raphael thought about all he went through to get Butterfly's attention. He laughed.

"Man, I ain't going through that shit again."

"Then you'll just have me and Reid," she said and looked up at him. "You like Reid, huh? She's intriguing."

"You're intriguing too," he told her.

58

Chapter 6

A FEW DAYS LATER, RAPHAEL WALKED INTO THE SHOP WITH MOON AND HEARD LAUGHTER COMING FROM THE OFFICE. He rounded the corner and found Candy and Butterfly laughing so hard it warmed his heart. But it wasn't Butterfly; it was *her* and her smile was so gigantic it was contagious.

"Hey, baby girl," Candy cooed, taking Moon from Raphael. "I'ma get her a popsicle," Candy said, heading toward the stairs to the apartment. Butterfly had made frozen yogurt on a stick to help with Moon's sore gums.

"Hey," he said, walking up to her and tilting her head back. He kissed her lips and she smiled up at him. He slid in the seat with her. "What's your name, ma?" he asked quietly; she quickly diverted her attention. "Baby," he called and pulled her face back in his direction and just that quickly she was gone. Butterfly smiled, melted into his arms and took a deep breath, inhaling his intoxicating scent.

"I missed you all day, baby," she said.

"I missed you too, ma," he said and kissed her.

Chapter 7

"Shit, Candy!" he said, jumping up. Reid was on top of him; she had started at his lips and was now at his chest softly and slowly teasing his body as she headed toward the bulge in his sweats. His dick was so hard it hurt; he fought to appear calm, but his body was on fire; she knew it and it made her move slower. He pulled her up and pushed her to the left of him; Candy rolled her eyes. They knew they weren't supposed to be doing that, but they insisted on disregarding her mother's rules. Raphael looked to see what Reid was doing; she was an alpha female and liked for everyone to bow down to her. But Reid was gone, and Butterfly was lying behind him smiling.

"See, this is why you can't answer your damn phone. And y'all doing this with the baby in here?" Candy questioned.

"She's sleep," Raphael said, looking toward the bassinet.

"Quincy said he's been calling you."

"You coulda knocked," he said. They had been spending more time at Butterfly's house; he was able to do that because it was summertime and he didn't have the responsibility of getting his siblings to school on time. Serena was working doubles this weekend to cover for an employee, so he made sure to be home.

"Whatever Phe," she said on her way out. When the door closed, Butterfly sat up in the bed.

"You finna leave, baby?" Butterfly asked.

"Nah, but let me see what he wants," he said, reaching for his phone on the nightstand.

"Yoooo!" Quincy said, answering his phone.

"What up?" Raphael asked. Butterfly was next to him with her leg thrown over his body and her nose buried in his neck.

"You said we'd have a makeup session for dinner, remember?" Quincy said. Kalia had been bothering him about getting to know the mysterious Butterfly and although Quincy didn't see the big deal, those closest to him seemed to be captivated by her. He didn't understand why Kalia was so eager to be around her when Butterfly showed no interest in Kalia. Even when they were together at Pappy's, she didn't really engage with Kalia; she was too busy being glued to Raphael, something Quincy told Kalia she should take note of.

"Yea, but not tonight," he said. They had gone out last weekend and he knew Butterfly wasn't going to want to go out again so soon because she didn't like to leave Moon behind.

"Just food, bro. Something simple to get out the house for an hour or two." That actually sounded good to Raphael.

Raphael looked over at Butterfly; she shook her head no. "I'ma call you right back," he said.

"Man, Phe," Quincy said. He thought Raphael was trying to get rid of him, but he was really trying to finesse his woman. Raphael hung up anyway so that he could talk to her.

"Baby, we just gon' go eat. An hour and a half, tops. I wanna chill with you."

"We're together right now."

"With friends, Butterfly. Come out with me for a little bit, please. Tell me what you want, and we'll trade." A smile crept on her face. "Tell me," he said, pulling her on top of him. She blushed so hard he began to smile.

"Kiss me...everywhere, then sex me until I get tired. Not when you get tired, not when Moon cries; do it to me until I can't take no more," she said.

"So I'ma fuck you while my baby crying?" he questioned.

"We can pause, get her settled, then we're back at it," she said.

"Okay," he said and kissed her succulently. He rolled on top of her and deepened the kiss. She spread her legs because she wanted to feel him against her; for now, it was enough to feel his hardness pressed against her center.

INSIDE THE DINER, RAPHAEL AND BUTTERFLY SAT ON ONE SIDE OF THE BOOTH WHILE QUINCY AND KALIA SAT ON THE OTHER. All Night Long was typically an after the club meet up. People would go to Pappy's then stop at the all-night diner for breakfast. Apparently, everyone was getting out tonight; Raphael figured Quincy knew that but forgot to mention it. Before meeting up with Quincy and Kalia, Raphael had been able to talk Butterfly into going to see a movie with him. She didn't mind that because it was just the two of them. She only made things hard when she had to share him with others.

"I don't know if I ever officially introduced y'all, but Butterfly this is Kalia; Kalia, Butterfly." Quincy introduced. The two girls smiled and nodded their heads.

"It's nice to meet you," they took turns saying. Soon, the waitress approached the table and they ordered their food.

"What are your black beans made with?" Butterfly asked the waitress when it was time to order.

"Um," she said and appeared to be thinking.

"Is there any meat in them?" Butterfly asked.

"No, I don't think so," she answered skeptically.

"Can you ask the cook?"

"Of course," the waitress said.

"Why would the beans have meat in them?" Kalia asked.

"The base could be made with beef broth or something. I don't eat meat or anything that has meat products in it," Butterfly explained.

"Oh, I didn't know that," Kalia said as the waitress walked back up.

"The black beans are boiled in water with garlic and lemon juice," she let Butterfly know.

"Thank you," Butterfly smiled. "I'll have the Belgian waffle, black beans and the fruit bowl."

"Black beans and waffles?" Kalia laughed.

"She's weird," Raphael replied and rubbed Butterfly's knee under the table. "A waffle, grits, and I guess I'ma try this turkey bacon," Raphael said and looked at Butterfly. She smiled, grabbed the side of his face and kissed his cheek.

"Maann," Quincy dragged out after hearing their order. "I want an order of pancakes, *bacon and sausage*, and scrambled eggs," he said and handed the waitress his menu.

"Same," Kalia said, handing over her menu.

The couples made small talk as they waited for their food; when it arrived, they dug in. Raphael felt a soft hand caressing his thigh and inching toward his dick, and he knew it wasn't Butterfly. She wasn't that bold. Raphael looked up and into Reid's tantalizing eyes. He watched as she bit into a juicy pineapple. "Gimme some," he requested, gripping the inside of her thigh. She put it in front of his mouth and he took a bite. Then he leaned in and kissed her, licking the maple syrup from the side of her mouth. His tongue stroking her face caused her pussy to twitch. They ended the kiss, opened their eyes and shared a brief peck.

"Damn, nigga," Quincy fussed.

"Kiss yo' girl," Raphael replied.

"We have manners," Quincy shot back.

Reid tapped Raphael's leg and then nodded down at her phone. In the Notes app she had typed: I'M READY TO GO.

They both knew they couldn't do anything at his house, but he understood that Reid found pleasure in breaking the rules. He was happy she had made an appearance, but he needed Butterfly to go home with him or else Serena was sure to put him out.

"Ma, we can't do shit at the house. You know that," he whispered in her ear. "I need you to respect that," he said. She scrunched her face and rolled her eyes.

"How long have you been doing nails?" Kalia asked with a big smile.

"Um. I started in school. We had a program for it," Butterfly said. Raphael smiled.

"I wish we had that," Kalia said.

"Girl, you barely passed art," Quincy joked.

"Baby, how much longer," Butterfly whispered to Raphael.

"Whenever you ready," he answered, figuring they would at least finish their food. He stuck his fork in his waffle, but before he could put the food in his mouth, he heard Butterfly calling the waitress.

"Excuse me," she said, waving the waitress over. "Can we have two to-go boxes?" she asked.

"Of course," the waitress replied.

"Really?" Quincy said, looking across the table at them. Butterfly didn't reply.

"That's her," Raphael stated, trying to eat more of his food before the waitress came back. When she did, Butterfly packed up their food while he paid. She stood, and he scooted out of the booth.

"Later," Raphael said, reaching over the table to slap hands with Quincy.

"Be safe," Quincy said.

"See y'all later," Kalia said. Butterfly smiled over her shoulder at her.

As they walked out of the diner, Raphael led the way. His hand was stretched back as he pulled Butterfly with him.

EBONY HAD COME TO THE DINER WITH A GROUP OF FRIENDS AND WHILE THEY WERE STANDING OUTSIDE TALKING TO GUYS, SHE HEADED INSIDE TO ORDER HER FOOD. Before she got to the steps at the entrance of the diner, she saw Raphael step out with a big smile on his face. Her heart rate increased; he had been on her mind heavy and she wanted to reach out but wasn't sure where things stood with him and his baby's mother.

"Hey," she greeted. Raphael looked over and saw her and his smile disappeared; not because he saw her, but because a mixture of thoughts involving Butterfly and Reid had him grinning and Ebony was interrupting that.

"What's up," he said as Butterfly stepped to his side. Ebony's eyes scanned Butterfly and then how firmly Raphael held her hand.

"I thought y'all broke up," Ebony blurted out. Immediately she regretted it, figuring she looked rattled by Butterfly's presence.

Butterfly didn't react physically, but Raphael knew he had fucked up. "We worked it out," Butterfly said and extended her hand. "I'm Butterfly." Ebony shook her hand and mumbled, "I'm Ebony."

"Later," Raphael told Ebony with a head nod and walked off.

On the train, he stood behind Butterfly with their right hands intertwined as he held their to-go bag with his left. He brought her hand to his mouth and kissed it. She smiled, looking over her shoulder at him.

The walk to his block was quiet until he spoke. "Your feet hurt?" She was dressed in a purple thigh-length, fitted skirt, a white crop top and closed-toe pumps.

"No," she answered with a pleasant smile.

"I could carry you," he offered.

"I'm good."

They climbed into the elevator, he leaned against the back wall and she leaned on him with her back to his chest. He kissed her neck. She smiled. He kissed it again, this time grazing his tongue against her. She reached back to cuff his face as he sucked on her neck. "Turn around," his hoarse voice requested.

The elevator dinged; she smirked over her shoulder as she walked off.

Entering his bedroom, she removed her shoes, then gathered her items and headed for the bathroom. He sat on the bed contemplating what to do. She was pissed but acting as if she wasn't. Reid hadn't appeared which he was thankful for; it was clear she had issues controlling her anger. He needed to explain the shit with Ebony. He didn't want to because it didn't mean shit, but it also didn't look good. He hadn't spoken to Ebony since that day at the park and the whole exchange had slipped his mind.

After several minutes, Butterfly hadn't come out of the bathroom, so he went to check on her. She was on the floor, sponge in hand, scrubbing the corners of the tub.

"Come on, ma," he said from the doorway. He knew this was her way of channeling her anger instead of arguing with him.

"This tub is dirty; Candy gon' be pissed."

He walked to her, bent down and scooped her up. Carrying her back to the bedroom, he sat her on the bed. After closing the bedroom door, he sat on the floor in front of her.

"What's wrong?" he asked. She stared at him. "Bug, what are you mad about?"

"You know," she finally said.

"But I want you to tell me so we can discuss it." She stared into his eyes, then lowered hers to the floor.

"Obviously you fucked her, but you shouldn't have been talking about me with her."

"How is it obvious I fucked her?"

"I saw how she reacted to seeing you with someone else, how she *questioned* you," she pointed out.

"I didn't fuck her. You already insinuated that I fucked someone while we were broken up, and I thought we shut that shit down."

"Ever?" she asked, looking up at him.

"I didn't say that," he answered after a deep breath.

"But you saw her recently?"

"I was at the park; she showed up."

"And why did I come up?"

"She was on some bullshit about us being friends again...like we were before anything happened between me and you. She was saying she'd talk to you about it to let you know she wasn't on bullshit and to make sure you were cool with it."

She gasped. "And you fell for that shit?"

"Fuck no; I walked her home and I haven't seen her since."

Butterfly huffed. "Walked her home?" He didn't seem to understand how something so simple could mean the world to a girl; especially a girl who liked him and who he had been intimate with. "Raphael," she sighed, shaking her head.

"It was getting late," he explained. She looked past him and shook her head.

"You think I cheated on you, Bug?"

"We wasn't together," she reminded him.

"You think I cheated on you?" he asked again.

"I think you walked a bitch home who got to the park perfectly fine without you, and then told her you were single. I think you was doing a lot while you and your girl were beefing."

"It was after our last argument. You had just talked to *your man* like you didn't give a fuck about what we were or could be—"

"Here you go; you wasn't on that before this. Now you're using it to justify your actions," she said and stood up. He stood up too, and when she tried to walk to the door, he blocked her.

"I'm still not on the shit but you're questioning my frame of mind, so I'm setting shit up for you. I wasn't out for no reason; I was clearing my mind."

"I don't care," she said, shrugging her shoulders.

"But you're cleaning the tub at 12 in the morning."

"It's dirty."

"You mad, Bug, and I'm sorry. I was in my feelings about you; that shit slipped because I was trying to end the conversation with her," he said, placing his hands on her hips.

"Okay," she said, about to go back to the bathroom. She had gone in there to shower, then saw some dirt on the tub and got irritated. Or, maybe she was already irritated and the dirt on the tub became her sparring partner.

"Okay what?" he asked, holding her in place.

"Okay, Raphael," she fussed.

"Okay, we good?"

"I don't like that shit, but we gon' always be good. I ain't tryna beef with you, especially not over that. It is what you say it is," she replied. *It is what you say it is*, he thought. He liked that.

"Cool, I ain't tryna beef either. I'm sorry. I'm in love with you," he said with his forehead to hers.

"I'm in love with you too." She smiled and pecked his lips. Then, she wiggled out of his embrace and went back to the bathroom.

After she got the water started, she heard a light tap on the door. She opened the door and Raphael walked in with his pajamas in his hand.

"No, Phe," she hissed, trying to push him back out.

"We're just bathing," he said, locking the door. "Everybody's sleep."

"They were sleep last time," she reminded him.

"We did more than bathe last time," he said while undressing. When he was done, he looked back at her before pulling the shower curtain back. He laughed while climbing into the shower. "Man, come on."

She got undressed and joined him. He smiled when she entered the shower.

"No funny business," she said. He squeezed her titty. "Phe," she whispered, popping his hand.

"Ouch! Man, stop," he said and pinched her pussy.

"Phe, you outta line."

"We gotta make up and this is all you like to do," he replied.

"Whatever. I'm good, we can do it tomorrow," she said.

"Then, too," he said, pressing her back to the shower wall.

"I want to, baby, but I'm scared," she admitted as he lifted her up.

"I know; just be quiet," he said; her titty was now in his mouth as he pushed inside of her. The showerhead rained down on them as they became completely engrossed in each other.

Swimming in the depths of her sucked all the energy from his body. Lazily, he pressed his body into her, but his stroke was still precise. Buried inside of her, he was in his favorite place and she was in her favorite state, their love thrusting from him to her, traveling through their bodies and exploding in a kiss. She bit into his shoulder blade to avoid screaming.

With her feet against the shower wall now, the weight of their bodies shifted back to him. Moving back and forth, she squeezed her vagina walls zeroing in on her G spot.

"Ah," he grunted. Her eyes popped open and she covered his mouth with hers, biting his lips.

"Be quiet," she teased. He kissed her face, neck and cheeks and groped her body, stimulating her beyond measure.

His ability to make love to her, every piece of her, always left her mesmerized. It took over every one of her senses. It tickled her ears and provided the most sensuous smell to her nostrils, which produced the sweetest taste on her tongue. Overpowered by its beauty, her eyes slammed shut. She felt it circulating through her body as she anticipated its eruption.

Chapter 8

TWO MONTHS HAD PASSED, SCHOOL WAS BACK IN AND AUGUST WAS CLOSING OUT. Butterfly and Raphael were at her apartment asleep on the couch when she was jolted out of her sleep by a violent rumble in her stomach. Leaning over him, she emptied the contents of her stomach and then fell back on the couch.

"What the fuck, Bug?" he said, looking from left to right.

"I'ma get it up." She huffed and rolled over on the couch.

"I'll get it," he said, untangling their limbs and sitting up.

"I got it, Phe," she fussed and finally hopped up.

"That's all those damn sweets yo ass been eating." He laughed. "You went from fruit to ice cream."

"It's still non-dairy," she replied as she dragged herself to the bathroom for a towel.

"Those Cinnabons and shit ain't." He continued to tease her. "Brother's every other damn day." He chuckled.

After cleaning up her mess and brushing her teeth, she washed her hands and climbed back over him to get in her spot on the couch. Lying on her back, she glanced over at him and then slowly placed his hand on her stomach. When their breathing was in tune, she rolled over on her side and he pulled her tighter into his arms. His hand fell to her stomach again; she placed hers on top of his. Understanding washed over him and caused his body to tense up for a moment. Then he rubbed her belly, buried his nose in her neck and drifted off to sleep.

"WHAT'S UP," RAPHAEL SAID, WALKING INTO THE APARTMENT. It was Monday morning, so he had to come home to make sure they got to school with no problems. Candy walked out of the bathroom and Jaquel headed in.

"Hey," Candy said, eyeing Raphael. "I thought we were on our own today," Candy said. She took Moon from Raphael and started bouncing her.

"Why would y'all be on your own? You think 'cause you're a senior you can take care of yourself?" he joked. He peeked into Kwame and Jaquel's bedroom and saw Kwame getting dressed.

"Mama told me about your conversation," Candy said as Raphael took a seat on the couch.

"What conversation?" he asked.

"The one where you accused her of not liking Butterfly," Candy said.

His face wrinkled. He couldn't understand why Serena was talking about that when it happened so long ago. They had never sat down to resolve the issue and it bothered him, but just like her, he had swept it under the rug and kept it moving.

"That was months ago," he said dismissively.

"Yea, but you've been moving different since you and Butterfly got back together."

"What you mean?"

"Y'all are more secretive; you go to her place more," Candy explained.

"If Mama told you the whole conversation then you should understand why," he replied.

"That doesn't mean Mama don't like her. Butterfly has her ways," Candy said.

"Yea, but she ain't did nothing to Mama."

"Not intentionally," Candy said. Raphael looked irritated.

"Not even unintentionally; you can go on with that," he said.

"Think about it. She cooks for you; you take care of her baby," Candy said. She wasn't on anyone's side, but Candy thought maybe she could explain how Serena felt better than she had.

"My baby," Raphael corrected, taking Moon from her and walking to his bedroom.

"You got that. My bad," Candy said, following him. "Maybe she feels threatened."

"Mama?"

"Yea 'cause you're her righthand and now you're missing in action. I know sometimes I feel a way."

"What you mean?"

"Arian don't take up all my time."

"Bug don't take up all mine. I work a full-time job too. Y'all gotta figure if I'm in a relationship, I'm gonna wanna put time into it," he said. Raphael was getting annoyed because he was tired of having to defend his relationship with Butterfly.

"You've been in a relationship before and it never changed our lives this much."

"I've never been in a relationship like this. Bug is family to me. The shit deeper than boyfriend/girlfriend."

"She's our family too," Candy told him. And she meant every word.

"Then what's the problem, Candy?"

"I'm just tryna help you see Mama's point, Phe, so there's no tension."

"I see it," he told her.

"Good; let me finish getting dressed."

Chapter 9

CANDACE WALKED INTO THE APARTMENT AFTER SCHOOL WITH A SCOWL ON HER FACE. Serena rounded the corner in just enough time to see her. "What's wrong with you?" she questioned; her face turned up too.

"I'm tired of school," she huffed and entered her bedroom. Serena chuckled and followed her inside.

"What happened?"

"Nothing; they just give us unnecessary homework. It's the weekend, let us live," she continued to complain. Candy was now seventeen; her birthday was at the beginning of the month and she had celebrated all week by going to lunch with her mother, dinner with friends, a special date with Arian and the arcade with Butterfly and her brothers. She had also received plenty of gifts. Her dad called her as he always did, but this time, he had also sent her some money. He had given her the Western Union reference number so that she could go retrieve it. She could tell Raphael wanted to say a lot about that, but since it was her birthday, he held his tongue. His birthday, which was in July, had come and gone as well; he was now twenty. While their dad had called him too, he hadn't sent him any money. Whether Phe not getting money had to do with the fact that Phe rushed the phone conversation with their father or not was beyond Candy.

"Well, it's your last year and you've already passed your SATs, so don't sweat it." Serena encouraged her.

"They need to stop sweating us." Candy laughed as she removed her backpack. "They're acting like we're freshmen."

"Speaking of, how has Jaquel been; he won't talk to me about it."

"You know he's good. People know him, so no one is going to mess with him," she said, now standing in front of her mirror taking off her jewelry.

"I'm proud of you," Serena said, looking at her through the mirror. Candy looked up at her and scrunched up her face in embarrassment. Serena's sudden display of affection shocked her.

"Ooookay," she chuckled and flopped down on the bed.

"I am. You're on track with everything. I admire you: your strength and your beliefs. You're a lot more centered and self-aware than I was when I was your age, even more than when I went to college."

"I'm not going to get pregnant," Candy replied, leaning up and crossing her foot underneath her. She figured that fear had brought on this impromptu heart-to-heart.

"I know," Serena affirmed with teary eyes. She knew Candy wouldn't get pregnant and it wasn't because of anything she had done or taught her. It was because of the woman Candy was. She created her own rules regarding boys, clothes, hair and her beliefs. She did what she wanted and what was in line with her goals for her life. Serena doubted that she taught her that. How could she when she was still learning it herself? And yet, Candy had learned.

"Why are you crying?" Candy fussed as her own tears built. She loved her mother more than words and knew that Serena's tears would only bring about her own.

"I just," Serena said, shaking her head. "I'm so proud of you and just honored, Candy, to have helped you along the way. I didn't know what I was doing, and most days I was terrified. Raising boys is easier. You teach them to respect themselves and women, and you make them work so they understand that if you don't work, you don't eat. Give 'em condoms," she laughed. "It was different with you. I had so much to instill in you and had no idea where to start. But looking at the woman you're becoming, I think I did a good job."

Candy was lost for words, so she pulled her mother into a tight hug and allowed the thump of her heart to speak for her.

They heard the front door open and close and pulled back from each other. Laughing, they wiped their tears.

Moments later, Raphael was in the doorway with Moon.

"Can you watch Moon in a few hours?" he asked Candy. "I'ma take Bug to Brother's for her birthday."

"Yea, but damn," she sighed, "I can't go?"

"You can go with us to Pappy's. Kwame and Quel are gon' keep her tonight," he let her know.

"I can watch her; that way everyone can go everywhere," Serena offered.

"Nah," Raphael said and walked out. Since the conversation with Serena three months ago, he had kept his promise and hadn't asked her to watch Moon.

Candy looked at Serena and took in her solemn expression.

"I didn't know that both you and Butterfly had birthdays in September," Serena said, trying to cover her sadness.

"Yup, Virgo nation," Candy said and pulled out her phone. "I'ma call Bug. I don't know what's up with him, but I know I want to go both places and I know Kwame wants to go to Pappy's."

"Let me know." Serena sighed, got off the bed and exited the bedroom.

Before the phone rang for Butterfly, Candy hung up. This could be a surprise and she didn't want to ruin it. Plus, she had a feeling that Raphael was still on his bullshit. He was acting like a kid and throwing a tantrum instead of talking to Serena. It would have only taken one conversation for him to let Serena know her words and lack of support had hurt him. She got up and went to Raphael's bedroom.

"Hey," she said, pushing open the half-closed door.

"What's up?" he said, turning back to face Moon, whose diaper he was changing.

"Butterfly work today?"

"Nah, but she's pampering herself, so I got Moon," he answered.

75

"Oh, so she knows where we're going?"

"Yea."

"She don't want the whole crew there?" she asked, easing into her pitch.

"She only cares if I'm there," he answered honestly, although it came off as cocky.

"Ssmmk," she smacked her lips. "Whatever. But for real, we should let Mama keep Moon. What's the problem with that? Bug don't want her to?"

"Butterfly don't have nothing to do with it," he said, picking Moon up. She wrapped her little legs around his waist and laid her head on his shoulder with her thumb in her mouth.

"You don't want her to? You still on that bullshit, Phe?" she questioned with her eyebrows furrowed.

"Mama don't like Butterfly." He walked out of the bedroom on his way to the kitchen.

Candy rolled her eyes. They had discussed this and while Candy thought they had come to an understanding, Raphael was still hurt because of how Serena attacked Butterfly's character.

"Yea she does; she just loves your black ass more. She was being overprotective, but she's off that now," Candy said. "I'ma call Butterfly," she said when he didn't reply.

"Leave her out of it," he rushed to say. Candy looked at him with her eyebrows lifted.

"I don't know what you're on, but Mama don't have a problem with Moon, and I trust her with Moon way more than Kwame and Quel. They don't even know how to change a diaper," she said, pointing at the shitty pamper in his hand. "I know Butterfly ain't going for that shit anyway," she said in regard to them changing Moon's pamper.

Unintentionally, he chuckled as he threw the diaper away.

"Ooohh," she said with a smirk as she crossed her arms over her chest. "You know if you leave her with them, Mama will get her; but this way, you can keep up this bullshit act of not asking her to."

"Get out my business," he said, walking past her.

"How long you gon' be mad about that shit?"

"What shit?"

76

"What Mama said about Butterfly."

"I'm not mad. I'm trying to respect her wishes."

"Cool; she wishes to keep her grandchild. I'ma tell Kwame and Quel that they're going. Quel is a freshman now, so we may as well introduce him to Pappy's. And I'll let Mama know you need her to watch Moon," she said and walked off. Raphael smirked as he made his way back to his bedroom.

AS SOON AS RAPHAEL SAW HER, HIS EYES ZEROED IN ON HER STOMACH. They hadn't spoken about it. He never asked questions and she never mentioned it, but he kept a close eye on her. She was dressed in a velvet, black skirt that rested on her thighs and was decorated in crystals and diamonds. She matched it with a blue blouse with deep red and purple designs along the arms of the shirt, and a black butterfly in the center that matched the high waist skirt. The shirt was tucked in allowing the skirt to accentuate her ass and hips. Her thick mahogany legs were oiled to perfection and her black open toed heels gave definition to her thighs and calves. Her 'fro was picked out to its fullest potential and could be seen a mile away.

"You look pretty," he said, kissing her when she was in arms reach. She had locked up the shop and made her way up the block to meet him. At the corner, it took a few minutes to hail a cab. Once one stopped, they hopped in and told the driver their destination.

"How you feel?" he asked her. Unsure of exactly what he meant, she stared into his eyes for a moment.

"Good," she finally answered. He nodded. She smiled. They looked in opposite directions out the window. Her hand was cuffed in his on her lap. He lifted it and kissed the back of it, then continued the drive in a peaceful silence.

"OH MY GOD," Butterfly said with a big smile when she walked into Brother's and saw Candy, Arian, Kwame, Josie and Jaquel. She hugged everyone and had a seat.

"Ms. Serena has Moon?" she asked Raphael. He nodded.

"I thought she knew about it," Candy stated, rolling her neck.

He laughed. "I thought I told you to stay out my business." Soon, they had ordered their food, and everyone was laughing and enjoying their dinner and each other's company. When it was time for dessert, Kwame ordered for Butterfly.

"Nigga, order for her," Raphael chastised him and pointed at Josie.

"I did; you didn't hear me order the German Chocolate cake?" he asked with a wink. Butterfly looked at Josie and they both shook their heads.

After leaving Brother's, they trekked to Pappy's taking a few breaks since all the women had on heels. When they finally made it, they found a table and enjoyed the music. It seemed as if as soon as they entered Pappy's, Butterfly tapped out and Reid appeared. She fussed with her hair in the mirror that took up the left side of the wall.

"It's beautiful," he told her, knowing she didn't like big hair. She was sitting on a stool and he was standing behind her.

"It's big and noticeable," she said, looking back at him. He brought his face closer to hers so they could hear each other over the loud music.

"It's a good thing you ain't killing nobody tonight," he joked and bit her earlobe. She looked at him and studied his expression; he had never joked like that before. Her eyes danced with amusement.

"It's all fun and games until you have to help hide a body," she said.

"Anything for you," he said. He saw her eyes go to the right and followed them. Quincy and Kalia were entering the club.

"I invited Quincy and Kalia," he told her. "They couldn't make it to Brother's because Quincy had to work," Raphael let her know.

"Kalia is best friends with Ebony, right?" she questioned.

"Yea but—"

"She's our enemy," she told him.

"Who?"

"Kalia," she answered. "By default."

"So is Quincy my enemy too?" he questioned sarcastically.

Her facial expression screamed 'hell yes'. "Y'all shouldn't have been doing dirt together."

"Man, that shit is old. I don't want Ebony; hell, I got my hands full. Please be nice, baby," he said as Quincy and Kalia approached them.

"Anything for you," Reid said with a fake smile before she kissed him.

After an hour of jokes and resting their feet, they were ready to dance. Reid led Raphael to the dancefloor, he wrapped his arms around her, and they shared a slow dance. Spinning around, she put her butt on his dick and then slowly rotated her lower body working her way to the floor. In the squat position, her ass cheeks expanded so wide that Raphael grabbed his heart before pulling her back up. With her back to his chest, he whispered in her ear, "You almost gave me a heart attack."

"This is why I don't wear skirts," she said.

"I couldn't see your flesh...the print was enough," he said. He looked up and spotted Melo on the other side of the club; they each threw their heads back as a greeting.

"Melo is here," he whispered in her ear while they rocked to the beat. "Did Butterfly tell you about him?"

"Yea; he was her favorite cousin," she said, rotating her ass on his dick.

"Say hi, baby," he said. "Green shirt, by the rail," he told her. She spotted Melo. Her smile broadened and she gave him a head nod. He lifted his drink to her and returned the smile.

"Thank you, beautiful," Raphael teased in her ear. That was the first time she had done what he asked with no push back. She playfully elbowed him, and they continued dancing.

"I want to fuck tonight," Reid told Raphael. She was now facing him. His hands were on her butt as she gyrated against him. "Y'all can get up early and go get Moon," she said, sucking on his neck.

"First thing in the morning," she added. "Please baby; it's my birthday."

"I got you," he said, lowering his face to kiss her lips.

"Thank you," she moaned into his ear as she continued to grind into him. "These crystals in the damn way. Only Butterfly would want to wear this costume," she complained.

"People stopped her on the street to say how nice it looks," he told her. Reid stopped dancing and looked up into his eyes.

"So."

He held her glare for a moment and then laughed.

"The fuck," she said and rolled her eyes. "You think I care what people said?" She leaned her head on his shoulder and resumed dancing.

"You care what I like?" He asked; his voice was full of lust.

"What you like, baby?" she asked. Her thick lips painted in the deep purple lipstick made his dick jump. She felt it and lowered her hand between them.

"Chill," he said when her hand ran down the length of his dick.

"Not until you tell me what you want," she said.

"I want you to throw all this ass to me, from the back in your heels," he said.

"We'll see," she said. Reid released his dick and turned around to shake her ass to the new song the DJ was playing. It took Raphael a moment to gather himself; she loved to tease him. That was something he had to get used to, because at that moment he wanted to take her to the bathroom and fuck her senseless.

THE NEXT MORNING RAPHAEL LEFT BEFORE SHE WOKE UP BECAUSE HE KNEW BUTTERFLY WOULD WANT TO SEE MOON. He ordered a Lyft to take him home then climbed the four flights of stairs to their apartment. When he walked in, he heard movement in the kitchen, so he ambled in that direction. Serena looked at him and then back down at the oatmeal she was preparing. Raphael took a seat at the counter and watched her for a moment.

"Thank you for keeping Moon last night," Raphael said. She smiled at him as she poured creamer in her coffee.

"I love Moon and you know that. You created the narrative that I have a problem with her," Serena told him. She took the oatmeal off the eye and set it to the side to cool.

"But you have a problem with Butterfly," he said, playing with his keys.

"I don't have a problem with her either, just because I mention my concerns..."

"It's not mentioning concerns, it's judging her unfairly. She hasn't done anything to you or disrespected you in any way. If she had, I would have checked that shit. I couldn't be with a woman that didn't respect my family unit and you know that," he said looking her in the eyes.

"All I said was that you're so...so taken by her that you overlook things," she said.

"I don't overlook anything," Raphael told Serena. "You have to understand that everything that happens in my relationship isn't your business. Maybe there is something about her that confuses you because it's not your business. You have to trust my judgement," he said. Serena bucked her eyes, chuckled and sipped her coffee.

"Butterfly came in and assisted me with the shit I have going on. That's what I needed because of the responsibilities I have. She couldn't be in competition with Candy for my love and attention, she had to get to know Candy and love her too. She moves like a grown woman and that's what I need because I move like a grown man. I always have, even before I made 18," he told her.

"I understand that, and I don't have a problem with that. But she never talked to me about how I want my house ran. She just took over," Serena told him.

"She isn't you, so she may do things different than you, but that doesn't mean it's done out of malice. She pays attention, like Kwame, and then she steps in. It's her way of showing love. She's not trying to take anything from you," Raphael let Serena know.

Serena figured that because Butterfly had been in foster care, she liked to make herself useful. She had heard of foster children wanting to be needed so their foster parents wouldn't get rid of them.

"Maybe I misjudged her," she said and looked up at Raphael. "It wasn't intentional. I just love you," she said. He smiled and got up.

"I love you too," he said and hugged her. Raphael held her until she pulled back and wiped her eyes.

"All you made was oatmeal?" he asked looking at the stove.

"Yea and there's only enough for me and Moon," she said, pouring it into a bowl. "Tell ya grown ass woman to cook for you," she said.

Chapter 10

"THIS IS NICE," KI'ANN COMPLIMENTED, WALKING INTO BUTTERFLY'S SHOP. Butterfly turned around to face her. Ki'Ann's eyes were dancing around the walls and taking in the décor.

"So," Ki'Ann said, finally looking at Butterfly. Her chocolate skin had a red undertone that made her glow so beautifully; that mixed with her huge smile made Butterfly feel safety wash over her. "You're the young girl slaying nails all over Monroe," she said. She was gorgeous from her smile, to her hair, to her eyes. She was dressed in light blue, mid-length jean shorts and a sleeveless crop top. She was also bra-less. Her B-cup breasts didn't need one—her nipples did. They were pressed against the thin material fully alert.

"What's up?" she said, flashing her unkempt nails. "I can't get my shit done?" Her voice was jovial and so was her spirit. Butterfly thought about what her mother, Stacy, had done to her. She wanted to hate Ki'Ann; she was supposed to, right? But Ki'Ann's energy was willing her in a different direction.

She had always liked Ki'Ann. Her sassy attitude and smart mouth excited Butterfly. She would roll her eyes and smack her lips with no fear of Stacy's consequences. She snuck boys in the house, stayed out late, and smoked weed in the bathroom. She was a rebel and unapologetic about it.

"During the week, I only do appointments. I'm waiting on my next client that's why the door is unlocked."

"Damn," Ki'Ann sang as a compliment. She was proud of her baby cousin.

"On Fridays, I do walk-ins, or you can make an appointment," Butterfly told her.

"Okay, Butterfly, I see you," she said with her hands on her hips. "An appointment, huh? For the cousin that used to eat your spinach for you?" she teased.

As a kid, Butterfly hated spinach and anytime Ki'Ann was there, she would eat it for her.

"Unless you want to come back after I close," she found herself saying.

"What time?"

"5:00," Butterfly answered.

"Okay cool. I got some errands to run, then I'll be back," she said with a smile.

"Okay," Butterfly said and walked her out.

HOURS LATER, KI'ANN WAS SITTING IN FRONT OF BUTTERFLY AS SHE USED HER DRILL TO FILE KI'ANN'S NAILS. Ki'Ann could tell she was the truth because even before she started filing them, her nails looked better than they ever did with her normal nail tech. She laid the acrylic perfectly using the brush to shape them and the drill to ensure they were flawless.

"Seriously though, you should come," Ki'Ann said as she smacked on her gum. For the past thirty minutes, she had been trying to convince her to come to Melo's birthday dinner.

"I don't know," she said with a shrug.

"I know you got issues with my mama and Aunt Faith. Hell," she huffed, "we all do, but shit, what could we have done? It's not like we knew what they were planning. When we came home and you weren't there, we asked questions and they lied."

"Where did y'all think I went?" Butterfly inquired.

"They just said you went to live with someone else; we assumed it was your dad or some other family member. It took Stasia getting drunk and cursing them out for us to find out the truth. Melo lost his mind; he moved out."

"Moved out?"

"Yup and he was only fifteen, but he was fucking with an eighteen-year-old. She had her own apartment in Marriot."

They were silent as Butterfly thought about the information she had just received and finished filing Ki'Ann's nails.

"You want designs?" Butterfly asked as she polished the long stiletto nails deep red.

"Naah, maybe next time. I like this," she said and did a little dance in her seat. "They won't be there," Ki'Ann said. Butterfly looked up at her. "The adults. I mean, they will in the beginning, but it's going to turn into a little kickback with just the cousins. You should come to that."

Before Butterfly could answer, Raphael walked in with Moon in his arms. Ki'Ann looked back and smiled at the gorgeous baby.

"You still working?" Raphael asked Butterfly with his face scrunched up knowing it was after hours. The aroma from the bag of food he held made Ki'Ann's stomach growl.

"This ya man?" Ki'Ann asked, smiling at him. Butterfly nodded.

"This is my cousin," Butterfly told him. "Ki'Ann; she's Melo's sister."

"You must be the dude that was grilling my brother at Pappy's," Ki'Ann joked in reference to the first time Raphael saw Melo at Pappy's.

"He was staring at my girl," he replied with a laugh.

"This y'all baby?"

"Yea," Raphael answered.

"She's beautiful," she complimented.

"Thank you," Butterfly and Raphael said in unison.

"I'm trying to get her to come to Melo's birthday dinner," Ki'Ann told Raphael. He looked at Butterfly; she made a face and then focused on her job. "I know she don't want to see our moms and that's cool. I told her she could come after they leave."

"When is it?" Raphael asked.

"Sunday; around nine or ten," she answered.

"Make sure y'all swap numbers. We'll be out Sunday anyway, call when they leave and if we haven't gone home yet, we'll stop through," he told her. Butterfly didn't look up once as she painted on the clear polish. Ki'Ann looked between them and determined that he had some type of control over her. That spoke volumes about him because she knew her cousin to be strong-willed, stubborn, and independent. It made her respect Raphael.

"We already did. I'll be sure to text," Ki'Ann gushed, "and if you don't answer, I will call and call and call again," she kidded.

"I'ma answer," Butterfly promised.

"It was nice meeting you," Raphael said to Ki'Ann as he headed for the apartment.

"You too," she replied.

"We'll be upstairs," he told Butterfly before disappearing behind the curtain.

"YOU GOOD?" RAPHAEL ASKED BUTTERFLY AS THEY MADE THEIR WAY TO KI'ANN'S APARTMENT. She had been quiet and very clingy since they got the call. She wouldn't let go of his hand and if she had to, she would grab his arm or hold on to him in some other way.

"Yea. I don't want to stay long," she told him.

"I know. We're just gonna say hi. You still cool with that?"

"Yea," she answered.

"Who all is supposed to be here?" he asked. He wanted to keep her talking so she couldn't create horrible scenarios in her head.

She shrugged. "I didn't ask. I'm assuming Melo and their sister De'Andrea. Of course, Ki'Ann, and maybe Faith's kids."

"Aight, well I'ma read your vibe so I'll know when it's time to go."

"I know," she smiled as they went up the two flights of stairs. When Ki'Ann opened the door for them, her smile was so wide it consumed her face. Her eyes were low as a result of the blunt she had shared with her brother. The red Solo cup in her hand was filled with a mixture of Hennessy and Pineapple Fanta. The combination had her floating.

"You came!" she sang and pulled her into a hug. Butterfly relaxed in her arms and hugged her back. "Cousin-in-law!" she greeted Raphael with a hug.

"What's up?" He laughed as he hugged her. They walked down the short hallway and into the living room.

"Family," Ki'Ann said, blocking their view. "I present to you, Butterfly "Grandma's Favorite" Reid!" she joked and stepped to the side. Melo was the first to hop out of his seat. He set the monopoly board he had been using to roll his weed on, on the floor.

"Yo!" he greeted. "What the fuck you doing here?"

"She's my present to you," Ki'Ann said.

"Well shit, thank you," he told her and then hugged Butterfly.

"Hi Butterfly," De'Andrea welcomed her with her arms outstretched.

"Hey," Butterfly replied after their embrace. Next, Bria and Brandon stood to hug her.

"Tia's too old for us now," Ki'Ann told her.

"Tell her I said hi," Butterfly said.

"Y'all have a seat," Melo said. "You smoke?" he asked Raphael and then looked at Butterfly, extending his blunt to them.

"Nah, we good," Raphael answered.

"Well shit," Melo said, taking a toke of the blunt. "We just watching movies and shit," he let them know as he sat back down.

After an hour of catching up, Ki'Ann asked Butterfly to follow her. Ki'Ann led her into her bedroom and told Butterfly to have a seat. She went to the dresser and dug into a jewelry box. Turning around to face Butterfly, she handed her a 24-carat gold ankh necklace.

Bewildered, Butterfly stood still as she stared at the ankh. She wanted to reach for it, but her limbs wouldn't move.

"You know what this is?" Ki'Ann asked. Butterfly looked up with agony etched on her face. "It's Aunt Olivia's," Ki'Ann added, figuring Butterfly didn't know. However, Butterfly did know, she had seen it on her mother in pictures.

"Why do you have it?" she finally asked through narrowed eyes.

"Grandma Bev was saving it for you," Ki'Ann told her.

"And how did *you* get it?" she continued to question her. Ki'Ann was thrown off; she had expected this to be a happy occasion, but Butterfly's whole demeanor had changed.

"Don't matter, I never wore it; no one has. I saved it for you," she said with a touch of attitude in her tone.

Butterfly took the necklace and stared at it as it laid in her palm. Ki'Ann smiled and turned to walk away. Butterfly grabbed her arm to stop her and Ki'Ann spun around. Butterfly hugged her tight and hard.

"Thank you," she said.

"You're welcome," Ki'Ann replied and walked out ahead of Butterfly. Butterfly took a few moments to gather herself before walking back to the living room. Raphael stared at Butterfly as she made her way to him. She eased back beside him, and he looked at her. She smiled and gripped his hand.

"We gotta get back home to Moon," he announced a few moments later.

"I can't wait to meet her," Melo said, standing up to walk them to the door.

"Yea, we gotta set that up," Raphael said, slapping hands with him. Butterfly hugged everyone and they left.

Raphael knew something was on her mind, but he had learned to be patient with her. They stopped to get Moon from Candy and then went to Butterfly's apartment.

After showering, they began to get dressed for bed. He threw on his boxer briefs and climbed under the sheets while she sifted through something on the dresser. He watched her slowly walk to the bed and climb in. Sitting on her knees beside him, she handed him the ankh.

"What's this?" he asked, holding it up and examining it.

"Read the back," she told him. Raphael flipped the necklace over and saw *D'Angelo and Olivia* engraved on it. When he looked up, she handed him a picture of Olivia wearing it.

"Oh shit; where'd you get this?"

"Ki'Ann saved it for me," she let him know.

"That's so dope," he gasped. He couldn't tell what she was feeling, but he knew it was intense. Raphael pulled her onto his lap.

"Come here. Come lay on your man and allow yourself to feel whatever you feel." Her stoic face crumbled as she lost the battle of fighting back her tears.

On his lap, she buried her face in his shoulder and cried. Moon began to whimper too.

"Now both of my girls are upset." He laughed and got off the bed to get Moon from her crib. He returned to the bed and they settled in each other's embrace.

With her mother's necklace clutched in her hand, her grandma's earrings next to her on her nightstand, her man holding her, their baby in her stomach, and their Moon latched to her breast, she slowly drifted off to sleep.

Chapter 11

"What's up my man," Melo greeted Raphael, walking into the barbershop. They slapped hands and bumped shoulders before Raphael locked the door.

"Damn it's dark," Melo said, looking around skeptically.

Raphael laughed. "It's late," he said, heading to the back. Melo saw a light on down the hallway and followed Raphael in that direction.

"Thank you for squeezing me in," Melo said, walking into Raphael's section. Melo was his last customer. EJ had already left for the day so only Melo and Raphael were in the shop.

"No problem, but shit, your normal barber ain't gon' run up in here is he?" Raphael laughed as he got prepared to cut Melo's hair.

"Man hell nah; his ass in jail. This shit happens at least twice a year. I'm done with his ass this time. Nigga be fucking up my plans," Melo said.

"Damn you sound like y'all breaking up." Raphael laughed.

"It be that way with a barber," Melo said. After Melo was comfortable in the chair, Raphael wrapped the cape around him.

"How's Butterfly?" Melo asked.

"Good; shit, busy," Raphael said.

"Man, sis told me about her whole setup. Said the shit was nice. I'm so proud of her." Melo beamed with pride as he thought about his little cousin finding her way.

"Yea, she do her thing," Raphael said with a smile.

"I need to stop by, bring my lady to get her nails done or something," Melo said. "She been hinting about getting them done since she saw Ki'Ann's," he said.

"Yea man; the girls go crazy over Butterfly."

"Her mom was into art and shit," Melo said, "so to see her pick it up and take it this far, man the shit just dope."

"Yea; she always talks about her mom, she even has a painting of hers. And y'all grandma too; she talks about the soaps and lotions she used to make," Raphael said as he cut Melo's hair.

"Yo, Grandma taught Butterfly all dat shit. She tried to teach my mama and sisters, but nobody was trying to hear that shit. I guess we thought we had time."

"Yea, her death really changed Butterfly's life. I'm glad she had her lessons though," Raphael said. Sadness washed over him; he hated the life Butterfly had to live, but he was happy she had overcome so much.

"I mean, shit, Butterfly was eleven when she watched Grandma get murdered. Shit, that woulda fucked me up too." When Melo heard the sound the clippers made, he reached back to see if Raphael had plugged his hair.

"Chill man, you good." Raphael laughed, turning the chair to stop Melo from touching his hair. He had plugged Melo's shit, but Raphael knew he could fix it. Melo's comment about Beverly being murdered threw him off.

"She talk to you about it?" Melo asked him.

"Not really, just bits and pieces. What happened?"

"Somebody tried to rob Grandma. Nigga was tweaking out his mind. Tried to kill Butterfly too," Melo informed him. He had no idea that Raphael didn't know any of this.

"She was right there?"

"Yes," Melo emphasize, punching his hand. "Nigga had them both on the couch. The police found Butterfly still on the couch with Grandma. Grandma had fallen into Butterfly's lap. She was rubbing her hair and singing to her," Melo said. Recollecting on the events had him emotional but he fought to remain calm.

"The fuck," Raphael mumbled. He couldn't believe all of this had happened to her and he didn't know any of it.

"Neighbors heard the gunshots and called the police. Them muthafuckas didn't show up for five hours."

"So, she sat with her," Raphael said, more to himself than Melo.

"That whole damn time," Melo said. He was in his head too.

"What the fuck," Raphael said. He was filled with anger. How the fuck could her aunts give her up after that shit? Why did Butterfly tell him Beverly died of an aneurysm? He wanted to put Melo out. He needed to go home and be with his woman. Plus, he was mad at Melo and his people; they were fucking savages.

"After that, Butterfly stayed with us for a few weeks." Melo continued to talk as Raphael tried to concentrate on the haircut. It was hard to focus on the job at hand because a tornado had been let loose inside of his body. "She started talking to herself but would stop talking when we walked in the room. We—"

"I'll be right back," Raphael said. He rushed to the bathroom just as the spew spilled from his mouth. He was hurt, not because Butterfly hadn't told him; he was hurt for her because she had to go through such a horrendous situation and then she was abandoned by the only family she had. Raphael was only picturing what happened, she had to live it. Hell, he would have created personalities after that shit too. It would be insane not to. She had to create a family to fill the void that hers left.

"You good?" Melo asked when he came back.

"Yea man. My bad." Raphael no longer wanted to discuss what happened that night because he was having a hard time containing his feelings. He wanted to take his anger out on Melo, but he knew he was a kid at the time too. Raphael needed some time alone so that he could organize his thoughts.

It took Raphael thirty minutes to finish Melo's cut. During that time, they lightened the conversation. They talked about sports for a while, but ultimately settled into silence. They each had a lot on their minds.

After Melo left, Raphael cleaned the shop and headed to Butterfly's apartment. He used the time it took to walk there to calm himself down. He didn't want to approach the situation by accusing her of lying, even though part of him felt that way. Raphael wanted Butterfly to feel safe with him. He figured that not feeling comfortable was the reason she kept holding things back.

REID HEARD THE DOOR TO THE SHOP OPEN AND CLOSE AND SWIRLED THE BLADE AROUND IN HER MOUTH IN CASE SHE NEEDED IT. The ninja rounded the corner and when she saw her love, she smirked and tucked it away.

"Butterfly forgot to lock the door," she said and rolled her eyes.

"I need to talk to her," he said. Reid took in his demeanor. He was trying to appear calm, but she saw the stiffness in his shoulders and the tightness of his jawline.

"Butterfly is resting; she's sick...you seem upset," Reid said, studying him.

"Y'all keep lying," he said. Raphael knew he had to wear kid gloves with Butterfly, but Reid was tough enough to handle his bluntness. Reid wasn't sure what he was referring to, but she knew Butterfly had told him all her truths, so he must have some things mixed up.

"Anytime you think she lied, you need to talk to me first because maybe I lied," she said, matching his attitude. She stood before him legs spread in a fighting stance with her arms resting at her sides.

"I only asked for honesty," Raphael said after looking Reid up and down. "I don't judge shit, Reid. We've talked, why haven't you told me everything?" he questioned. His tone was softer and his body was relaxed. Raphael knew he had to loosen up in order for her to. He sat in the pedicure chair and she came to stand in front of him.

"What Butterfly tells you is her truth. It's the truth as far as she knows it. And you have to respect the truth that I created because it's what keeps us in sync and balanced. Now what are you pissed about?" she asked.

"How did Beverly die?" Raphael asked.

"Who have you been talking to?" she questioned.

"I told her I was cutting Melo's hair tonight. She didn't think it was wise to tell me? When he said that shit, I was so thrown off, I fucked up his cut," he told her. Reid smiled and eased in the chair with him. She was between his legs perched on her knees.

"Yea but you the best, baby, so I know you fixed it," she said, rubbing his shoulders.

"Reid," he said, pushing her back. She stood back up and stared at him for a moment. He stared back refusing to break eye contact.

She huffed. "She was murdered, baby," she said with a shrug. "Some crackhead."

"And you handled him?"

"No; the hood did...she was beloved," she said emotionlessly. He stared at her; she sucked her teeth. "Your love is transparent...it holds no lies or secrets. I can respect that and I can give you that. But with Butterfly, we have to be more careful. She needs a different type of love; one that protects her...foresees the future and keeps harm from her. She's our foundation; if she isn't okay, we aren't okay."

"I got it."

"So you come to me first. And you trust me if I say she doesn't need to know something, okay?"

"Okay," he agreed.

"She needs to believe it was an aneurysm," Reid told him.

"Tell me what happened."

"A robbery. Butterfly let him in...she wasn't supposed to open the door, but she knew him. He shot her grandma in the head, aimed the gun at Butterfly and barely missed. She peed herself and played dead. She thought she died that day. Until she met you, she wished she had." She chuckled. "You have no idea how much you changed her," she said. He smiled and she continued her story. "We kept her calm through the entire process, didn't let her see the bad. In foster care, before we were placed in a home, we had to stay in a detention center. That's where I created the aneurysm story," she said with a shrug. "I got it from listening to the guards. Butterfly was fucking up in there; she's love," Reid said.

"I know," Raphael interjected. Butterfly was loving, caring and nurturing. Raphael could see how that would make them vulnerable.

"We couldn't really have that," Reid retorted.

"I understand," he replied.

"We had to tighten up in order to survive."

"So, you became the dominant?"

"For a while...apparently I had too much rage. Jiu jitsu helped."

"And the other personality; what's she like?"

"She's more quiet; calm and observant, less trusting. She's good for us."

"Can she mimic Butterfly?" he asked.

"She does a flawless Butterfly; whenever I try, even before you knew, you could tell something was off with Butterfly," she answered.

"Was it Butterfly or her when we met her cousins? I wanna know who I'm with, Reid. I'm not with all the secrets."

"My loyalty lies with them, Raphael. It has to; letting people come between our bond will fuck everything up. In due time, you'll know everything. Please trust us," Reid said.

"She's not sick...she's pregnant," he told her.

"I know."

"Does she?"

"Yes, she's very in tune with her body," Reid said. "She's worried that you're worried. Are you good with it?"

"Of course. She hasn't said anything so I'm letting our vibe do the talking. She knows I know, and she knows I love her."

"True," Reid replied.

"What were you doing?" he asked, pulling her to him. She sat on his lap with her knees in the seat and thought for a moment.

"Research," she finally said.

"On?"

"D'Angelo."

"Why?"

"I want to know more about his wife and Edee. He came by; did she tell you?" Reid inquired.

"Yes."

"Well, I have a new gun," she said.

"So gangsta," he said, shaking his head. "She told me that too, but I don't think you need a gun with him."

"Too late."

"Reid!"

"He can't sit here and watch us. We aren't his possession," she voiced.

"Technically," he said. "I mean, you're his daughter," Raphael told her.

"Butterfly is and she doesn't want to see him," she said, correcting him.

"What did you do?" he asked her.

"I just went outside with the gun and told him if she wants to see him, she'll reach out to him."

"You said she?" he asked.

"No, Phe, of course not. She interjected though," she said, shaking her head. "Started crying." She took a deep breath, wondering if all of this was too much for him. They were piling a lot on him and she knew he needed a way to release it. "It's important that you know the same rules apply...what she told you about whatever we tell you is between us," she said. She raised his face and they were looking into each other's eyes.

"I know that, Reid."

"I just know how close you are with your family."

"Yea, but I'm protective of our relationship," he said.

"I know," she said. "But this is a lot so maybe you need a confidant. I'm your confidant," she said and kissed him passionately. He caressed her body, igniting more fury in the kiss.

"Let's go take a shower," he said, breaking the kiss. Before she could refuse, he lifted her up and carried her upstairs.

"HE WANTS TO SPEND TIME WITH YOU TO GET TO KNOW YOU BETTER," REID SAID.

"We have spent time together; he knows me."

"He wants to know it's you," Reid pushed.

"He knows when it's me," she replied.

"Oh my god! He wants confirmation, okay?" Reid yelled.

Raphael woke up to what he used to think was Butterfly talking to herself. In the past, he never truly heard what was being said, so he assumed she was praying. But there had been a few times that he had walked up on her having a full conversation and she was the only one talking.

He and Reid had ravaged each other's bodies until Moon began to cry. He got up to get her while Reid showered, and then Butterfly got the baby while he showered. They had all climbed in bed to watch TV and he had fallen asleep. Now, it was the wee hours of the morning and the apartment was dark. The streetlight and the sound of her voice revealed that Butterfly was sitting on the couch. Moon was in her lap bouncing and cooing completely comfortable with her mother, Reid and *her*.

"Jada!" Reid yelled when Moon started to whine. *Jada,* Raphael thought and smiled to himself.

"My bad," she replied.

"Lower your voice!" One of them chastised. He noticed that it was difficult to tell Butterfly and Jada a part. Someone started to hum and Moon settled down.

"I don't think it's a bad idea. You said he's good for us, you wanted this," Reid said.

"And we have it."

"Raphael likes to know everything. He just does…like Reid. Just talk with him so he knows you're real; he won't force anything."

"He brought up the pregnancy," Reid revealed.

"What'd he say?" Jada asked.

"He's fine with it," Butterfly said.

"How do you know?" Reid questioned.

"I met him first; I know him."

"I spend the most time with him."

"Are we really about to fight over him? He's all of ours; that was the agreement," Reid said. That made Raphael smile.

"Are you going to talk to him? As yourself?"

"If it'll make you happy. But I like my life how it is."

"It doesn't have to change."

"Butterfly," Raphael called. Eavesdropping on their conversation felt deceptive so he put an end to it.

She cleared her throat. "Yes?"

"What time is it?"

"Late; Moon couldn't sleep. She's just now going back to sleep."

"Come lay with me," he said. She eased off the couch and walked to the bed. She slipped into the bed with Moon on her chest and then slid Moon to her left with her back to Raphael so that she could pat Moon's back. Raphael turned to her and pulled Butterfly's back to his chest and rested his hand on her stomach.

"Did you hear?" she asked.

"A little. Her name is Jada," he said.

"She'll explain everything," she said.

THE NEXT MORNING, RAPHAEL WALKED INTO THE KITCHEN AND INSTANTLY KNEW SHE WASN'T BUTTERFLY OR REID.

"Hi," she said, moving the bangs from her afro out of her face.

"Hey," he said, "can I kiss you...hug you?" he asked.

She laughed. "You have before." He kissed her cheek and hugged her tight. He let her go and took his seat. Raphael did recognize her; her vibe was so peaceful and mysterious. It lured him to her and made him want to stay forever. She placed his food in front of him; there was a bowl of breakfast casserole and a plate of French toast. She then fixed her plate and sat next to him at the island.

"I don't want to force anything on you, Jada. I know you're more laid back and observant; it's your way of protecting Butterfly and I respect that. I just wanna know every piece of her. When it's you, I wanna know it's you. When it's her, I wanna know it's her. That's all I ask."

She nodded her head. "I just like to meditate. It allows me to be in complete peace. That's where I like to be."

"But you're with my family. Doing Candy's nails, talking to her about Arian...bossing the boys around and helping me keep them in line," he said. He knew it had to be her because Reid had already alluded to the fact that Butterfly didn't really care for his family; her focus was him and Moon. "Ma look, it don't have to be a relationship. I just want to get to know you on some friendship type shit," Raphael said, but couldn't help but smile because he knew that she knew that was the same way he got Butterfly. She smiled too.

"Just be good to them, Raphael, and I'll be good to your family," she said. "I tried with your mom..."

"Please don't stop trying; she'll come around," he said.

"I won't; I know she's important to you."

"So, you're only the way you are with them for me?" he wanted to know.

"No. I like them. They feel safe; solid," she explained.

"But you don't really like me," he asked while forking his casserole.

"I love you, Raphael," she said, looking up into his eyes. "For everything that you are, your patience...for helping me with Moon... the delivery. I love how you are with your family. I met you first. I brought them to you," she told him. "I—I made love to you the first time," she said bashfully.

"Thank you," he said with a smile. He wouldn't trade his relationship with them for anything in the world. "I love you too."

"I'll keep taking care of your family and you keep taking care of mine."

"Agreed," he said with a lazy smile. "Come see me every once in a while, though," he said.

"I was with you at Ki'Ann's for a while," she said.

"I thought so," he replied. "And on your birthday too, huh?"

She nodded and leaned over to kiss him.

Chapter 12

IT HAD BEEN ABOUT A MONTH SINCE HE'D SEEN HER. He figured being quiet and still, almost like meditating, brought her out. That and placing his hand on her belly not in an overt way...something covert like a simple graze or kiss. They hadn't said much as they sat on his bedroom floor for the past hour. He walked in and she was feeding Moon; when she was done, he pulled her to him. He didn't press her or question her, he just vibed with her and she responded to that. She was on his lap, her flat stomach, which poked out when she ate, pressed against his. Their hands intertwined. Words were a distraction when they were in their trance...they were almost disrespectful. In moments like this, they allowed their energy to wash over each other and they bathed in it.

After thirty minutes of kissing off and on, Raphael thought about her and how good she was with his family. She provided what they needed before they could even ask...sometimes before they knew they needed it. If someone in the house was sick, she added more garlic to their food. It was a natural antibiotic, so she healed them and avoided the other housemates getting sick without having to say a word.

She had fallen in love with him because of the closeness he shared with his family. Their love for one another had made her feel safe; it made her believe in family again. He felt obligated to offer her that same thing with her own family. Raphael had talked to Melo, and Melo had asked if they could hang out. Raphael thought it could be good for her.

"I saw Melo," he said to her, finally breaking their silence. But he kept their hands intertwined because he wanted to stay connected to her.

She smiled. "You cut his hair, right?"

"Yea."

She smiled again.

"He wants to see you," he informed her.

"I-I don't want to, baby."

"I think it'll be good for you. What if you could have what you have with my family with them?" he asked her.

"What if I can't? Your family is so close, your friends' families are close, so you're naïve to the fact that—"

"Naïve?" he questioned through furrowed brows. *Optimistic*, he thought, *yes. But naïve? Hell no.* He was well aware of the fact that some family units didn't work, but he thought hers, at least with her cousins, could.

"Yes baby," she answered lovingly. That didn't stop him from being offended.

"I understand dysfunction. My family isn't perfect, neither are my friends'. My father left and you know that," Raphael told her.

"You're not trying to rekindle with him," she pointed out.

"He's not trying to rekindle with me. Melo is trying; I feel bad having you the way we do, seeing you with my family, even when you won't be with me," he joked and pinched her side. She smiled. "And not being able to give that to you," he said seriously.

"But you have given it to me, Raphael," she expressed. She loved that he was always trying to give her more, but she wished he'd be at peace with what he provided. To be confident that what he had given her and was continuously giving her was enough.

"I'm fine with seeing Melo out and saying hi, and I'm glad we did the meetup at Ki'Ann's because I was able to get Mama's necklace," she said, picking it up and kissing it, "but that's all I want from them. Everything can't have a happy ending; sometimes you have to just move on."

"But they didn't—"

"But they remind me of it, Phe," she said, raising her voice. She couldn't understand what he couldn't understand. "It hurts me," she stressed and laid on his shoulder.

"I'm so sorry, baby. I didn't think of it that way. I won't bring it up again," he said, rubbing her back. He looked down and kissed her cheek. "Let's lay down," he said.

REALITY TUGGED RAPHAEL FROM HIS SLUMBER AND HIS EYES LANDED ON HER. She was sitting up in the bed looking down at him. She giggled as she watched him stretch.

"You like to go out, huh? To hang with your friends, meet new people?" she asked.

Raphael looked at her; he studied her face and mannerisms. She was pulling one of her two strand twists and wrapping it around her finger. She wore a tiny pair of spandex shorts and her legs were gapped open. His eyes roamed the print of her pussy and his dick jumped.

"And you want your girl to do those things with you," she said.

"What's your name?" he asked, placing his hand on her thick thigh and rubbing it. She giggled.

"Alexis. When you asked Jada to go out with you that time. With your friend...ummm Quincy," she said, "and his girlfriend, you asked what she wanted to trade," she said, trying to jog his memory.

She giggled. He laughed. "That was Butterfly, but yea I remember." She looked confused then shrugged it off.

"Maybe I'm wrong. Anyway. I answered," she admitted with a big smile on her face. He had never seen any of them smile so much; it warmed his heart.

"Your smile is so pretty, baby," he said.

"Thank you," she said. Her sisters had chastised her for being so happy and smiling so much; they said it attracted unwanted attention.

"She doesn't really care about sex; I mean she loves it when y'all do it, but it's enough for her to smell you and feel you; she's weird," Alexis said.

"You like sex?" he asked. She blushed but didn't answer. The crop top that she wore, which exposed the bottom of her breasts, was very sexy. She seemed more youthful than the others; she actually acted like a teenager.

"I don't come out much...too friendly," she said and rolled her eyes to the ceiling.

"What's wrong with that?"

"They don't like friends. We have too much to hide," she informed him.

"How many more are there?" he asked.

"Just us."

"So, four?"

"Yea."

"Okay."

"It's overwhelming," she said nervously. If he started to pull back, the others would blame her.

"It's cool."

"I know you like to hang out and have fun. You can't take Reid because if someone pisses her off, she'll slash them with her blade. And Jada just wants to be up under you all the time; she wouldn't even talk. She'd just stare at you and hypnotize you to get you to leave early, but you like for everyone to interact and have a good time. I can be your date!"

"Oh yea?"

"If you want..."

"Yea, I want that," he said with a smile.

"Good. Where are we going?"

"To meet up with Melo. You think Butterfly will be cool with that?"

"Yea; as long as she can be at peace; she prefers to be there."

"Then we can go to Pappy's," he said; she looked sad. "What?" he asked.

"Reid likes to go to Pappy's with you," she told him.

"Maybe you can ask—"

104

"No," she said, shaking her head. "It's best that we keep a schedule. Everybody has a job; things get messed up when we get outta sync. But if you go somewhere else after Pappy's, I could come," she said.

"We can go have breakfast with Quincy and Kalia," he said.

"Okay," she beamed.

"Butterfly likes braids, Reid likes her hair pulled back, and Jada likes her 'fro...what do you like?" he asked.

She giggled and shrugged. "I don't care; I just like to have fun."

They spent the next few hours around the house playing with Moon and entertaining his siblings. Like always, Candy had no problem watching Moon while they went out. So, they got dressed and left the house around 8pm. Alexis looked sexy in a baby blue blouse that exposed her supple breasts and skin-tight, ripped jeans. Raphael was proud to have her on his arm.

They arrived at Melo's apartment and he was rolling a blunt and watching TV. His girl was still at work but would be joining them shortly.

"Y'all want a drink?" Melo asked as they took a seat in the living room.

"N—" Raphael started to decline his offer at the same time that Alexis was saying yes. They looked at each other and she cheesed.

"Well, I do," Alexis said.

"Cool; I got Henny and coke or Cîroc and pineapple juice," he said, walking toward the kitchen.

"Umm," she said, trying to decide. She had never had a drink before, but always wanted to try it.

"We're good," Raphael said, looking at her sternly. Melo looked from him to her and decided to give them a minute to decide while he made his drink.

"I want a drink," she said, rubbing his knee.

"You're pregnant," he reminded her.

She giggled. "No, I'm not; Butterfly is." He took in her facial expression; she was completely serious. He thought about it and realized Reid never moved like she was pregnant either. They'd each mentioned sharing a space before; he took that to mean a body, but did they understand that?

Melo came back into the living room with his drink and set it on the table when he took his seat in the recliner. "Oh shit," he said, jumping back up. "Let me go get the photo album and embarrass your ass," he said. When he left, Alexis grabbed his drink and took a long swig. Raphael grabbed it from her hand, wasting a little on her shirt and the table. Her face was turned up, both from his action and the nasty taste of the Hennessy. She couldn't understand what all the hype was about.

"What the fuck is wrong with you?" Raphael seethed.

"Why are you being mean?" she said, her eyes filling with tears.

"The same way y'all share me, y'all share a baby; you can't fuckin' drink," he hissed.

Melo walked back in the room. He hadn't heard the conversation but knew they were beefing by the suffocating tension that now filled the room.

"Y'all good?" he asked, looking at the Hennessy on the table. She looked down at her shirt and tried to wipe the brown stain off.

"Yea man," Raphael said. When she snuggled under him and rested her head on his shoulder, he knew it was Butterfly; Raphael kissed the top of her head.

"How much longer, baby," she whispered, looking up at him. Her beautiful big eyes tugged on his soul.

"We just got here, baby. Please chill," he said. "His girlfriend is on the way."

"Why are we even here?" she questioned. He didn't feel like going back and forth with her. Too much was on his mind. His anger with Alexis was at the forefront of his mind, then there was the nagging feeling of anxiety hovering over him. How was he going to get them to understand that they were all pregnant and had to protect their body?

"Look man," Raphael said, standing up. "My bad. She ain't feeling too well...we gotta go," he told Melo.

"Damn, I got the photo album," he said to Butterfly, holding it up with a big smile. She stood, intertwined her arm with Raphael's and looked up at him.

106

"Another time, man. I promise; and I'll make sure we ain't beefin'," he joked.

Melo didn't want to see them go, but he knew what it was like for your girl to have an attitude in public, so he let them off the hook.

"Aiite man, cool," he said. He slapped hands with Raphael and went to hug Butterfly, but she didn't even look at him.

Raphael and Butterfly trekked up a couple of blocks before they made it to the bus stop. Melo lived in Abraham and they were going to Raphael's neighborhood in Royal City, so the bus ride would be about fifteen minutes. Butterfly seemed unfazed. She held on to him as they walked up the block, waited for the bus, and then climbed on when it arrived. She slid into the seat and he sat next to her. She looked at him and smiled as she placed her hand on the side of his face preparing to kiss him. He turned his face forward before she could.

"Damn," she said.

"You couldn't just pretend to have a good time for 30 minutes, Butterfly?" Raphael fussed.

"No," she said unapologetically. She looked out the window for the duration of the bus ride.

At home, she peeked in on Moon who was sound asleep in Candy's bed. She entered Raphael's bedroom, and he was sitting on the bed removing his shoes.

"What happened at Melo's; why did we even go over there?"

"Alexis agreed to go," he said.

"Alexis?" she questioned with an attitude.

"Yea," he said, getting up to place his shoes in the shoebox. He thought about the fact that he knew nothing about Alexis; she had just appeared out of nowhere and he had to flow with it. That was fine, but shit, couldn't they flow with him sometimes? "How many are there?" He hadn't meant to raise his voice, but it was hard to hide his discontent on the outside when so many unanswered questions floated around inside of him.

"Why are you yelling?" she asked.

"I'm asking you a question. Y'all can never answer a damn question," Raphael fumed, using his hands to emphasize his point.

"Yo, why are you cursing, and why are your arms waving the fuck around?" Reid wanted to know. Her voice was calm but the look on her face said she was ready for war, so did her stance.

"Because I'm trying to have a conversation and y'all keep switching out!" he replied.

"What are you mad about!" she yelled.

"Y'all good?" Candy asked, opening the bedroom door.

"Candy, I have asked you over and over to knock," Raphael said.

"You not mad at her, so don't take it out on her," Reid said.

"Thanks sis," Candy said before rolling her eyes at Raphael and closing the door.

"I met Alexis tonight," Raphael told Reid in a lower voice.

"What did she do?" Reid stayed stoic, seemingly unmoved by his new discovery.

"Nothing...she drank," he said, pacing the small room.

"You're not her father. She likes to have fun; y'all have that in common."

Raphael's face contorted into a look of bewilderment. He felt like he was in the twilight zone. "You can't drink if you're pregnant. The same way y'all share me, y'all share the babies," he tried to explain.

"No, we don't," she said.

"What about Moon?"

"They don't trust me with Moon."

"Why not?"

"Some shit the therapist said," she shrugged, "'bout me have sociopathic traits."

He looked at the door and then at her. Reid didn't seem to care if anyone heard. He figured if they did, they wouldn't believe it anyway.

"Y'all share a space, so if someone is pregnant, y'all all have to protect that baby. That's the only way to explain it. That means Alexis can't drink and you have to go easy on the exercising," he said.

108

"Got it, drill sergeant," she said sarcastically.

"How many are there?" he asked, taking a seat on the bed.

"Four," she answered. Her arms were now crossed over her chest and she bore a look of impatience.

"And that's it?"

"Yes."

"Why do you have an attitude?" he asked.

"I'm not the one that has gotten into an argument with three people. Four, if we count Candy. Maybe you should sleep on the couch," she said, working her neck as she spoke.

"The couch?" he questioned as if the word was foreign.

"Fine; I'll just go home," she said.

"It's late," he replied.

"I can protect myself," she said, grabbing her bag.

"Reid," he called in a defeated tone. She looked back at him.

"Come relax me, baby. I'm sorry." His surrender excited her. She dropped the bag and a sexy grin covered her face.

She walked over to him then lowered herself to her knees in front of him. The bulge in his pants made her pussy jump and her mouth water. Reid released Raphael from his jeans and twirled her tongue around the head of his penis before licking up the sides of his shaft.

"Hmm," he moaned. She covered his manhood with her mouth and allowed saliva to build as she bobbed up and down. She could feel his body relaxing and that turned her on. She gazed into his eyes and let the spit ooze from her mouth as she continued to slurp on his shaft. He was captured by her beauty and mesmerized by her freakiness. The door flew open. Raphael jumped; Reid looked back. It was Candy again. Candy was shocked by the act and confused by the abrasiveness that Butterfly showed. She thought Butterfly would be embarrassed about being caught in that position, but Butterfly smiled instead.

Her hand gripped Raphael's dick and started caressing it. The wetness of her saliva allowed her hand the glide up and down his shaft with ease. He grabbed her hand to stop her and she looked back at him. He was stuck; Candy watched them stare at each other;

she was frozen by Butterfly's boldness. When she saw Butterfly's hand start moving again, Candy closed the door. Outside of the bedroom, she stood in shock for a moment. Candy had never seen Butterfly in that light; she had never seen her brother so...weak.

"She'll start knocking now, baby," Reid said and lowered her head back down on his dick. She gathered more saliva in her mouth and let it run down his shaft. Then she moved her head up and down taking more and more of him in until his toes curled. Reid tightened her cheeks and increased her speed as his dick slipped farther and farther down her throat until she gagged and produced more lubrication.

Raphael was lost in a trance by her cockiness and skill. He tried to pull out of her mouth, signaling that he was about to release but she sucked harder; she didn't stop sucking until he had nothing left. Reid pulled her shirt over her head and then unclasped her bra. With her breasts free, she stepped out of her pants and panties. He watched her, still lost by her dauntlessness. He was like a zombie controlled by her penetrating gaze. Finally, he began to get undressed. He removed his shirt as she climbed on the beanbag chair, spread her legs, and began playing in her pussy.

He kneeled before her and ran his tongue up her center. He took her clit into his mouth and played with it with his tongue. Reid didn't like the control he was having over her, so she pushed him back and walked to the bed.

"On the floor, baby; the bed makes too much noise." He said, praying Serena didn't hear them because he couldn't stop what was about to happen even if he tried.

"Sit on the beanbag," she directed. He did and Reid sat on his dick in the reverse cowgirl position. With her hands planted on the floor, she began to ease up and down his dick rolling her body slowly and putting him back under her spell. Before long, she was bouncing up and down; her ass crashing against his pelvis leaving the mark of her juices on his lower stomach. He bit his lip; it was too much, too good, too wet. He let out a low growl then chastised himself for it. The smacking noise their bodies made, and the sound of him plunging into her wetness filled the room.

"Fuck," he mumbled when she started throwing her ass in a circle. He began to play with her clit and that really made her go buck wild. Before he knew it, she was coming and he was right behind her.

They took turns showering and then he climbed in bed with Butterfly. She snuggled under him, deeply inhaled his scent and drifted off to sleep.

THE NEXT MORNING, HE WOKE UP TO HER LEG TOSSED OVER HIS WAIST AND HIS HEAD BURIED IN HER CHEST WITH HER ARMS WRAPPED AROUND HIS HEAD. He ran his hand up the side of her shirt; she squeezed him tight and kissed the side of his head. He kissed her arm and rolled over.

"Candy might have a attitude today," he told her, placing his feet on the floor and checking the time on his phone.

"Why?" she asked, getting out of the bed to go get Moon.

"She walked in," he said. She looked confused. "On me and Reid last night. Reid didn't stop," he told her. She rolled her eyes.

"What?"

"You let Reid do whatever the fuck she wants, that's what," she said, walking out of the room. Raphael could only shake his head; he had as much control over Reid as they did...none.

"GOOD MORNING," SHE SAID WHEN SHE ENTERED CANDY'S BEDROOM.

"Y'all have to be more respectful of my mother's house," Candy said. Her deep-set eyes were squinted, and her lip was curled up.

"I understand," she said, picking up Moon.

"Where was your understanding last night, Butterfly? I walk in the room and you don't even bother to stop? That's disrespectful. She lets you come here and stay the night and the only thing—" Candy continued to fuss, getting up from her desk.

"Heard you," she said, cutting Candy off and exiting the bedroom. After preparing Moon's bottle in the kitchen, she walked back into Raphael's bedroom. He was lying back in the bed; she climbed in bed with him. He turned to look at her as she got ready to feed Moon.

"I'm not trying to beef with you today, Butterfly," he said. Yesterday had been a roller coaster of emotions on behalf of him and his women. He felt drained and wanted to chill and be in peace. He wished he could ask for Jada, but he knew that wouldn't go over well.

"I'm not trying to beef with you either," she said, but her tone said otherwise.

"You mad about some shit that I can't control."

"Your recklessness with one can fuck things up for us all," she stated.

"Making love?"

"If the rule is not to do it here."

"The new rule is don't get caught," he said and smiled. She didn't find it funny.

"Changing the rules for Reid isn't smart. The more control you give her, the more she wants," she told him.

"And what about you? We've been out before and you were cool, but last night you wouldn't even look at Melo. Is my acceptance lessening your consideration?"

"Why was my shirt wet?" she asked.

"Why did you do that?"

"I didn't want to be there; I didn't agree to go," she told him.

"But we were there, so the least you could have done was chill for a minute. I know it's you; I know you don't like to be out a lot. Trust that I got you," he told her.

"You just don't wanna talk about Reid," she said, shaking her head.

"I'll talk to Reid about Reid."

They both looked at the door when they heard a knock.

"Yea?" Raphael called out.

"Can I come in?" Candy asked.

"Yea," he said. He wanted to smile because Reid was right.

"We need to talk," Candy told him. He could tell she was beyond pissed; she didn't even look at Butterfly.

"Here I come," he said. She closed the door and left without saying anything further.

"After I feed her; we need to head home."

"I'll take y'all," Raphael replied.

"Nah, worry about fixing things with your sister," she said. "We need a few hours apart." He didn't reply because she was right. He rolled out of bed to go handle his hygiene. When he was done, he knocked on Candy's bedroom door.

"Come in," she said. He walked in and took a seat on the bed. She was sitting at her desk with a scowl on her face.

"What's up?" he asked.

"You can't keep disrespecting Mama's house," she told him.

"If you would have knocked, you wouldn't have known what was going on," he let her know.

"Then the way Butterfly behaved," she said, standing up and pacing the floor.

"Yea, I know," was all he could say.

"You are so crazy about her. She has you wrapped around her finger! It's like you never had sex before! Why are you acting like this?"

"It's not the sex. I'm in love with her. We were sharing a very private, a very intimate moment together. It was bigger than us," he told her.

"And if I was Mama, would you have stopped then?" she questioned, stopping in front of him. She crossed her arms over her chest and waited for his reply. He rubbed his face and mumbled...

"I hope so."

"Then when she came in here, she had an attitude with me!"

"We're going through a lot right now, Candy. It ain't about you. She loves you...she just...she's mad at me."

"She didn't seem mad last night."

"Like I said, we were caught up in the moment. You didn't hear nothing, right?"

She hadn't, but she didn't answer him.

"See, I learned my lesson. I'm in a relationship now, Candy, so you can't just bust in my room."

"Don't try to blame me for the disrespectful shit you're doing," she said and rolled her eyes.

"And you don't blame her. This shit is on me, but I got it under control now," he said.

"Whatever, Phe. You can go now," she said, sitting back at her desk and putting her headphones on. He shook his head and left her bedroom.

Back inside his bedroom, Raphael saw Butterfly packing their things while Moon was strapped in her stroller.

"Let me walk y'all down," he said.

"We're taking the elevator; we're fine," she told him.

"Let me kiss her, Butterfly."

"Hurry please," she said with an attitude. He kissed Moon and then kissed her. She sucked her teeth and then left.

Chapter 13

"REID IS DOING TOO MUCH," JADA SAID.

"Reid is right here," Reid said.

"Can we all please calm down," Butterfly said. The ladies had been going around and around discussing what had happened with Raphael. Everybody had something to say, but no one had any solutions. When Butterfly first met him, something deep in her spirit resonated with him. She wasn't afraid for him to know every single thing about them; although, she knew she had to reveal one thing at a time. But she hadn't accounted for the pettiness that came with the women having to share him. "Raphael is supposed to add peace to our lives, not chaos," she reminded them.

"It's not about him; it's about order," Jada said. Reid knew that comment was about her, but in her opinion, if it wasn't directed it wasn't respected. Her glare fell on Alexis; she was scantily clad as per usual, looking as if she hadn't a care in the world. She lived in LaLa Land.

"Alexis, who even gave you permission to come out?" Reid asked.

"I matter just as much as y'all," she said. Reid knew she was reciting what Butterfly had told her. "We like to have fun; we have that in common," she told the ladies. Alexis felt that she had sat on the sidelines long enough; when she saw a void in him that the others weren't filling, or even trying to fill, she happily jumped in.

"You fucked up though," Reid said.

"Plus, I thought we didn't want to put too much on him," Jada said. "What did you do anyway?"

"He can handle it," Butterfly interjected, massaging her temples. She had more faith in Raphael's ability to handle her sisters than she had in herself.

"But can we?" Jada said, "I'm not trying to go backwards. What happened, Alexis?" Jada asked, getting back on topic.

"We went to Melo's."

"I told him I didn't want to see them," Butterfly said.

"Well, I thought as long as you're at peace…"

"See, she needs to be monitored at all times," Jada said, throwing her hands up in frustration.

"What's the big deal?" Alexis said, hitting the counter. She was tired of their disrespectful dismissiveness and was ready to demand her respect.

"They are triggers!" Reid and Jada yelled.

"What else happened?" Butterfly wanted to know.

"I asked for a drink and Raphael said no. I just wanted to taste it, so when Melo left his on the table, I took a sip. Raphael snatched it from my mouth and wasted it on my shirt and the table," Alexis explained.

"Yea, he said something about because we share a space, we all have to protect your baby," Reid told Butterfly. It made sense to Butterfly; plus, she liked for them all to be in sync. No one should be drinking alcohol because they didn't know what it could trigger.

"Well, y'all do help with Moon," Butterfly reasoned.

"Y'all won't let me touch Moon," Reid said with a chuckle.

"That was in the beginning; you were very negative," Jada reminded her.

"What about me?" Alexis said. Her hand was on her hip as she tapped her foot.

"You can help with Moon, Alexis," Butterfly said. Alexis smiled big and clasped her hands together in excitement.

"What about this sharing space shit? He wants me to chill on exercising; I need that," Reid said.

"Let's just trust him. If he's saying that; let's go with it. You can still exercise, just not so hard," Butterfly said.

"We still have to come to an understanding with him. If it's us or him we have no choice," Jada said.

"So, you really want to give him up? I just got to spend time with him," Alexis pouted.

"Exactly. So you don't know what we should do. Be quiet and let us figure it out," Reid said.

"I deserve to create a bond with him too, right, Butterfly?" Alexis said.

"Right," Butterfly said. She didn't want to give Raphael up; he had added to her peace and she felt that he could lighten her burden when it came to juggling the girls.

"We need to stay in sync... getting our wires crossed isn't good," Jada said.

"Our wires aren't crossed," Reid said.

"You fuckin' in his mother's house. Candy said you didn't even stop when she walked in," Jada replied.

Reid chuckled. "She needed to learn a lesson."

"Keeping his family happy is important...they are important to him. We have to keep him balanced too," Butterfly said.

"First, we have to be balanced," Alexis said.

"Look at you, making valid points," Reid teased.

"I'm not dumb," Alexis replied.

"No one said you were," Butterfly said.

"I have the personality. I got us the job when we were homeless; I built our clientele," Alexis said.

"No, my art did that," Jada said.

"It takes all of us. We all work together to create harmony," Butterfly said.

"Harmony doesn't always work," Reid said.

"It has to between us," Butterfly replied.

"She got a taste of him, now she wants to hog him," Jada said to Butterfly while glaring at Reid.

"Girl, I come out, fuck him, check him and go. Your jealousy is our biggest problem," Reid replied.

"I wanna fuck him," Alexis mumbled.

"Alexis, stop!" Jada said dismissively.

"He wanted to fuck me," Alexis said matter-of-factly.

"Yea, 'cause you probably had all your ass out," Reid said with a laugh.

"You dress sexy," Alexis retorted.

"But I'm covered," Reid replied. Reid liked form-fitting clothes that displayed her figure and teased onlookers.

"How does this help us?" Butterfly said. "We have to be aligned; y'all know that's the only way this works. Y'all wanna get back on medicine? 'Cause we have Moon now, and she is my main priority. I'd rather Raphael take care of her while we sleep all day than to have her experience us...like that," she told them.

120

Everyone was quiet. They each thought back to how it was before the medicine; they were so paranoid they couldn't even trust each other. It was like they were trying to kill each other in order to be the last one standing. The medicine helped to relax them, but it took away their creativity and made them sleep all the time. So, they learned the importance of a schedule; they each had a role and they trusted each other to fulfill it. Reid needed Jiu jitsu to calm her and strengthen her skills as the protector. Alexis needed her openness and bubbly personality to build relationships; she thrived on human contact. Jada's art ensured that they weren't homeless while calming her spirit, and Butterfly's lotions and oils reminded her of her grandmother and kept her at peace while securing a higher paying customer base.

"I don't want to give him up," Jada admitted. Even though she had been the main one talking tough, she loved Raphael.

"Me neither," Alexis said.

"He needs me," Reid replied.

"I need him," Butterfly said.

Later that night, Raphael made his way to Butterfly's shop. He always spent the night with her and Moon on Saturdays because neither of them worked on Sundays, but this time he was a little apprehensive. They hadn't spoken since their argument that morning, so he wasn't sure how his presence would be received. When he made it to the door, it swung open.

"Hey," he said, stepping inside of the shop.

"Hey," she said, falling into his arms.

"I needed you the other day," he said, holding her tight.

"I heard a lot went on," she said.

"I need to apologize to Alexis," he said.

She smiled. "She'll love that." She let him go and locked the shop, then he followed her upstairs. "Raphael," she said and turned to face him.

"Yea," he said. She stood on the step above him; he placed his hands on her hips.

"Part of your job is to help keep us in sync," she told him. Her voice was calm; she made sure she didn't sound accusatory. They were all in the learning stages of this relationship and she never wanted him to feel like she was expecting too much.

"I'm trying. I—"

"I know," she said, placing her hands on the sides of his face. "And you're doing a great job. Just remember we're four girls in love with one man."

"I know."

"We're trying to make it as easy on you as possible. Reid and I are pretty low maintenance; she likes the physical stuff, me the peaceful stuff..."

"Y'all are all low maintenance really. If I put you all together, it's like having one girlfriend." He laughed. "...With different sides to her."

"I hoped you'd see it that way. We don't wanna stress you; we just all need different things," she explained. "We try to match them to your needs. Everything isn't coinciding the way we want yet."

"That stuff takes time. And you know I'm a patient man," he said with a big grin.

"Yea, baby. I know," she said and kissed him. They continued up the stairs. He walked into the apartment and smelled food; his stomach growled; she hadn't cooked in a while. A genuine smile covered his face.

"We planned an easy-going night for you," she said, matching his expression.

They ate, vibed and chilled with Moon. After she put her to sleep, Reid took over the nightly duties; then he fell asleep with Butterfly. In the middle of the night, she woke him up with soft kisses on his face. She pulled him on top of her and their lips attached like magnets at the same time that he pushed inside of her.

"Shit, baby," she cooed as he lifted her legs and drilled inside of her.

RAPHAEL WAS IN A DEEP SLUMBER, MILES AWAY IN A STATE OF EXTREME PEACE; IN HIS DREAM, MOON WAS RIDING A BIKE DOWN THE SIDEWALK AND A LITTLE BOY WAS ON A BIKE BEHIND HER. He never saw his face, but he knew it was his son. Moon turned to look back at him.

"Look, Daddy," she said, taking her hands off the handlebar.

"Moon, no," he said sternly. He looked up at an apartment and Butterfly was sitting on the balcony in a long, floral dress that flowed down to her ankles. His eyes roamed to her protruding belly and he felt proud.

"Daddy, Daddy," the little boy said, tapping on him. He was too mesmerized by her beauty to look away. When he finally turned to look down at his son, he was pulled from his dream, but the tapping continued. He slowly opened his eyes and the first thing he saw was her gigantic, infectious smile.

"Good morning," she said and giggled. He stretched and turned his face from her.

"Good morning," he said and rolled off the bed.

"I—" she said, scooting to the edge of the bed. "I thought you were looking for me."

"I was, baby," he said with a smile. "Let me brush my teeth."

"Oh, okay," she said beaming.

He peeked in on Moon as she slept in her crib. She was on her back with her arms stretched out. He hurried into the bathroom and handled his hygiene. When he came out, Alexis was standing near the couch in a rainbow-colored thong with her thick thighs and luscious ass on full display and a white half shirt. She blushed as she watched him take in her body.

"Butterfly said you wanted to talk to me." She walked over to him and ran her hands along his broad chest. He only wore a pair of burgundy boxer briefs.

"Yea. I'm sorry about the shit at Melo's. I wasn't trying to waste the drink on you, and I didn't mean to scare you. I just…"

"Don't want me to drink. Butterfly said it's probably best, so I'm sorry too," she said and smiled so big the sun chose that moment to shine brightly through the window.

"I wanna take you out today…maybe we can go eat," he suggested.

"Umm, what about a movie?" she suggested; going out to eat was boring.

"But we're gonna have the baby," he said to her.

"Why can't Butterfly?" she asked.

"I…she," he stuttered for a moment. "I told her I'd watch her."

"Oh, okay. Well, they want me to step up more with her so that's fine. But why can't we go see a movie still?"

"She might cry."

"She might cry at a restaurant too, right?"

"Yea, but the movie is loud; it might scare her."

"Oh, right. Okay," she said jovially. "We can go eat."

"No, I want to take you somewhere you'll like. I know you like to have fun."

"What about the carnival? We could meet up with Quincy and…" she said, trying to remember his girlfriend's name.

"Kalia."

"Yea Kalia, and they can keep Moon if we wanna ride a ride together," she said.

"Okay," he said with a big smile. "Let me call Quincy."

A FEW HOURS LATER, THEY WERE AT THE ENTRANCE OF THE CARNIVAL WAITING FOR QUINCY AND KALIA. Alexis still had on the crop top from earlier, although Raphael had to remind her to put on a bra, a pair of denim jeans, and a baby blue bubble jacket.

"You know they're gonna call you Butterfly, right?" he asked her.

"Yea, baby, I know," she said, making funny faces at Moon.

"And they're gonna think Moon is your baby, so you gotta play the part. But still with your personality, though."

"I know. I got it."

"What's up?" Quincy said as he and Kalia approached them.

"Hey," Alexis said and gave him a brief hug. That shocked Quincy.

"Hi," Kalia gushed.

"Hi. I like your purse," Alexis said and hugged her too.

"Thank you," she said. "Aww, your daughter is so cute," Kalia said, squeezing Moon's hand.

"Come on man," Quincy said jokingly, pushing her away.

"Boy, I'm not trying to get pregnant," Kalia said, hitting his hand.

"Yea 'cause you scared of your daddy," he teased.

"No, you're scared of him. Phe, you should hear him stuttering every time my daddy asks him a question."

"Quincy, I know you ain't going out like that," Raphael said, grabbing Alexis' hand.

"Whatever," Quincy said as they made their way inside the carnival.

"YOU KNOW EBONY IS MY BEST FRIEND," KALIA SAID AS SHE AND ALEXIS WALKED TO FIND THE GUYS WHILE EATING COTTON CANDY. They had separated from them to ride a roller coaster together. Afterwards, Alexis saw the cotton candy line and couldn't resist.

"Uh. Yea," Alexis said, even though she didn't know that; she didn't even know Ebony.

"But I like you too. Quincy said you're super shy, but you are so fun. I think we have good chemistry," Kalia told her.

"I mean, I'm shy sometimes, but I also like to have a good time."

"Ebony gets a little upset when we meet up with y'all. But Quincy and Phe are best friends, so what can I do?"

"Why does she get mad? Does she feel left out because y'all are so close?" Alexis questioned.

"Yea, I guess," Kalia said.

"Well you should bring her next time. I'm sure we would all have fun together," Alexis said.

Kalia looked a little confused and then smiled. "You cool as hell, girl," she said as they approached the guys.

"We're watching the baby while they ride the Ferris Wheel; then we're next," Quincy told Kalia.

"Okay, cool," she replied.

"Just go right there, Quincy," Raphael told him, pointing at the station with the basketball net. "Win your girl a prize."

"Man, you don't have to keep giving me instructions. I'm not going to lose your baby," Quincy said, pushing the stroller away from them.

IN THE LINE, ALEXIS WAS TURNED TO FACE RAPHAEL AS HE LEANED AGAINST THE RAIL.
"You having a good time?" he asked.

"The best time, daddy," she said and moved her face closer to his. He leaned in and kissed her. The motion of his tongue overwhelmed her for a moment, and she pulled back; then she giggled and kissed him again. "Can I stay with you tonight?" she asked innocently. He looked into her big, beautiful eyes and fell in love.

"Yea," he said and kissed her again.

"Good," she said and then moved up in line.

She was standing in front of him and he had his arms around her as they periodically moved up in the line.

"Oh baby, who is Ebony?" she asked, turning to face him.

"Umm...she...why?"

"Kalia brought her up, said she was jealous because we were spending time with them. I told her to bring her next time," she said with a shrug. She walked up a few steps, and finally they were at the front of the line. They were directed to their seat and when they sat down, Raphael turned to her.

"Nah, baby, she can't come," he said.

"Why?" she asked as the attendant pulled the bar down to lock them in.

"We used to date," he told her.

"You still like her?"

"No, not at all."

"Then why can't she come?" He was so shocked by her response that he stared at her for a moment. He didn't care if Ebony came, but if Ebony still had feelings for him, she'd get hurt watching him be affectionate with Alexis. But then he thought about the others. They wouldn't like it.

"It's not a good idea, baby. Not because I like her, but because the other girls may not like it."

"Oh, okay," she said and shrugged.

"I'll tell Kalia it's not a good idea, and if she says anything else to you about it, just tell her I said no."

"Okay," she said. She rubbed the back of his head and leaned in to kiss him.

"LET'S RIDE IT ONE MORE TIME," ALEXIS SAID. She had said the same thing after they finished their first ride, but he had to say no this time.

"No Alexis; we gotta go get the baby. It ain't that fun," he laughed.

She blushed. "I like when you kiss me at the top. And when we're going down," she admitted. He smiled, grabbed her hand, and led the way to find Quincy.

LATER THAT NIGHT, MOON WAS SOUND ASLEEP. They were in bed; Raphael had kissed every inch of Alexis' body and was now on top of her. Her breasts pressed against his chest and his dick roamed at the entrance of her wet tunnel. His first thrust inside of her was so deep, she gasped.

"Oh baby," she said.

"You good?" he asked, looking down at her.

"Yea; keep going, daddy," she said and kissed him passionately. She sank her teeth into his bottom lip as he gyrated his hips in a circular motion dancing between her walls and driving her crazy.

"Damn, Alexis, this pussy so fuckin' wet," he said, lying his head on her shoulder and working his dick inside of her. She pulled something different out of him; the submissiveness in her eyes triggered the savage in him. He wanted to punish her body and the way her pussy was reacting to him told him she wanted that too. Her hand was on his butt pushing him farther inside of her; her mouth was agape and her legs were sprawled as wide as she could stretch them.

He looked down at her and she sucked on his juicy lips as she began to match him thrust for thrust.

"Fuck," he groaned. Her head fell back, and he sucked on her neck. He eased up on his knees, pressed her legs into the mattress and attacked her G-spot with fury.

"Whose pussy is this, Alexis?"

"Yours daddy; fuck me, Phe," she cooed. Now her feet rested next to her ears on the mattress; he was knee deep in her pussy awe-struck by the flexibility of her body and the fact that she didn't try to slow him down.

Initially, Alexis did feel pain, but the pleasure aroused her so much she couldn't stop; she relaxed her body, surrendered to his power and opened herself completely to him allowing him to swim the depths of her. The more she welcomed him, the better the sensation. Raphael began to tease her, pulling his dick out of her and ramming it back in.

"Daaaddyy," she whined. She had wanted to experience sex for so long and she was finally getting it; her mind was blown. "Make me come, Phe," she pleaded. He buried his dick inside of her, pounding against her flesh until she exploded all over the bed.

When he came, he collapsed on top of her.

"Did I do good, daddy," she asked after a few moments of silence.

"Hell yea," he replied breathlessly.

She let out a deep breath. "Good, baby. I wanted to please you." That sentence made his dick jump.

Chapter 14

"SEE PHE THIS IS WHAT I'M TALKING ABOUT," REID SAID, WALKING TOWARD THE COUCH. He came over after work to get her and Moon so they could spend the night with him. Reid was in the bedroom getting dressed while he texted Candy to see what she was cooking. He had already lied and told her Butterfly wouldn't be cooking tonight because she was sick. He looked up at Reid and she wore a pair of panties and a black sports bra; she was holding a pair of jeans in her hands.

"Me slowing down on my exercises has me gaining weight. I just wore these jeans not too long ago and now I can't fit them," Reid fussed as she stood at the arm of the couch. He looked at her forming belly and then up at her screwed-up face.

"Ma, it might be because you washed them. You wear 'em so much you probably shrunk them," he said, standing up and moving toward her.

"No, I didn't! These are my favorite jeans. I don't have anything else to wear. I don't even wanna go now," she told him.

"Over some jeans?"

"My workouts are important; I have to be able to protect us!"

"Maybe I could protect us for a while," he said, putting his hands on her butt and pulling her to him.

"It's not funny," she said as he sucked on her cheek.

"We just gotta get through the pregnancy with Butterfly," he told her. He was now standing up straight and talking in a more serious tone because he didn't want her to think he was dismissing her feelings.

"See and I feel like you're making our world revolve around her, and that ain't fair," she said, throwing the jeans on the couch.

"When you get pregnant, all of our worlds will revolve around you," he said. His tone was flirty and that made her smirk. He planted a simple kiss on her lips.

"Stop playing. I'm not having kids," she informed him.

"Why not?" he asked.

"You would want me to?" she asked.

"Yea. Not right after Butterfly, but down the line."

Her lips curled up as she lifted her left eyebrow. "Hell no," she said and playfully hit him. "It ain't gon' happen; my body is important to me," she said. Reid tried to walk back into the bedroom, but Raphael stepped in front of her.

"It's important to me too," he said with a mischievous grin.

"Whatever. I have autonomy over my body, not you and not a baby."

"Autonomy?" he questioned.

"Look it up," she said, walking toward the bedroom.

"Baby, just wear some tights or a dress," he suggested when he heard her flop down on the bed.

"A dress?" she spat.

"You wear all those tight ass clothes, but you can't wear a dress?" he asked, standing in front of the bed.

"No," she said and rolled her eyes. Raphael rubbed his hand down his face. It was a full-time job trying to safely get through this pregnancy. Whereas he used to spend the majority of his time with Butterfly, he was now spending more time with Jada, but most of his time was spent between Reid and Alexis, who he constantly had to remind to move like they were pregnant.

Raphael decided to give her a moment while he made sure Moon's bag was packed. After a few minutes of sitting on the couch with Moon on his lap and her bag beside him, he called out to Reid.

"Beautiful?"

"Yea?" she replied

"Are you getting dressed?"

"I don't wanna go," she said.

"Ma, we just going to my house. Just wear something comfortable."

"I wanna stay home. Butterfly has an early appointment in the morning anyway."

"You want me to take the baby?" he asked.

"She's yours," she replied.

After kissing Reid goodbye, Raphael made his way down the stairs with Moon. Downstairs in the shop, he pulled out his phone to call Candy.

"Yea?" she answered.

"You started cooking?"

"Damn Phe, I barely finished my homework," she fussed.

"Well look, we can get dinner. Meet me at that shop Bug likes; the one on Jefferson Ave. I need your help picking out some jeans for her."

"Can I get a pair?"

"Yea Candy," he said, shaking his head.

"Cool. I'll meet you there," she said and hung up. Raphael pulled Moon's stroller from the office and put her inside before locking up the shop and leaving.

RAPHAEL MADE IT TO THE CLOTHING STORE AND SAW THAT KWAME WAS INSIDE WITH CANDY.

"Where's Quel?" he asked as he approached them.

"He didn't wanna come," Kwame said. He reached out his hand and he and Raphael slapped hands. Raphael hugged Candy and then she took Moon from the stroller.

"What she need new jeans for? And why ain't she with you?" Candy asked as she led them through the store.

"She got an early client tomorrow; plus, I told you she's sick. I wanna find some like the ripped ones she always wears," Raphael said.

"She's starting to cook less and less," Kwame said. He laughed. "Now that we love her, she like fuck y'all."

"She's like that with Phe too," Candy said, eyeing him. "Is everything good with y'all?" she inquired.

"Me and Reid?" Raphael asked. His attention was on a pair of jeans and before he knew it, he slipped up.

"Reid?" Candy questioned.

"My bad." He laughed. "Butterfly," he said, correcting himself. Candy looked skeptical. "Reid is her last name," he told her.

"I know. I just never heard you call her that. Why you gotta give her so many nicknames?" she said, looking through the rack of jeans.

Kwame laughed. "He probably got one for every mood swing."

"Fuck you know about mood swings?" Raphael said. He wanted to get the subject off Butterfly and her many names.

"Shit, all girls have them," Kwame said.

"Boys too," Candy said, pulling out a pair of jeans and handing them to Raphael. They were a perfect match to Reid's favorite jeans; he checked the size then put them back and got a bigger size. He noticed Candy staring at him.

"What?" he asked.

"Nothing," she said.

"Boys don't have as many as y'all," Kwame said, walking in front of them. He was now holding Moon as they searched for jeans.

"That's what you guys like to think," Candy replied.

"Yea we good," Raphael told Candy getting back to her original question. "Why you ask that?"

"Y'all argue a lot more."

"More like debates," Raphael told her.

"They locked in, Candy; don't trip," Kwame told her.

"Why would I trip?" she asked, holding a pair of black jeans against her body.

"'Cause you love her and don't want him to fuck it up," Kwame said; they all shared that sentiment.

She laughed. "She's alright," she joked.

"He learned his lesson from the last time," Kwame teased Raphael.

134

"She learned hers," Raphael replied.

"Say that when she's around," Kwame challenged.

"Hell nah!" Raphael said and they all laughed.

They spent another thirty minutes in the store before they were done shopping. On the way home, they stopped to get food.

Chapter 15

THE CRISP DECEMBER WEATHER CAUSED RAPHAEL TO SHIVER A BIT. His hands were shielded by gloves and stuffed in his pockets. The hood attached to his coat was pulled tight around his head, which he kept low throughout his trek to Butterfly's house. When he finally made it to the stoop, he heard, "It's about time." He looked up at Candy as he walked into the shop. She had come to get her nails done and was waiting for him to show up because Butterfly had gone upstairs to tend to a cranky Moon.

"What you still doing here?" Raphael asked her as he slapped hands with Arian.

"Bug wanted us to let you in. She went upstairs," she answered. After putting on her coat, she hugged her brother goodbye and they left. Raphael locked up the shop and darted up the stairs. He heard the shower going and wanted to peek in on her, but he had to check on Moon first. She was in the center of Butterfly's queen-sized bed sleeping. When he appeared in the bathroom doorway, Butterfly had gotten out of the shower. She quickly grabbed her towel to hide her stomach. She was now five months pregnant. They hadn't talked about it, they had just vibed about it in the way they did when words weren't powerful enough. He wrinkled his face and then walked to her and pulled the towel down. Her naked body stood before him, its reflection in the mirror.

"You know I know you're pregnant, right?" he questioned and then handed the towel back.

"You never say anything," she mumbled, dabbing her body dry.

"*You* never say anything," he replied, smirking as he watched her.

"Because." She paused and shrugged. "I don't know how you feel," she said. She was now facing him as she leaned against the sink.

"You know how I feel," he said, rubbing her belly. She did know but she thought he would have said something about it by now. He lowered his head and kissed her, slowly, passionately. "Get back in the shower," he requested.

Inside the shower, the water rained down on them as they kissed. He swept her into his arms. She wrapped her legs around his waist and her arms around his neck.

"Be careful," she panted as he entered her.

"I got y'all," he promised as he pumped deep inside of her.

"WE GOTTA TELL MY MAMA," RAPHAEL TOLD BUTTERFLY A FEW HOURS LATER. They were on the bed eating vegetable soup and crackers while Moon laid on her back playing with a toy.

"You tell her," Butterfly said, swinging her feet as they hung over the edge of the bed.

"You scared?"

"She's gon' be mad. I'd rather you handle it. She already don't like me," she said, chewing her food.

"She likes you," he said, glancing over at her.

She chuckled. "Whatever, liar."

"I want us to live together," he let her know. She smiled and looked at him. That was good news; it was something she also wanted but wouldn't bring up. She wanted to grab his face and kiss him but held her composure.

"Me too," she said, holding back the gigantic grin that was fighting to be revealed.

"Our building has some five-bedrooms," he said. She stiffened. She thought he would move in with them. That made more sense to her.

"You could move in here," she suggested as if it were no big deal.

"You know my mom needs me right now, Bug. I ain't tryna miss shit with y'all, either. Your place is too small...the four of us won't fit. Well shit, I guess it's seven of us."

"You already said we equal one; we can fit," she told him.

"But with a five-bedroom, our kids could have their own room," he explained.

"Y'all should move here...to Georgetown," she suggested.

"Shit is too expensive," he said, dismissing her idea.

"Okay," she said jovially. "We can just use this as our love nest," she said with a smile. With his hand cuffing her face, he kissed her tenderly. "When you gon' tell her?"

"You're showing now, shit. I might as well tell her now."

"I wasn't this big with Moon," she said, looking down at her belly.

"I don't want you to hide it anyway," he said.

"I got pregnant fast. She's going to—"

"Stop," he said and kissed her temple. He knew she was worried about what Serena would say, but it was too late for that. "It's gon' be okay," he assured her. "I'ma handle it," he said, kissing all over her face. "Why are you crying?" he asked when he tasted the tears on her cheeks.

She laughed and wiped her tears. "It's my hormones. I'm happy," she said with a smile.

"Me too," he replied as they resumed eating. "What's the plan?" he asked. She looked confused. "As far as the baby," he added. Still, she looked befuddled. "You never mentioned going to the doctor; we don't know the sex..."

"I know how to check the heartbeat and my blood pressure," was all she said.

"And?"

"And I want it to be like it was with Moon."

"We're not delivering this baby, Butterfly. Period."

"Why not?"

"We got lucky the first time. Some shit could go wrong," he fumed. She focused back on the TV. "We're gonna find a midwife at least," he said, calming down a little. "You don't wanna know the sex?"

"No, I want it to be like with Moon... but I'll get a midwife," she said with a slight attitude.

"Cool," he said, standing to go put his bowl up. She rolled her eyes at his back, then began to wonder how she was going to get out of moving into Serena's house.

"THAT FELT SO GOOD," REID SAID. They were laid out on the living room floor after exercising. Over the last week he had been exercising with her which she loved because they got to spend more time together, but she also felt like he was trying to monitor her to make sure she didn't over do her routines.

"Did you exercise when Butterfly was pregnant with Moon?" he asked, trying to find a way to discuss what was on his mind.

"Yea," she answered. He watched her guzzle down half a bottle of water. She was dressed in a pair of his Ethika boxer briefs, a sports bra and a dropped armhole tank top.

"A lot?" he asked.

"That was a crazy time, Phe. We had so much going on; I don't remember how much exercising I did." They were silent for a few moments.

"The first pregnancy was different," he said, sitting up and rubbing her belly. "Come here," he said. She moved so that she was sitting between his legs resting her back on his chest. "Y'all weren't around anyone, but with this one y'all will be around my family. So, they'll touch your stomach," he said.

"They'll touch Butterfly's stomach," she corrected him.

"I know to each of you, you look different. And I know to you guys, Butterfly is the one who's pregnant. But when people see y'all, they see this," he said, showing her a picture of Butterfly in his phone. "So, they'll see her stomach," he tried to explain. She stared at the picture of Butterfly; she had never thought about it that way although it made sense. When she was acting as the dominant, people still addressed her as Butterfly *because that's who they saw.*

"What do you look like, beautiful?" he asked, pulling her from her thoughts.

"What?" she asked a little confused.

"Are you my shade?" he asked, holding out his dark chocolate arm, "or lighter, darker?"

She put her arm next to his and smiled. "We're the same color."

"What else?"

"My body is very toned. I have an athlete's body, but because you restricted my workouts—"

"I'm sorry, baby," he said and kissed her. He could tell by the way her voice started to rise that she was getting upset. "You'll get it back."

"I have small breasts," she said, touching them. He tried to picture her with small breasts instead of the double D's she was blessed with. "My eyes aren't as round as hers," she stated, looking at Butterfly's picture. "And they're a little lighter," she said. "I have full lips," she said. He turned her chin so that she faced him and kissed them. "I have hips. They come from my rigorous workouts." She ran her hands over them then circled to her butt. "And a—," she started.

140

"I know you got ass," he said. She laughed and winked at him. She took his phone and studied the picture of Butterfly.

"You see me as her?" she asked him.

"Not anymore, beautiful," he replied with his face buried in her neck; even after a workout she smelled good. She blushed.

"Stop tryna turn me soft," she said, pushing him away.

He laughed. "I'm tryna prepare you so you won't cut nobody."

"You told them?"

"Not yet. Tomorrow," he said.

"If they're gonna have an attitude, don't take her over there; wait 'til they calm down," she warned.

"They won't have an attitude," he said.

"Good 'cause I don't wanna cut nobody," she said, making him laugh.

BUTTERFLY WALKED INTO SERENA'S HOUSE AND AUTOMATICALLY KNEW RAPHAEL HAD TOLD HER. The energy in the house was off and the tension was thick, which immediately altered her mood. She loved his family, but the fear of being judged always made her defensive. She inhaled deeply and bit her bottom lip as she made her way to Raphael's bedroom.

"Hey." She heard from behind her. She turned and saw Jaquel smiling at her.

"Hey," she said with a forced smile. He hugged her and walked out the door. She took a seat on the bed and waited for Raphael. When the bedroom door opened a few minutes later, she looked back and saw Candy entering the room. She approached the bed with Moon in her arms, both wearing a big smile on their faces.

"Congratulations," Candy said, sitting with her.

"Thank you," Butterfly said, taking Moon into her arms. She kissed her cheeks as Candy rubbed her belly.

"Whoa," she said, astounded at the size of her hard, round stomach. "How far along are you?" she asked. When Raphael announced that she was pregnant, Candy figured she was no more than a few weeks.

"Five months," she answered.

With a big grin, Candy said, "Y'all love keeping secrets. Do you know what it is?" she asked.

"No, we'll find out when I have the baby."

"What do you want?" she inquired.

"A boy, but I'm cool either way," she shrugged and then added, "we're gonna have more." The nonchalant tone in her voice made Candy's jaw drop. "Not anytime soon," Butterfly rushed to say with her face wrinkled.

Raphael walked in; his eyes lovingly fell on Butterfly who couldn't hold the grin that covered her face.

"I'll give y'all a minute," Candy chuckled and took Moon from Butterfly before she exited. Butterfly stood and walked to Raphael.

"You told them I see," she said.

"Yea, I had a conversation with my mama first, then I told my siblings," he told her.

"What'd she say?" she finally asked.

"She was cool," he lied and walked over to the bed.

"Don't you lie to me," she said, turning to face him. He pulled her to him and kissed her stomach.

"I want y'all to be moved in before the baby gets here," he told her.

"I thought we were getting a five-bedroom?" she mentioned, to buy herself some time.

"We are, but Mama said that could take a while. I'ma go talk to the super tomorrow," he let her know.

"How does she feel about us moving in?" she questioned.

"She understands," he answered. That wasn't enough for Butterfly; it was important that she and her sisters felt comfortable in their home. The fact that Serena didn't like the situation let her know that they wouldn't be. *She understands*, she thought and then chuckled slightly as she sat on the bed.

In addition to the issues with Serena, there were other issues to consider, such as Reid needing room to exercise and Butterfly liking to take long, quiet baths. And what about sex? Would they have to be quiet from here on out? She didn't feel that he was thinking clearly; he knew everything that she came with and yet he was trying to confine them to a crowded living space with a woman who didn't like her. Plus, Reid wouldn't cower to Serena. How would that work?

"It's gon' be fine," he said, standing in front of her. He could sense her reservations, but he knew that she and his mother could work it out. They both loved him, Moon and the future baby and because of that, they would find common ground. Once they did, that energy would be passed on to Reid, Jada and Alexis and they could live in harmony...or close to it.

Serena and Butterfly had more in common than they knew and because of it, Raphael knew that when they finally built a relationship, it would be untouchable. Until then, he had to play the middleman and keep the peace.

"Y'all should talk...build a relationship," he suggested.

"We talk," she retorted. Her tone let him know that she felt that talking wasn't going to solve anything. "I tried."

"Y'all make small talk here and there, but y'all should get to really know each other," he said.

"I'm open to her, Phe," she fussed. "As open as I can be. Who I am is enough for everyone except her." In Butterfly's opinion, their lack of a relationship wasn't her fault. She hadn't pushed Serena away; it was the other way around.

"She doesn't know that you're open...maybe that's why she has reservations."

"Is that what she said?"

"You're guarded, Bug." He saw the expression on her face and rushed to finish his thought. "For good reason, but since she doesn't know any of that, she just feels...like you're sneaky." He could tell by the frown on her face that he wasn't making it any better. He sensed an intense argument on the rise, so he took a moment to gather his thoughts.

"I get it, and you don't have to tell her anything. I'm just saying, she can tell that you always change the subject. She feels like she doesn't know anything about you and that makes her hesitant," he explained.

"As long as you know everything," she whispered. He smiled and sat beside her.

"Don't misunderstand me, Bug, I'm not saying go tell her everything or even anything at all; I'm just trying to get you to see it from her perspective."

"I get it."

"I'm not trying to make you uncomfortable," he told her. She was looking down at the floor. He took her chin into his hand and pulled her face to his, "I like being your secret keeper," he said against her lips.

"I know," she said with a smile. "I want to build a relationship with her, but she's going to have to judge my actions to know that I'm good for you," she said.

"You just gotta spend time with her. Like you do with Candy," he said.

She wanted to be cool with Serena, but she was a natural introvert, so she didn't like trying to think of conversation topics or forcing relationships. Her relationship with the others seemed to form naturally, but with Serena it was hard work. It felt strained from the beginning. Cooking for her hadn't worked, and neither had lightening her load. But she knew the importance of forging a relationship with her, so she would put her reservations to the side and try again.

THE NEXT DAY, SERENA, CANDY, JOSIE AND JADA WERE IN THE KITCHEN MAKING DINNER. Butterfly was supposed to be doing this because she agreed to mend the relationship with Serena. But since Raphael had accused Jada of taking advantage of his acceptance and no longer trying to get along with others, she saw this as an opportunity to prove him wrong.

They had decided on steak and potatoes for dinner, so she was busy peeling and slicing potatoes and watching her pot of beans while Serena seasoned the meat. Josie was making broccoli rice casserole using her family's recipe and Candy was grilling vegetables.

"How many months are you, Butterfly?" Josie asked. The cat was out of the bag about her pregnancy, but she and Serena still hadn't discussed it.

"Five months," Jada answered.

"Daanng," Josie sang and looked up at her.

Candy laughed. "She loves keeping secrets."

"I don't love keeping secrets," she said, slightly annoyed. "I'm just a private person," she mumbled.

"I thought we were best friends though," Candy teased.

"She don't hear, see or care about no one but Phe," Serena commented. Although Jada knew how important it was to Butterfly that Serena saw how much she loved Raphael, that statement felt more like a dig.

"I hear, see and care about a lot of things," she uttered.

"Yea, as long as it's centered around Phe. Kwame told me how you hog him," Josie said and looked at Serena. They both threw their heads back and laughed. Part of her knew they were playing with her and that she shouldn't take it seriously, but another part felt attacked. They all laughed, clearly oblivious to the fact that she hadn't so much as smiled. When she was done with the potatoes, she washed her hands.

"I'ma go lay down for a while," she told them, already heading to Phe's room.

"See," Candy said, and they all laughed. "Come on, Josie, we can watch a movie while the food cooks," Candy said, leading Josie to her bedroom.

Inside Phe's bedroom, she paced the floor for a few minutes trying to calm down. She was fighting hard not to overreact, but she was upset about being the butt of their jokes. She wasn't sure why it bothered her so much; maybe because of the pressure they felt to make Serena like them. She grabbed her bag and started shoving their things inside.

"What are you doing?" Alexis asked her.

"Leaving," she said.

"But Phe expects you to be here. I'll take over," she said.

"No; it's not me, it's them. I'm not about to kiss their asses," she fumed.

"No one asked you to; you're being too emotional. They were joking with you," Alexis tried to explain. "His family always jokes," she added.

"They have an issue with the way I love Phe," she replied.

"No, they don't; you're overreacting."

She sat on the bed for a moment and tried to relax. But her spirit wouldn't settle, so she grabbed Moon and her things and darted out the front door without saying goodbye.

RAPHAEL DRUG HIS TIRED BODY INTO THE HOUSE AFTER A LONG DAY AT THE SHOP READY TO EAT AND CHILL WITH HIS FAMILY. He opened his bedroom door and they weren't there, so he ambled towards Candy's bedroom expecting to see Butterfly when he opened the door.

"Where she at?" he asked Candy through furrowed brows.

"She went home," she answered.

"Why?"

"I don't know. I grilled vegetables for her and everything, but when I went to get her, they were gone."

"Did something happen?" he asked. Butterfly was supposed to be there when he got home; she knew it and he knew it. She hadn't even called to say she was leaving.

"No," Candy shrugged. It never dawned on her that their jokes had offended Butterfly. She loved Butterfly and would never purposely hurt her, she figured Butterfly knew that.

"Aiite," he said, closing her door. He sighed as he strolled back to his bedroom. Blowing out a frustrated breath, he pulled out his phone to call Butterfly. "Where are you?" he asked when she answered.

"Home."

"Why?" he asked, annoyed.

"You don't have to come," Jada said, sensing his irritation.

"You couldn't tell me you were leaving?" he asked. She was silent, something he noticed she did as a way of apologizing when she knew she was wrong.

"I'm on my way," he said.

"I—" she started, but abruptly stopped when she heard the double beep which let her know he had hung up. She stuck her hand in the big cup of ice she had been eating and tossed some in her mouth.

RAPHAEL ARRIVED AND THEY DIDN'T SPEAK AS SHE LED THE WAY BACK UP THE STAIRS. Alfredo pasta topped with a crunchy chicken breast cut into thin slices was waiting for him. He washed his hands and sat down to eat as she poured his drink and set garlic bread and a salad next to him. He still didn't speak.

"Good night," she said and headed to the bedroom. She crawled into bed and counted down the moments until he would join her.

She heard him clean his dishes: *three*, she thought. She listened as he started the shower: *two*, she thought. Twenty minutes later, the shower stopped and a few minutes after that, the bathroom door opened. "One," she said and exhaled deeply. Within moments, he was kissing Moon's cheek and crawling into bed with Jada.

"I'm sorry," she said.

"What happened?"

She shook her head before she answered. "They were making fun of me."

"Who?"

"All of them: Josie, Serena, and even Candy," she answered.

"Making fun of you how?" he questioned. Candy had told him she didn't know why Butterfly was upset and he knew she wasn't a liar.

"Just saying that I only care about you."

"What?" he asked, raising up on his elbow and staring over at her. He couldn't see why that offended her so much when Reid had even said that she only cared about him and Moon. She looked back at him feeling a mixture of stupidity for getting mad and misunderstanding that he too couldn't empathize with her feelings.

"It's the way they were saying it," she mumbled, rolling back over. "And it was all of them...laughing and... I don't know, I felt," she stopped and smacked her lips. "Just forget it."

"Baby, they were playing; and what's so bad about loving me?"

"They kept saying that I only love you and that I do things only because of you."

"Don't y'all want my mama to know how y'all feel about me?"

"Not like that, Raphael."

"Well, then how?"

"You don't understand," she accused. He could tell he wasn't going to win this battle. She was pregnant and he didn't want to further upset her, so he conceded.

"I get it, baby," he said, lying behind her and wrapping his arm around her. He rubbed her belly as their baby kicked and soon, they all drifted off to sleep.

Chapter 16

"GET HIM ON THE PHONE," REID SAID, STORMING INTO THE APARTMENT. Raphael looked at her confused; she had been downstairs in the office "working on something" as she told him. Now, she was barging into the apartment enraged. Reid had fire in her eyes, glaring at him as if he was the enemy.

"Yo, chill; Moon is asleep," he said, walking toward her.

"Get him on the phone," she said again. She paused after each word.

"Who, Reid?" he asked, placing his hand on her side. Her body was hot.

"Her father," she replied.

"And why am I—"

"Raphael!" she said, cutting him off. "Call EJ, get his number and hand me the phone," she instructed.

"Reid!" he said, matching her tone. She leered at him. "I'm not who you're mad at, so don't take it out on me. Calm down and tell me what happened. What is this about?"

"Her mother," she answered. He could tell she was trying to do as he asked; he respected the fact that she had relaxed her body and softened her eyes. Raphael pulled out his phone and called D'Angelo; he already had his number so that when this moment came, he wouldn't have to go through EJ.

"Raphael!" D'Angelo greeted. "Meh so happy ya called." D'Angelo's loud voice boomed through the phone.

"She wants to speak to you," Raphael said.

"Glad ta hear it," D'Angelo said. Raphael could tell he was smiling from ear to ear; unfortunately for him, this wasn't a happy occasion. He handed her the phone.

"I thought you handled Edee," she said.

"What?"

"You told Raphael that you handled it," she reminded him.

"I did," he replied.

"She's alive," Reid retorted. She reported the news as if it was information he couldn't possibly have. Because if he did, how could he consider her handled?

"Okay," he said. D'Angelo was old school, so talking over the phone was a no-no for him. Still, he was on the phone with his daughter and he didn't want to mess that up. He felt that it was the first step.

"Olivia is dead and she's alive; you didn't handle shit," she spat venomously.

"Trust me, 'er life has been hell. Dere are tings far worse than death," he tried to explain as discreetly as possible.

"Like?" Reid asked.

"Let's meet up," he said cheerfully. He was currently in Kemet, but a trip to Alexandria to see his daughter would be his pleasure. "Some-tings shouldn't be discussed over de phone," he said.

Reid hung up without replying. She wasn't interested in seeing him, and the fact that he brought it up felt like a con to her. He wanted what he wanted...Butterfly. She wanted death to come to Edee; that meant they had nothing else to speak about. Raphael watched her pace the floor for a few seconds before his phone rang. He looked down to see D'Angelo calling back and silenced it.

"I'm going to see her," Reid said to Raphael.

"No."

"What?" she questioned. Her nose was turned up; she loved him, but he wasn't her boss. She only told him her plans out of respect. She wasn't asking for permission.

"That's not safe right now," he said, placing his hand on her belly. It was non-existent to her, but she knew what it symbolized.

"I would never hurt Butterfly or anything attached to her. I just want to see Edee. I'm not going to do anything," Reid told him.

"I don't trust that," he admitted. That was like a blow to the face to her.

"Why would I lie to you?" she asked.

"You may feel differently when you see her," he explained.

"I think logically, remember? I need to see her, then I will plan, next I will execute."

"Wait until we have the baby." He didn't want her to do anything at all, but figured he'd cross that bridge when he got there.

"To execute?" she asked.

"For any of it," he answered.

"To execute," she said as a statement this time.

OVER THE NEXT COUPLE OF DAYS, RAPHAEL HAD BEEN WATCHING BUTTERFLY LIKE A HAWK. He wanted to make sure Reid didn't get the chance to go see Edee. But the fact of the matter was he had to work, so he couldn't watch her 24/7.

Finally, the opportunity presented itself for Reid to sneak away for an hour. With Moon in tow, she traveled by train to the address she had for Edee in Marriot projects. She prayed the address was still current because she didn't have time to go on a wild goose chase. She arrived at the Marriot projects and attempted to take the elevator to the ninth floor where Edee stayed, but it was broken. She was thankful that she had ditched Moon's stroller or else she would have to climb the nine flights of stairs with it.

At Edee's apartment, Reid was disappointed. No one answered after she had knocked five times and when she put her ear to the door, she didn't hear anyone moving around. The last thing she wanted to do was ask a stranger about her. Reid looked at her watch and knew this was a failed mission; she had to get back to the shop because Raphael was coming over after work.

"Butterfly!" She heard a woman call out as she reached the seventh floor. She turned to see who it was but didn't recognize her. She was a beautiful, brown-skinned woman with long, blonde extensions and the body of a video vixen. She looked familiar, but Reid couldn't place her. Then it hit her; the woman who taught Butterfly to do nails.

"What are you doing here?" Sienna asked and pulled her into a hug. When she did, she felt Moon who was strapped across Reid's chest. She pulled Reid's coat open and looked at the baby. Moon cooed and Sienna gasped.

"Oh my... is she yours?"

"I...yea; she is," Reid said. In her mind, she was trying to figure out how to make this moment work for her. She didn't think it was a coincidence that she ran into one of the women who had nurtured Butterfly. Sienna had gone as far as to allow Butterfly to stay at her shop and work there rent free. Reid knew she could use Sienna's love for Butterfly to her benefit.

"She's beautiful; are you with the dad?" Sienna asked.

"Yea," Reid said; thinking about Raphael made her smile and that made Sienna smile.

"What are you doing here?" Sienna asked.

"What are you doing here?" Reid asked as they descended the stairs.

"You know I'm a project baby! I have a non-profit now; we come out here twice a month to feed the residents. I was delivering a couple of plates to people who can't make it to the food truck," she explained.

"Oh," Reid said. Her mind immediately went to Edee. If she was truly in the shape that D'Angelo alluded to, she had to be at that food truck.

"Ya man from Marriot?" Sienna asked.

"Nah. My mom's old friend. I was looking for her, but she didn't answer," Reid said. She switched her tone and demeanor to match Butterfly's.

"What's her name? I know everybody out here," Sienna said.

"Edee," Reid said. She noticed that Sienna's body tensed, and she looked worried.

"Your mother ran with Edee back in the day?" she asked.

"Not really; they were acquaintances," Reid replied.

"Oh, well she's different now. She got into an accident some years ago. Had acid thrown in her face and fell off the fire escape on the fourth floor. She's crippled now...has a limp. The acid scarred her face and caused her to go blind," Sienna said. "If you saw an old picture of her, that's not her anymore. I want you to be prepared. She's not mink coat, fly clothes-wearing, hair-always-perfect Edee anymore."

"It's cool. I didn't really know her then. I just want to see her, not talk to her. If she's too bad off, I'll just head home," Reid said.

Sienna led her to the picnic area in the back of the projects. Some people were sitting down eating and others were in line at the food truck. When Sienna saw the long line, she picked up her pace; she needed to go help her workers.

"That's her," Sienna said over her shoulder. "Come see me before you go," she said, heading to the food truck.

Reid positioned herself on the other side of the table and watched Edee. She didn't want to look suspicious, so she played with Moon so that she would look like a young mother tending to her baby. Edee's face was burned from the acid and those burns had turned into scars that turned into keloids. Her short, thin hair was pulled back into a ponytail. Her clothes were raggedy and the coat she wore was two sizes too big with holes along the bottom.

Ten minutes passed before Edee grabbed her cane and struggled to stand. People saw her helplessness as she grabbed her trash, but no one tried to help. She limped to the trashcan using the cane as her guide and threw the plate, cup and napkin away.

After tying a sleeping Moon onto her back, Reid put her coat back on to shield Moon from the cold and any evil acts she may not be able to stop herself from committing. She discreetly followed Edee into the building and up the stairs. Edee fumbled with her key trying to get it in the keyhole. Reid touched her hand, steadying it, and helped her ease the key into the keyhole. Edee smiled; no one had helped her in a long time. People treated her like she had the plague. Even her family, who she had once taken care of, had abandoned her.

"Who are you?" Edee asked; she smiled revealing her stained teeth. One of her front teeth was chipped.

"You don't know me." Reid's voice was low and sinister as she squeezed Edee's fragile hand. Edee immediately became terrified. "But you killed someone very valuable to me," Reid said. Fear paralyzed Edee; she couldn't run or scream, not that anyone would help her anyway. "Because of it, I'm going to kill you," Reid whispered in her ear. The hairs all over Edee's body stood as she shook with fright. Tears ran down Edee's face. "Wait for me," Reid said and walked away.

RAPHAEL WAS SITTING ON THE STOOP WHEN SHE WALKED UP THE BLOCK WITH TWO GROCERY BAGS IN HER HANDS. Moon was strapped to her chest lying her head down with her thumb in her mouth.

"Why didn't you call, Jada?" he said, making his way to her.

"I stopped to get one thing and then I had a basket full," she said with a smile. "Kiss me," she said because he grabbed the groceries and started walking to the apartment.

"My bad, baby," he said and turned around to kiss her. They entered the shop and made their way up to her apartment. He sat the groceries down while she untied Moon. She was bouncing up and down ready to see Raphael. He grabbed her and kissed her.

"Hi, fat mama," he said.

"What did you do today?" he asked, looking at her skeptically.

"Nothing. Work. I had two clients, then I went to the grocery store," she answered.

"Has Reid…said anything?" he asked. He didn't want to say too much; he knew Reid had to protect Butterfly, and that there were certain things he needed to keep between himself and Reid.

"About what?" she asked as she put the groceries away.

"I don't know," he said. He figured he had said too much. Raphael had never asked for one of them specifically, but he was considering it. He really needed to make sure he and Reid were on the same page.

"Are y'all fighting?" she asked. "Do you want her?" He heard the attitude in her voice and changed his mind about asking for Reid.

"I'm just asking if she's done anything," he said.

"No," she answered truthfully. But she wouldn't know if Reid had done anything unless Reid told her.

"Okay. Damn, calm down," he said, hugging her from behind. She looked over her shoulder at him and they kissed.

RAPHAEL: CAN YOU COME TO THE SHOP?

Butterfly: You want food?

Raphael: D'Angelo is here.

"Why is he telling me that D'Angelo is there?" Jada said.

"D'Angelo is where?" Reid asked.

"At the barbershop," she answered.

"I'll handle it," Reid said.

"What's going on, Reid? Butterfly won't like this."

"Leave her in peace. Nothing is going to happen to him. Let me play my role," she said.

After getting dressed in black jeans and a black sweater with Monroe written across it in red, she parted her hair down the middle and braided it back. She grabbed her black trench coat and Moon's bag and reviewed the list that Butterfly had created to make sure she had everything, then she ran down the stairs. She pulled the stroller out of the office, set the alarm and with Moon strapped in her stroller, Reid rushed out of the shop.

Reid made it to the barbershop and entered through the back so that she could give Moon to Raphael before she went to the front to talk to D'Angelo. She was surprised to see D'Angelo sitting in Raphael's room. He wore a pair of slacks and a collared shirt. His leg was crossed over his knee as he talked to Raphael without a care in the world. When he saw her, he stopped talking and smiled.

"Meh girls are 'ere," he said and stood up. "And one on de way," he said, looking at Raphael. Raphael laughed and rubbed her stomach.

"Baby, will you watch her while I talk to him outside," Reid asked.

"You don't have your gun, do ya?" D'Angelo joked.

"Always," Reid replied.

"Talk in here," Raphael said. He kissed her cheek and took Moon from the stroller. She watched him walk out of the room before turning to face D'Angelo. He wanted to hug Butterfly but nothing about her demeanor said that was okay.

"She's still alive because..." Reid asked.

"Edee had a lot of enemies, but as long as she was attached to me, she was protected. But she took some-ting that meant every-ting to me, so meh took meh protection. Meh neva told no one to do nothing to 'er; that was 'er karma," he said, taking a seat.

"She's alive; she enjoys food, she can walk and talk and *breathe*," she gritted.

"She's broke, Butterfly, and ugly and alone. Money, beauty and popularity, that was all she ever cared about and now it's all gone," he said.

"She's blind; how does she know she's ugly?"

"How do ya know dat?" he questioned, crossing his leg. She didn't reply; inside he was beaming, she was his daughter through and through. "Trust me, meh know Edee. She wakes up and touches 'er face every day. She feels de scars. She gets disability, lives in the projects; she always thought she was better than dat. She hates her life; meh know dat."

"If she hates it so much, why hasn't she killed herself?"

"She isn't brave enough. Killing 'er is doing her a favor; you're taking her out of 'er misery. Let her wallow," he said. His words really resonated with her; plus, she related to his cold, calculated demeanor. She rolled her eyes and left the room.

Raphael was right outside the door. Moon, who had begun to walk, was waddling back and forth clapping at her progress.

"You good?" he asked.

"Yea," she answered.

"Meh see ya later," D'Angelo said, exiting the room. "Hey, pretty girl," he said, kneeing down to Moon. "Can you say Poppa? All ya cousins call me Poppa," he told her. Moon smiled and wobbled away.

"We need to talk," Raphael said when D'Angelo disappeared up the hall.

"I know," she said. She pulled Moon's stroller out of his room and into the hallway. He placed her inside.

"Be there when I get home," he said. She nodded and made her exit.

"WHAT HAPPENED?" Raphael asked, later that night.

"I went to see her; that's it," Reid said.

"And?"

"She's in bad shape like he said," she replied. She had just finished her nightly workout when he arrived. Now, they were sitting at the counter eating the takeout he had brought. He wasn't staying the night; he just needed to see her.

"Is that enough for you?"

"Not really," she replied.

"We have a family," he said. He didn't want to get upset; he knew how she thought and why she thought that way, but he needed her to be on a different type of time now.

"I don't have that thing that other people have. That...feeling that says, 'this is wrong; don't do it'. That impulse. I just know to protect Butterfly," she told him. She stood from the counter and walked to the trash to throw away her half-eaten food container. He finished his last bite and did the same. After kissing Moon, Reid walked him out.

"Do you trust me?" he asked at the front door of the shop.

"Yes."

"Then let me be your impulse," he said. He kissed her and left.

Chapter 14

THE MISEDUCATION OF LAURYN HILL PLAYED THROUGHOUT THE APARTMENT EMITTING A TRANQUIL ATMOSPHERE AS SHE COOKED FOR RAPHAEL. She was making fish tacos with brown rice and black beans. Raphael went from playing with Moon to kissing on her and rubbing her stomach then back to Moon to build blocks and back to her for a quick slow dance in the kitchen as "Can't Take My Eyes Off Of You" played.

"What?" she asked when he looked at his ringing phone skeptically.

"It's Melo," he said.

"That's your friend, right," she sassed. "Answer it."

"What up," Raphael said, answering the phone. He looked up and she mouthed speaker.

"Chilling man; I'm calling with an invitation," Melo said with a chuckle.

"Mannn, you know my lady don't act right," he said, winking at her. She smiled and jokingly started swirling her neck.

"I know, but it's a happy occasion. We link up every year to celebrate Grandma's birthday," he said. Raphael looked up at her when he heard the metal spoon hit the tile floor. She looked discombobulated.

"I...um." His mind had left the conversation and was now on his woman. She picked up the spoon and rinsed it in the sink. Her hands shook. "I don't know, Melo."

"I wanna go," she said with her back to him. He muted the phone.

"Jada, are you sure?"

"Tell him, baby," she said, now stirring the beans.

"Come on, man," Melo was saying when Raphael tuned back into him.

"The family gon' be there?" Raphael asked, more to warn her than to get information from Melo.

"Yes. It's time," Melo said. She agreed.

THE DINNER WAS ON A SUNDAY, SO NEITHER RAPHAEL NOR BUTTERFLY HAD TO WORK. They had eaten breakfast and then spent the afternoon in the bed, talking, vibing and playing with Moon.

"Are we taking Moon?" he had asked that morning.

"Yes," she had answered.

"IS THIS WHERE SHE USED TO STAY?" he asked her as they approached Stacy's walk-up.

"Yup," she answered.

"Cousin!" Ki'Ann cheered when she opened the door for Butterfly and pulled her into a hug.

"Hey," Butterfly said with a smile. She liked Ki'Ann's energy. "Cousin-in-law," she said, hugging Raphael. "Oh, and my beautiful baby cousin," she said, taking Moon from him. Moon kicked and started to whine. "She's a daddy's girl, I see," Ki'Ann said, handing her back to Raphael.

They entered the apartment and hugged all of Butterfly's cousins.

"Mama and Aunt Faith, Butterfly is here," Melo announced. They had been in the kitchen but came into the living room as Butterfly hugged Tia. They expected a hug next. She looked up at them; they smiled nervously.

"Hi," Butterfly simply stated and took her seat. She looked at Melo as if to ask, 'what's next'. Everyone looked at each other; they saw Butterfly's rejection; hell, she didn't try to hide it. Stacy and Faith were dumbfounded for a moment; they looked at each other and then at their children for answers. No one had any. Raphael sat next to Butterfly on the sofa without speaking. He felt bad about coming into their home and being rude; Serena would chastise him for it. But they owed his woman an apology; they knew that, and once it was done, he would show them more respect.

"How old is Moon?" Bria, Faith's daughter, asked.

"She turned one a couple weeks ago."

"She's beautiful; she looks a lot like you," Stacy said. Butterfly smiled politely.

"Do any of y'all have kids?" Raphael asked her cousins.

"Tia has three and De'Andrea has one," Ki'Ann said. "Melo will have one in another few months."

"Ya girl pregnant?" Raphael asked him.

Ki'Ann laughed. "No, but she will be."

"Don't listen to her," Melo said.

"Speaking of kids, let me go back here and make sure they are playing nice," De'Andrea said.

"I gotta run up the block to the store. Raphael and Brandon, y'all wanna walk with me?" Melo said.

"Nah," Raphael said, looking over at Butterfly.

"It's okay, baby," Butterfly said.

"You sure?"

"Yes." She reached for Moon, but she snatched away.

"She in her bag today," Raphael said with a laugh.

"Yea, but she always wants her mama," Butterfly said, looking at Moon as if she was mad. Moon grabbed her face and kissed her but didn't leave Raphael's arms.

"It's cool; I'll take her," he said, getting up.

After they were gone, Stacy and Faith joined the girls in the living room while the food continued to cook.

"How many months are you?" Stacy asked Butterfly when she eased out of her coat.

"What happened to her apartment?" Butterfly asked, looking from Faith to Stacy. Beverly had lived in a co-op with the option to buy. She would tell Butterfly the importance of owning her home, and how one day their apartment would be hers.

"What do you mean?" Stacy asked.

"She was buying it, right? Are y'all renting it out?" Butterfly asked.

"We sold it," Faith said. "She died in there; did you expect us to keep it?" Without them knowing anything had changed, the mention of Beverly's death brought Reid out. The transition happened effortlessly as they looked on.

"We couldn't keep up with the mortgage payments anyway, Butterfly, we had to sell Mama's apartment," Stacy said.

"What did you do with the money?" Reid asked.

"Why?" Faith asked. She didn't mean to be so on edge with her; they had talked to their children who had urged them to talk things out and try to resolve their past issues. Stacy and Faith had agreed, but Butterfly being there reminded Faith of what she had done. While at the time she thought it was for the best, over the years she regretted their decision. Seeing Butterfly in the flesh made Faith happy; she looked healthy, the kids said she was successful, and Raphael clearly loved her, but Faith could see the judgement in Butterfly's eyes. She could feel the resentment and hatred she held for them; she could taste it; it was palpable.

"How long have y'all been doing this?" Reid asked. He tone was more friendly, but her undertone was plagued with contempt.

"About five years," Bria said; hoping to lighten the mood.

"Oh wow, so while I was in foster care grieving her death alone, y'all were here celebrating with family." Reid looked at Ki'Ann.

"You see why I don't give a shit about family?" Before Ki'Ann could reply, Reid turned her attention to Faith. "Did you ever go to college?"

"I, um... I—"

"Just kept making excuse after excuse after excuse, huh?" Reid said.

"I wasn't making excuses, life kept happening," Faith said.

Now, Butterfly was back in control. She wanted to have this conversation and she didn't need Reid speaking for her. Butterfly felt that getting this off her chest would help her to move on. One of the things that was restricting her peace was the nagging feeling of abandonment at the hands of her aunts. Everyone else who had left her had come back to her.

"Don't flatter yourself. Life happens to everybody, not just you. You're not special. Raphael's mother got pregnant in college and lost her track scholarship; she still finished. And now she's working on her master's degree with four children. Sienna, my nail tech instructor, was a prostitute. Her boyfriend made her do it, and she turned that into a very lucrative career as a nail tech. You didn't finish because you're lazy. You need to admit that," Butterfly told her.

"Look, I know you're upset because we didn't take you—" Stacy tried to interject.

"Take me? You had me...you didn't keep me!"

"I understand that it's easier to blame us, Butterfly, but think of the situation we were in," Faith pleaded.

"You were jealous! Of my mother first and then of me...just admit it. Sending me to foster care felt good to you," Butterfly stated.

"Look Butterfly, I understand that you're upset, but you're talking to my mother," Tia interjected. She was sitting at the edge of her chair as if she were ready to attack.

"Fuck you and your mother," Reid fumed. *When I need your help, I will ask for it*, Butterfly said to Reid. Reid was fighting hard to ignore her. She didn't want Butterfly present in case they said something that Reid was protecting her from.

"There is no need to be disrespectful," Stacy said. "We invited you here…"

"You asked me to come," Reid said to Butterfly. Stacy assumed she was asking her if she told Melo to invite her. *And when I am ready to tag you in, I will!* Butterfly fumed in response to Reid. "Melo invited me," Butterfly replied nonchalantly to Stacy as she took back over.

"This is my house! If you wanna talk about what happened, we can do that. But you will respect my house and my sister."

"What happened, Stacy?" Butterfly asked, crossing her hands on her lap.

"I had three kids to feed. I was already living paycheck to paycheck; shit, their fathers were barely there. I was stretched too thin already," Stacy said with tears in her eyes. She hated that Butterfly felt that they gave her up out of spite; the truth was, they couldn't see how either could make it with another child.

"A question that I always had," Ki'Ann said. She didn't want to go against her mother or aunt, but she too felt that they could have done more. They were family, so if they had to struggle even more to keep Butterfly with them, she felt that they should have.

When everyone looked at Ki'Ann, she continued to talk. "What about her father? Did anyone look for him?" she asked.

"What is the point of this? It's done and over with; we're either going to move on or we aren't," Tia fussed.

"Without us, your life still turned out perfect," Faith told Butterfly. Flashes of all she had gone through raced through Butterfly's head; when she got to Henson, she tapped out and gave the control to Reid. *She said my life turned out perfect anyway*, Butterfly told Reid.

"Did it? You stupid bitch!" Reid fumed, jumping up from the couch. Just then Raphael and Melo reentered the apartment. "You have no fucking idea what I have been through!"

"Baby," Raphael said, stepping in front of her. She looked around him so she could see Faith.

"Being bounced from foster homes to the detention center to being homeless. That's your definition of perfect? Is that what you tell yourself so you can sleep at night?" Reid swiftly bent down, and

Raphael knew she was going for the box cutter in her boot. He pulled her up and shoved Moon into her hands to keep her hands occupied.

"We're gonna go," he said as he grabbed Moon's diaper bag.

"No," Reid said and shook her head repeatedly. "I'm waiting for Stasia; she's coming, right?" she asked Melo.

"Well, we don't know what time she'll be here," De'Andrea said, figuring it was time for Butterfly to leave.

Reid dug into Moon's bag and pulled out a bottle of vodka. "Tell her I brought her favorite drink. That should put some pep in her step." She looked around the room and everyone was shocked into silence.

"Butterfly," Raphael said, reaching out his hand for her. When she didn't take it, he grabbed hers and pulled her toward the door.

"No," Reid said. "I want to talk to Stasia," she told him sternly.

"We have our baby with us," he said. He was saying it to trigger Butterfly. "What about our baby in your belly?" he said, touching it.

"No," Reid said, pushing away from him. He saw tears fall. Reid didn't cry; she couldn't, so he knew Butterfly was trying to come out. Just then the front door opened. Reid handed Moon to him as Stasia walked in. Reid's face was covered with a smile so big it reminded Raphael of Alexis. She wiped Butterfly's tears before she spoke.

"Stasia," she said jovially, "it's so nice for you to join us."

"Butterfly," Stasia said with a big smile. She was at the entrance of the living room, and Reid was about ten feet away in the center of the floor.

"I brought you a gift," Reid said and held up the vodka.

Stasia frowned. "I don't drink anymore," she said.

"Oh really?" Reid said.

"Yes, I'm sober...two years."

"Sober? Umph," Reid said, slowly swaying the bottle trying to tempt her. "And what made you give it up? Your daughter couldn't, your sister's death didn't, your only granddaughter being an orphan and sent to foster care didn't. So, what made Stasia get her shit together?"

"It was all those things. It just took me a while," Stasia told her.

"Took you a while?" she said. Reid looked down at the bottle of vodka. She was holding it by the neck. Quickly, she tossed it up in the air and caught it around the body. "I didn't have a while! I needed you right then. Fuck you!" She hurled the bottle at her. Stasia watched the bottle somersault through the air before she ducked. It crashed against the wall.

"Hold her," Raphael said, giving Moon to Ki'Ann. Raphael grabbed Reid around the waist and pulled her to him. "Butterfly," he called.

"No, Phe," Reid screamed, clawing at his hands. At that point, she didn't care which one of them she got her hands on, she just wanted to hurt someone. Too much rage was inside her body, she had to release it somehow.

Raphael pulled Reid into the bathroom and slammed the door. "You gotta chill. We got the baby. We need to leave; I don't know what type of shit they are about to be on. What if they call the police?"

"You had to know this would happen," Reid said, pacing the floor.

"I brought Butterfly. She was supposed to speak her mind," he said.

"She only wants peace. So, when shit needs to get handled, who do you think is going to do that for her? She let me out; she told me the plan before we even came. Fuck them; you need to choose a side," Reid said.

"I don't need to choose shit! You know how I'm coming. But, we have our daughter with us. That's her crying outside the door. Now ain't the time. You throwing bottles and shit, all this yelling. She's scared, but I gotta be in here with you. You can't hear her?" He was looking at Reid but talking to Butterfly.

He opened the bathroom door.

"Let me see her," he said to Ki'Ann. After being in Raphael's arms for only a second, Moon's cries turned to sniffles and then she was completely calm.

"I'm sorry," she said. He looked up and into the eyes of Butterfly. She took Moon and smothered her with kisses. They exited the bathroom. Butterfly was holding Moon and Raphael was holding her hand.

"Butterfly," Stasia said as Raphael grabbed Moon's bag and Butterfly's coat and kept walking to the front door. "I wanna have this conversation with you. I'm sorry for everything that happened. I wasn't in my right mind."

"Your apology isn't needed. At this point, it's pointless." She shrugged. "I'm happy you're better now," she said as Raphael opened the front door.

"I didn't agree with Beverly keeping you from your dad. But she was my sister, so I helped her. If I hadn't, you would have never been in foster care. You'll never know how sorry I am," she pleaded. Raphael and Butterfly continued to exit the apartment as if she hadn't said a word. In the hallway of the apartment building, Butterfly put on her coat and gloves, bundling up to face the cold weather. Raphael and Moon had never taken off their coats, but he pulled her hood over her head and slid the mittens on her little hands before they exited the building.

"THE FUCK DID SHE MEAN BY THAT? She helped Beverly keep me from my dad?" Butterfly hissed when they got to the bus stop. Throughout the five-minute walk that was all that was on her mind. Raphael knew that, so he hadn't interrupted her thoughts.

"When I saw him at EJ's, he said she moved; I told you that. EJ used to deliver money from D'Angelo to your grandma. One day y'all were gone. He said he saw Stasia and she said y'all moved to East General," Raphael told her. They were silent for ten minutes as they waited for the bus to arrive.

"And you believe that shit? They're lying," she said to him. They were now on the bus and had just taken their seats.

"All of them? Maybe she thought she was doing the right thing," he said, referring to Beverly's actions.

"Yea, 'cause she thought his wife killed my mom," Butterfly said. She needed something to right Beverly's wrongs.

"But she didn't," he said. Throughout the rest of the ride that echoed in her head. *But she didn't.*

"DID YOU CALL REID TO COME OUT? Did y'all have a plan?" he asked later that night. They were in the tub together surrounded by the perfect temperature water. The steam relaxed their bodies and created a feeling of serenity that was sorely needed after the way their evening had played out. The only light in the apartment was from her candles. He ran his finger down her arm; the oil in the water made it feel like silk on her skin and the combination of those things made her tingle.

"Yes," she answered.

"Why?"

"Because they needed to know. Plus, she needed it," she said.

"Why does she need it?"

"She has a lot of pent up rage; I can feel it. She'll explode, Raphael; you can't control her."

"I'm not trying to."

"Is something going on with y'all? You asked about her," she said. Butterfly had been thinking about it since it happened but didn't want to ask. She figured he would tell her what she needed to know.

"No," he said and kissed her. Now, his mind was on other possibilities. Butterfly was asking about something that she shouldn't know about. He had asked Jada about Reid; had they talked about it? *Maybe it made Jada mad and she discussed it with Butterfly*, he reasoned.

Butterfly could feel him disconnecting from her. She knew his mind was somewhere else, but she wanted it wrapped in her as she was wrapped in him. She turned and sat on his lap; they were chest to chest, belly to belly. She kissed him deeply, taking her time to enjoy the taste of his tongue and the feel of his lips. Then, she adjusted herself and slowly rocked until he filled her. He groaned. She moved up and down, grinding into him as their lips locked. In her mind, she was willing him to her, telling him how much she loved him, cherished him, needed him.

He was overcome with emotion as he gripped her ass and plunged into her from the bottom. She held on to him and moaned in pleasure as they connected mentally, physically and emotionally.

Chapter 18

THE NEXT DAY AT WORK, RAPHAEL COULDN'T TAKE HIS MIND OFF BUTTERFLY. Who was Butterfly? Was she the girl who only wanted him, or the girl who loved his family, took care of them and by default lightened his load?

Jada was in the kitchen when Melo called; she said she wanted to go. But it was Butterfly who went with him; she called out Reid. He thought back to his first encounter with Alexis: *When you asked Jada to go out with you that time. I answered.* He corrected her and told her that happened with Butterfly. *Maybe I'm wrong,* she had replied. But maybe she wasn't. *Jada just wants to be up under you all the time,* Alexis had told him.

As Raphael cut Lonzo's hair, he went all the way back to the beginning when he first met Reid.

"She don't like to dance, and she don't like your friends." That was what Reid had told him. He had assumed she was talking about Butterfly; now he thought maybe it was Jada.

"Yes, she does."

"No. She likes you and Moon."

"And Candy," Raphael had told Reid. He had seen their relationship firsthand; that couldn't be fake.

"Nope." Reid had replied with such confidence.

"Yo, this shit looks good!" Lonzo said, looking in the mirror. Raphael hadn't even realized he had finished the haircut, cleaned him up and taken the cape off. Lonzo dug in his pocket and paid Raphael. They slapped hands and Mikey hopped in his seat.

Back in his zone now, Raphael continued to piece the puzzle together. At one point, he didn't know Jada's name; he knew there was a third personality but didn't know anything about her. He thought about the description Reid had given him about her:

"She's more quiet; calm and observant, less trusting. She's good for us." Now he understood; she didn't like anyone because she didn't trust anyone.

"Can she mimic Butterfly?" He had asked this question about Jada because Reid told him that she herself had mimicked Butterfly on many occasions.

"She does a flawless Butterfly," was Reid's reply. So, Jada was quiet, less trusting and could mimic Butterfly. She didn't like people, not even his family, only him and Moon. He thought about all the times he thought Butterfly was snuggling under him, wrapping her body around him and squeezing him tight. It was Jada. *So, who is Butterfly,* he wondered as he spun the chair around to finish Mikey's haircut.

"You want the part again?" he asked Mikey.

"Yea," he said, removing one of his AirPods.

"Aiite," he replied. Mikey put the AirPod back in and resumed watching his movie.

Alexis had told Raphael that Butterfly wouldn't mind them meeting up with Melo as long as she could be at peace. *She prefers it there.* Alexis had told him. *Where is peace?* He wondered.

"Her mom and her grandma," he said aloud.

"Huh?" Mikey said, removing his AirPod.

"Nothing man, my bad," Raphael said. Butterfly liked to meditate; that was why she liked candles, that was also why words always seemed to disrupt their time together. She was Moon's mother; she breastfed her, and she was now pregnant with his baby. That was why rubbing their stomach brought out who he thought was Jada but was actually Butterfly; she was his peace. He had them mixed up. Butterfly allowed him to think Jada was her so that she could go be with her mother and grandmother.

Butterfly saw him first, she had the connection with him; she knew he could and would take care of, love, and protect them and as a display of reciprocity she had done the same for him and his family. She had studied him and then told them each how to bond with him so that he'd have everything he needed even in her absence.

When he finished Mikey's hair, he took a lunch break. His next customer was waiting so he didn't want to take too long. But he had to see her, and he knew it would be her because she loved oils and lotions; she loved giving massages and relaxing people the way her grandmother had taught her.

THE DOOR SWUNG OPEN AND BUTTERFLY ROUNDED THE CORNER COMING FROM THE ESTHETICIAN ROOM WHERE SHE WAS GIVING A FACIAL. She saw the look on his face and was worried.

"One moment, Ms. Laten," she said and pulled the curtain. He stepped outside and waited for her on the stoop. Quickly, she wrapped her coat around herself and met him. He stared at her for a moment taking in her face and her energy, as if for the first time.

"I thought Butterfly did nails and anything involving the shop. But Butterfly likes the oils and massages and spa type treatments," he said.

"Baby, it's all the same," she said. She wasn't sure where the conversation was going, but she wasn't trying to reveal another secret while she had a customer waiting.

"No, it's not. Butterfly takes care of my family through meals and just..." He paused to think. "Her energy. Like her grandmother taught her. Butterfly had a hard life; she likes peace, so she meditates and through that she transitions and gets to spend time with her mother and grandmother," he said. She gasped from the shock that he had read her so clearly.

"I had it wrong. I had you and Jada mixed up, but I got it now," he said with a smile. He grabbed her face with both hands and kissed her. She was apprehensive of the kiss at first. She didn't understand that he was telling her that he knew what she needed, he knew who she was, and he accepted it; she didn't have to hide it anymore.

"What's wrong?" he said with his forehead pressed against hers. Tears ran down her cheeks as love traveled in and around them. She felt seen and heard and loved despite her flaws.

"Nothing," she said and kissed him.

"I'll talk to Jada," Raphael let her know as he walked away. Butterfly gripped his hand. She didn't want him to leave; she wanted to be engulfed in the energy of his love as he caressed her from the inside. He came back to stand in front of her and kissed her again.

"We have to work," he said and smiled. "I'll see you later though."

RAPHAEL HAD TEXTED JADA TO LET HER KNOW HE WAS ON HER BLOCK, SO WHEN HE GOT TO THE SHOP AND THE DOOR WAS UNLOCKED, HE KNEW IT WAS ON PURPOSE. He locked the door and ascended the stairs to the apartment. When he walked in, she was in the kitchen fixing his plate. Jada looked up and smiled so big her beauty made him pause.

"Hey baby," she said as he approached her.

"Hey Jada," he replied. She froze for a moment and quickly tried to regain her composure.

"I, no," she said, lowering her head to focus on pouring gumbo into his bowl.

"Yes. I had it wrong at first," he said, lifting her chin so that she looked him in the eyes. "Butterfly loves to cook and nurture; she loves family. You just love me and Moon," he said and laughed.

"Oh, baby," she said, falling into his arms. She felt so free now that he knew who she really was. "She told you?" Jada asked.

He chuckled. "No. I figured it out...it took me long enough."

"It's so exhausting being her when all I want to do is be with you," she told him. They shared a passionate kiss. "It was supposed to be her that day with your mother, Josie and Candy...when I got mad because of their jokes," she said to him. "I was trying to show you that I wasn't taking advantage of your kindness; I failed," she said.

"Oh," he said as he thought back and laughed. They kissed again. "Moon sleep?" he asked.

"Yes," she said.

"You cooked?" he asked as he washed his hands.

"No, she did. I mean I can...not as good as her because it's not my thing," she said, setting his food on the table.

"Art is your thing, right?"

"Right," she said and blushed.

"I'm gonna get Candy to watch Moon this weekend and take you to the museum," he said. Her face lit up.

"Actually baby, there is an art show this weekend. I saw a flyer for it," Jada told him as she took her seat.

"Where?" he asked. He swallowed a big spoonful of his gumbo as he looked up at her.

"Downtown at the Alma Thomas Center," she replied.

"When is it?"

"Sunday."

"Okay, we can go there," he said.

"Thank you, baby," she said and turned her attention to her food.

"Why'd y'all keep it a secret?" he asked. He thought he had figured it out, but he wanted to make sure.

"She just wanted to keep things the way they were," she answered, eating her food. Her gumbo consisted of onions, bell peppers, celery, garlic and okra on top of white rice while his included fish, shrimp and crab meat.

"And you were cool with that?"

She shrugged. "I'm used to being her," she answered.

"I'm happy I get to know you now," he said.

"Me too," she said. "I'll do better with being around people. Not," she paused for a moment. "Not like I want to go hang out, that can be you and Alexis' thing. I just mean if I happened to be there or if we run into someone."

"Thank you, baby," he said with a big smile. She blushed and they continued their meal in silence.

AFTER DROPPING MOON OFF WITH CANDY, RAPHAEL AND JADA WALKED TO THE TRAIN STATION. When they were traveling from neighborhood to neighborhood in Monroe, they always took the bus, but because they were going to the Alma Thomas Center in downtown Alexandria, they had to take the train.

They exited the train station and walked the five blocks to the gallery. Jada looked up at the skyscrapers in amazement as they passed popular theaters, high-end designer boutiques, and fancy restaurants. While she attended the private school in Henderson County, she never toured downtown. She went to school and back home; now she was regretting the fact that they never stopped to enjoy the view. She was dressed in a black jumpsuit with a long mustard yellow peacoat, gloves and a scarf. Raphael wore black jeans, a white, long-sleeved button down and a tan, knee length bomber coat as he held her hand leading her through the busy sidewalks.

The couple walked into the Alma Thomas Center and checked their coats. Raphael ran his hand down his untucked shirt to smooth out invisible wrinkles before grabbing her hand. They moved around the gallery from piece to piece. Raphael had never seen her look at something with such passion and adoration, besides him. Jada couldn't touch the artwork, but she would stand in front of a piece ogling at it. Her eyes scanned each line like his did when he read a good book. Certain colors made her eyes pop out as if she hadn't expected it. That reminded him of the climax of a book, one that took a reader by total surprise. Or when he read one of James Baldwin's books. If Beale Street Could Talk was one of his favorites. He loved how Tish and Fonny got together.

After she finished studying the work, she would tell him her interpretation of the piece before they moved on to the next one.

"Is this the type of art you want to make?" he asked her as they walked hand in hand to the next masterpiece.

"I always wanted to put more time into painting. At the private school, I worked with acrylic mainly, but I also took a painting class. I liked it. But after everything that happened, I just wanted to stick with nails," she told him. She stopped in front of the next painting ready to dive in; she didn't want to think about the private school because it reminded her of *him*, and *he* had almost taken the pleasure of art from her.

"And now?" he asked. He stood behind her with his arms wrapped around her cradling her in his embrace. "Do you still only want to do nails?"

"I...can sketch too. Maybe I'll start back with that."

"I'm sure there's an art store around here. After we leave, we'll find one and get you some supplies," he said. She didn't reply, but she was so thankful for the way he loved her.

Chapter 19

JADA WAS EXHAUSTED AND COUNTING DOWN THE SECONDS UNTIL SHE FINISHED HER LAST CLIENT OF THE DAY. Moon, weighing in at twenty-three pounds, was tied to her back as she worked. This was the only way she could get her to settle down and allow her to get some work done. At some point, Moon had fallen asleep, but she was now up tapping her little fingers on Jada's back.

"Okay, Kierra, slide your hands in here so your nails can dry," Jada said, standing from the table to stretch. She stood for a moment massaging her neck while Kierra relaxed against the seat. Tired was an understatement; the pregnancy had been draining Butterfly of all her energy and it was affecting them as a whole. Where Jada used to lie in bed for thirty minutes to an hour before falling asleep, she now fell asleep sitting up on the couch.

Butterfly decided it was best not to complain to Raphael; he'd only insist that they take time off from work, or worse, make them move in with his family. They wanted to live with Raphael, but Butterfly felt that the cramped apartment would cause more harm than good. She wanted everyone to feel at ease in their own home. They had spent too much time in foster care and in other people's environment; she never wanted them to experience being a burden in someone else's home again.

Within the next thirty minutes, Kierra was gone, the shop was straightened up—since she was off the next day, she would do a thorough cleaning then—and Butterfly was preparing a bath for herself and Moon.

When the water was perfect, they sank into the tub. She leaned against the back wall while Moon sat on her lap splashing water and giggling. When droplets of water landed on Butterfly's face, she smiled and forced herself to open her eyes.

Gathering all her strength, she quickly bathed herself and Moon, wrapped them in a big towel, and headed for the kitchen. Leftovers from the night before were on the menu because she had no energy to cook. Usually, she would spend the weekend at Raphael's, but she wasn't in the mood for that either. Jada had texted him earlier in the day and he had agreed to come over.

RAPHAEL MADE HIS WAY DOWN THE STREET ON HIS WAY TO BUTTERFLY'S. He had to stop by the house after work to get some clothes, and then he ate since Serena had cooked meatloaf, one of his favorites. Now he laughed to himself because he realized that he would have to force himself to eat at least half of whatever Butterfly cooked so she wouldn't get that pouty look on her face. The one where her nose flared and either her hand or foot tapped impatiently while she tried to keep an unbothered expression on her face. It never worked, though; her eyes betrayed her, and her right eyebrow would lift slightly, confirming her irritation.

"Fuck, Bug," he hissed after having knocked and waited for at least three minutes. He had called her phone multiple times with no answer. Now, he was bouncing from side to side trying to keep warm. She had called him to make sure he was coming so why now, all of a sudden, was he unable to reach her? He knew she wasn't in danger because no one could get into her shop unless she let them in. Losing patience, he began to beat on the door. He waited then he called and called and beat some more. An entire hour passed; his fingers were numb before he cursed under his breath and headed home.

178

BUTTERFLY WOKE UP FROM A DEEP SLEEP CONFUSED BECAUSE SHE DIDN'T FEEL RAPHAEL'S BODY PRESSED AGAINST HERS. Figuring he had gotten up with Moon, she turned and looked toward Moon's crib. She was asleep. Butterfly sat for a moment, then grabbed her phone. It was 6:32am and she had over twenty missed calls from Raphael. He had also rang the doorbell; she knew this because she received an alert on her phone whenever the doorbell rang. "Shit," she cursed while simultaneously wiping the drool from her mouth. She quickly called him, but he didn't answer. She huffed knowing he was asleep. She texted him letting him know she had been asleep and apologized for not answering.

Lying back down, she was unable to fall back to sleep. She felt anxious about missing his call; she had yearned for him all day and with Saturdays being so busy for him, she knew she wouldn't be able to see him until later that night. Butterfly tossed the covers back and headed for the kitchen. After she cooked herself something to eat, she called him again, but he still didn't answer.

When 3pm rolled around with no word from Raphael, she knew he was pissed and was purposely not talking to her. After a brief conversation, Candy agreed to watch Moon while Butterfly ran some errands, so she dressed herself and Moon in warm clothes and they left the apartment.

BUTTERFLY WALKED INTO RAPHAEL'S SHOP AND LEANED AGAINST THE DOORFRAME. She noticed he had someone in the chair and someone up next, but she was willing to wait. He glared up at her as she stood in the doorway, but he didn't speak. She nervously shifted her weight from one leg to the other, but otherwise waited patiently.

"Hold on, man," he said to his client and walked towards her. Placing his hands on her hips, he guided her into the hallway. "What, Butterfly?" he questioned, clearly agitated.

"You're not answering the phone," she told him.

"You weren't answering the door," he retorted.

"I was sleep," she explained.

"Okay."

"I was tired, Raphael; running a shop and taking care of Moon is a lot," she fussed.

"Ms. Kaufman offered to watch her while you work; you said no," he said. Ms. Kaufman was a family friend who had lived in their building for as long as they had. One of Jaquel's best friends was her great-nephew who lived with her. She was a retired kindergarten teacher and so bored at home that she had begged to watch Moon for them. "I gotta get back to work," he said when she didn't say anything else.

"Why are you so mad?"

"I was tired too, Bug. I came all the way to your house and stood outside for an hour waiting for you." What Raphael wasn't saying was that he was worried that Reid had done something to Edee. But he couldn't say that to Butterfly; he couldn't even hint at it, because she was his peace and he had to protect hers.

"I'm sorry."

"What was you doing?" he found himself asking. Deep down, he knew she wasn't doing anything foul, but during the hour he sat outside many thoughts had ran through his mind. Alexis could have come out and with her need for human contact and flirtatious behavior she could have met someone else. He knew that was bullshit, but he still thought it because thinking that Reid could be out with Moon committing a murder was far worse.

"What does that mean?" she said with her eyes squinted and her nose turned up. He could have reminded her of her sneaky ways and prolonged the argument, but he knew it would only be his fury speaking.

"Nothing, shorty," he said, looking away from her. She took a moment to control her anger before she spoke again.

"I just came by to bring you this," she said and pulled out two keys. "This one is to the shop. The passcode is here," she said, flipping the key over. A piece of tape was on the key with six digits written on it. He quickly recognized them as the month he was born, the day she was born, and the year Moon was born. "Memorize it and throw it away. This is to the apartment; even when the shop is locked, I still lock the apartment door."

His eyes bore into her making her shift. "I'm sorry," she said again.

"Where she at?" he asked, referring to Moon.

"I took her to Candy."

"I'ma finish them two and then I'ma stop by the house. Wait for me there."

"Okay," she said, and he walked away.

STANDING IN THE DOORWAY OF HIS BEDROOM, RAPHAEL SAW THAT BUTTERFLY WAS ASLEEP, LYING ON HER BACK WITH HER FEET PROPPED UP ON SOME PILLOWS.

"Her feet are swollen," Serena said in passing, stopping briefly to place her hands on his shoulders. From her tippy toes, she looked over him at Butterfly. Raphael immediately felt bad that she had come to his shop to apologize, figuring that couldn't have helped the issue. When he sat on the bed, she stirred from her sleep. He rubbed her belly as she woke up.

"I'm sorry, baby; I was tired, and I sleep so hard now," she apologized.

"Because you're not giving your body time to rest," he replied. She rolled her eyes and shook her head. "Look at your feet, Bug. And you walked to the shop," he fussed.

"You weren't answering your phone," she replied.

"Still," he huffed. "You're not listening to your body."

"I was listening to my heart." He could tell she was still sleepy by her lazy grin and the way her eyes kept closing.

"You're not working next week, period. You need to call and let your clients know. Your body is tired; you of all people should know to take better care of yourself and our baby. I'm not interested in discussing it," he said with finality and got up from the bed. "Get some sleep and be here when I get off," he said and exited the bedroom.

She smiled, relieved that he had taken charge. She knew she needed to rest, so she pulled out her phone and sent emails to her clients. Then, she made a post for her Friday walk-ins on Instagram. She was sorry to disappoint them, but she had to do better by her baby.

"I'm sorry," she said, rubbing her belly and rolling over to fall back to asleep.

"BUTTERFLY." She heard someone calling her name, pulling her from a dream that included both Beverly and Olivia. She rarely got those and always relished in them when she did.

"Sleep like this," Serena said, helping her roll over onto her back, "so you can keep your feet elevated and the swelling will go down," she said, adjusting the pillows.

"Okay," Butterfly said, letting her eyes slowly close hoping Olivia and Beverly were waiting for her.

"I know you don't like doctors. I'm just a nurse." Serena laughed. "I'ma check the baby's heartbeat and your blood pressure," she said. "Raphael is worried. I told him you're just tired from a one-year-old, a pregnancy, work...and him, of course," she laughed again.

Butterfly smiled, seesawing between reality and her dream. Beverly was telling her to slow down on the babies. *That boy ain't going nowhere,* she fussed.

"Do you like him?" Butterfly asked them both.

"He's cute," Olivia said and giggled like a teenager. "In an odd beauty kind of way," she added, tilting her head left to right.

"He works hard, and he loves you; we like him," Beverly said.

"He's so good with Moon," Olivia added.

"He's going to be crazy about that boy," Beverly stated and glided her hand over Butterfly's belly.

"It's a boy?" she asked excitedly. She must have said it aloud because Serena answered.

"I think so—just by how you are carrying, but boys are normally easier on you."

"It's a boy," Olivia confirmed.

"He's not taking all your energy; you're just spreading yourself too thin," Beverly chastised.

"Everything is good," Serena said, removing the rubber cuff from Butterfly's arm. "Just get some rest. We got Moon," she said and left.

"She don't like me," Butterfly complained.

"She likes you," Beverly said.

"Butterfly, you're kinda standoffish," Olivia said as if she were breaking bad news to her. "You're kind to people; but if they don't pull you to them, you won't go to them. Maybe she's waiting on you."

"Shit, if somebody tries to pull Butterfly and she don't wanna be pulled, she's going to kick their ass." Beverly laughed.

"Yea, so it's risky," Olivia agreed.

"I'm worth it," Butterfly said.

"Damn right, baby," Olivia cheered.

"I miss y'all," Butterfly admitted.

"We miss you too. Go to sleep, baby," Olivia said, raking her hand through Butterfly's hair.

BUTTERFLY WOKE UP A FEW HOURS LATER FEELING MUCH BETTER. She laid still for a few moments listening to the rumblings of the house and gathered that everyone was in the kitchen. Soon, the smell of food travelled to her nostrils taunting her stomach, which growled its displeasure. She got up and made her way to the kitchen.

"Hey sleepyhead," Jaquel said. "I checked on you and you was slobbin' all over yourself," he teased. She playfully punched him as she continued toward the smell of the food. Candy was sitting at the counter eating with Moon on her lap. Moon looked up at Butterfly smiling as she mashed a carrot to her face trying to get it in her mouth.

"The meat is over here," Candy explained, pointing to her other plate that was out of Moon's reach. "I'm only letting her eat vegetables. Raphael says he does it too," she quickly added.

"What did y'all cook?"

"Vegetables, mashed potatoes, and beans for you. Mama said you need a hearty meal." She laughed. "She was tryna make rice too."

"You're up," Serena said, reentering the room. "I didn't want to wake you, but we cooked for you. Candy made sure I used the right ingredients," she told her.

"Thank you," Butterfly said, sincerely moved by Serena's efforts.

"I was gonna make your plate," Kwame said, walking into the kitchen. He held his empty dish that he was about to load with more food. He took the plate from Butterfly and finished piling food on it. "You can go lay down. Raphael said you ain't 'pose to be up," he dismissed her.

When Candy saw the retort forming on Butterfly's face that would soon spill from her lips, she interjected. "We'll eat in Raphael's room with you," she said, gathering Moon and her plate. "Will you get that one?" she asked, tilting her head back. Butterfly grabbed the plate with fried chicken on it and followed Candy.

RAPHAEL WALKED INTO THE HOUSE AND HEADED TO HIS BEDROOM. He was surprised to see Butterfly and Candy on the bed eating with Jaquel and Kwame in comfortable spots on the floor enjoying their meal.

"I told her you said she couldn't get out of bed," Kwame said. "But really, it was Ma who said it." He laughed. Jaquel and Candy joined in the laughter.

"See," Candy said with a giggle, "everyone knows you only move for Raphael." Butterfly laughed and shook her head. Jada had told her about the incident with Josie, Serena and Candy. At the time, Butterfly understood but now she was realizing Jada had overreacted as she looked at Raphael who seemed to have known it all along.

"What's that?" she asked, referring to the large duffle bag over his shoulder that she usually kept in her closet.

"I brought y'all some clothes," he said, setting the bag down and walking out of the bedroom. When he came back, he had fixed his plate and squeezed in the spot behind her on the bed.

"Did you do what I asked?" he questioned.

"I took off for a week," she answered.

"Cool. There's enough clothes in there for that. Y'all staying here," he let her know.

"Okay," she simply stated. He couldn't lie, he had expected more of a fight.

"That's it?" he replied.

"Yup," she said with a smile.

"Took you long enough," he chuckled and leaned back against the bedpost.

Chapter 20

THREE DAYS LATER, BUTTERFLY FELT REPLENISHED, REFRESHED AND STIR CRAZY. Everyone was either at school or work, leaving her and Moon alone and bored in the apartment. As Butterfly made her way around the apartment, she realized they had been a little lax on the cleaning and the refrigerator was practically empty. She quickly decided she would do some cleaning and then head to the market so that she could cook a big dinner to thank them for taking care of her.

"IT SMELLS GOOD IN HERE." Candy's voice was the first one she heard. Butterfly smiled from the kitchen, waiting for her to enter.

"I wanted the food to be ready when y'all got here," she told her. "But it'll be maybe thirty more minutes," Butterfly told Candy as she continued cooking.

"SO, YOU CLEANED, WENT SHOPPING AND COOKED?" Raphael asked later that night. She had made his plate and was now sitting at the island with him as he ate.

"I was tired of laying around. I feel so good, baby. I've had time to do my yoga, so my joints aren't stiff," she explained. He was unmoved. "I cleaned, then rested. We went to the market, then we took a nap. Then I cooked," she said. He smiled. "Crazy boy," she joked and pulled him to her for a kiss.

Chapter 21

"I DON'T GET IT; Y'ALL MIGHT AS WELL STAY. You been here this long, so you know what it's going to be like," Raphael said to Reid. He knew he needed to get her on board with the move to ensure things ran smoothly.

"Yea, but aren't we supposed to get a bigger place?"

"We are, but a five-bedroom isn't available yet."

"So, we wait until it is," she replied.

"What if the baby comes first?" he asked. She sat quietly.

"I don't want to live here, Raphael," she finally admitted with a huff. "On top of everything we come with, ya mama don't like me. Yes, she has been nice during this time, but what about when things get back to normal? What about when there is no pregnancy and Butterfly is cooking, cleaning and getting on her nerves? Or when Jada is antisocial? We need to feel comfortable, like we belong...not like we're visiting."

"What has she done recently?"

"It's what she's done in the past. Butterfly is on eggshells around her. I want to live with you; just not under her roof."

"So, you don't want to live with my mother?"

"This apartment is too small for all that; any apartment in New York would be too small if we don't get along well enough," she stated unapologetically.

"Sorry to intrude," Serena said, announcing her presence. She had been on the way to the bathroom when she heard Butterfly say, with finality, that she didn't want to share a home with her. Family was important to Serena and she wanted to keep a strong bond within hers. She had vowed never to do to her kids what her parents had done to her. She would voice her concerns and opinions but ultimately, she would support them in whatever decision they made.

She had been trying to build a relationship with Butterfly, to be more relatable and compassionate with her, so to hear her say any apartment was too small for them to share, hurt. Butterfly was taking her son from her whether she realized it or not. Why did a son have to leave his mother for his wife? Why couldn't he blend the families? Serena believed that's what a man should do, so that's what she taught her boys.

With all that she was trying to instill in her children, she prayed that they would find partners that cherished family and worked to keep them close. She never feared the way she raised them because she had faith that other mothers were doing the same with their kids. She assumed other mothers were raising their daughters with the values she had instilled in Candy, and that because of shared values, her kids would find those kids.

Butterfly seemed oblivious to the fact that as the matriarch of her family, she had the power to strengthen or weaken Serena's bond with Raphael and it enraged her.

"But as you stated, this space is small. I do like you, Butterfly, and I am really trying to mend our relationship, but you have to try as well. My son doesn't ask you for a lot—he doesn't ask anyone for a lot, but he gives plenty. I don't think you recognize that and if you do, I don't think you realize how to show your appreciation. If you don't want to be here, that's fine," she let her know. "I know you'll go with her," she said, now looking at Raphael. "And that's fine too." She left the doorway.

"I should have closed the door," Raphael said in the way of an apology. "I didn't know the conversation was going to go there," he added.

"We're going home," Reid said, jumping off the bed. She wanted to do so much more, but disrespecting his mother wasn't an option.

"I thought you were staying a week?" he said.

"Five days is long enough," she said, throwing her things into the duffle bag.

"Butterfly and Candy are supposed to be going out," he reminded her. She didn't acknowledge his comment because she was too riled up and it was too late to calm down.

Reid had wanted a few moments alone with Raphael while Butterfly waited for Candy to finish getting dressed. Instead of doing what he knew she wanted to do, he brought up the conversation about them moving in. Now, their plans had gone to shit.

CANDY WAS DRESSED IN PEA GREEN JEANS AND A WHITE, LONG-SLEEVED SHIRT. She walked out of her room while pulling on her ankle length peacoat to tell Butterfly their ride was outside. When she saw the duffle bag in the hallway and Butterfly stuffing things into Moon's diaper bag, she looked confused.

"We still going to eat?" Candy questioned.

"No, I'm going home," Reid said, not making eye contact.

"Why?" Candy questioned and looked at Raphael. "What did you do? She's pregnant; stop pissing her off," she fussed.

"I ain't do shit," Raphael spat. "That's her," he said in a defeated tone as he got Moon settled into her car seat and then attached it to the stroller.

"Bug, I already ordered a Lyft; y'all can figure that shit out when we get back," Candy said with a smile on her face. Candy had told Butterfly how important it was to her that they spend time together today; she never expected Butterfly to disappoint her. She had some urgent things she wanted to discuss with her, and she couldn't do it within earshot of her brothers. They had planned this, and she had waited for it all week.

"We'll talk later, Candy," Reid said and charged out the door, pushing Moon's stroller with Raphael carrying her bag and following them.

"THE PROBLEM IS, YOU DIDN'T DEFEND HER," BUTTERFLY SEETHED. Reid was pissed because she knew there were certain things she couldn't say to his mother, so in moments like that, she felt that he should speak up for her. As soon as they exited his apartment, she retreated and sent Butterfly to deal with him. They were now at her apartment, Moon was asleep, and they were in the kitchen.

"Defend her? She was talking shit about her; my mother just gave her opinion. Your problem is, you don't like for people to tell you shit," he fumed. He felt that she had instructed Reid on how to handle the issue of her moving in because she liked peace. She was a co-conspirator in the situation, so there was no use in pretending that it was all on Reid.

"The problem is, you're a mama's boy," she spat.

"With what you've been through, I would think you would want me to cherish and appreciate my mother," he replied, glaring at her.

"And I do," she retorted, "but I don't force relationships. If a person don't fuck with me, then I don't try to make them."

"No, you're unrealistic."

"Unrealistic?"

"Nobody is perfect. But if a person does something to you, intentionally or not, whether they actually did it or are guilty by association, you put them out of your life. That's not cool; people make mistakes, but that doesn't mean they aren't meant to be in your life," he told her. "You have to learn to forgive. Not just move on as if the person doesn't exist," he raged.

"I said we could all move to Georgetown," she reminded him.

"Georgetown is more expensive."

"I have money. Y'all can pay what you've been paying, and I will pay the rest. The schools are better and the neighborhood is safer."

"They're in high school, Bug. I'm not going to ask them to switch schools and leave all their friends," he huffed, appalled that she had brought that up again.

"It's a twenty-minute bus ride," she raged.

"That they would have to take twice a day for what?" he yelled. "So you can have your way?"

"It was just a suggestion," she mumbled, turning back to the stove to finish cooking.

"That you keep making. I'll be back," he said, grabbing his coat and heading for the door.

"Tonight?" she humbled herself enough to ask.

"Yea," he said, closing the door behind him.

"REID, WHO THE FUCK TOLD YOU TO BLOW UP?" Butterfly fumed after five minutes to make sure he was gone.

"Blow up?" Reid hissed. Butterfly had heard about her blow ups, so why she categorized her leaving Serena's house that way was beyond her. "I didn't say shit while she went on and on about us not appreciating him. She made it sound like we were savages who couldn't love, and I ate that shit," Reid said.

"You could have just had the conversation with him," Jada said, fixing herself a cup of ice.

"I was! She came in. Just like Butterfly said, if we live there, we won't have any privacy," Reid replied.

"Maybe we can find an apartment in a building close to them," Butterfly said.

"Or we could do what he asked since he always does what we ask," Alexis said and bit into her apple. The room was silent after that.

RAPHAEL MADE IT BACK TO THE APARTMENT AND WATCHED ALEXIS PLAY HIDE AND SEEK WITH MOON FOR A MOMENT. Alexis would hide where Moon could easily see her and when Moon peeked at her, she would playfully scream causing Moon to erupt into fits of laughter. When she saw Raphael, she scooped her up and stood up. She wasn't sure how receptive he would be because he was mad at Reid and Butterfly, but secretly she was on his side and didn't want to fight.

"She made you chicken fried rice," she said.

"Did you eat?"

"Not yet. I was waiting for you," she said.

He smiled. "Come on." They sat at the table and ate with Moon on Alexis' lap. She listened intently as he told her about some of his favorite books. He really liked Walter Mosley, so he told her about the books he had written making her guess what she thought happened or why she thought certain things happened.

They sat talking for two hours and along the way, Moon fell asleep. After laying her down, Alexis went into the living room with Raphael. She was about to sit down but he stopped her in front of him. With his hands on her hips, he looked up at her. The innocence that she possessed aroused him. He unbuttoned and unzipped the cut off shorts she wore, then worked them over her hips.

He started with a kiss on the mound of her pussy. She squirmed standing on the sides of her feet before placing them flat on the floor. He moved down farther kissing her pussy through her thin, silk panties, running his tongue up the center as he massaged her ass. Her wetness started to seep into the seat of the panties making them stick to her pouty lips. Raphael pulled them down and she stepped out of them along with her shorts that were around her ankles. He lifted her leg on the sofa and ran his tongue up her slit parting her lips before he hungrily took her clit into his warm mouth.

"Ahh," she moaned as her heart rate increased. He pulled her to him, her pussy was sitting on his face as he worked his tongue over the pot of gold between her legs. She began to throw herself in his face. He stiffened his tongue and entered her love tunnel.

"Oh my god," she moaned. Her nipples were hard from the tingling sensations running through her body. Raphael looked up at her as he tongue-kissed her center. Her eyes were closed tight, her face contorted as she gripped his head and rode the waves bursting through her body until she couldn't take it anymore and her essence spilled on his tongue. Slowly, she opened her eyes and bashfully looked down at him. Pure bliss was in her eyes. He smiled up at her.

"What...what do you want me to do, daddy?" she asked breathlessly.

"Lay down, ma," he said. She laid on the couch as he took off his clothes. He laid on top of her lifting her shirt and taking her breast into his mouth. He teased the nipple before sucking on it. Raphael bent her legs back and dove deep inside of her. It was his turn to slam his eyes shut and scrunch up his face.

"Fuck," he said. She was so wet and tight. Her walls swelled when she was aroused so they had his dick in a chokehold. He started to roll his body slowly into her. She couldn't do anything but take it because of the way her legs were pinned back. If she were to thrust into him even once, he wouldn't have been able to take it. Her pussy was too good. She watched him grind in and out of her and the movement of his body made her pussy throb. He was so sexy.

"Shit, Baby Girl," he said, resting his body on top of hers and lazily throwing his dick into her. She placed her feet on the couch and started throwing her pussy at him, swallowing his manhood deep into her love tunnel.

"I'ma come. Fuck," he hissed.

"Come, daddy," she encouraged him, "This pussy yours, Phe, come in it," she cooed. He did just that and collapsed on top of her. They fell asleep in that position and then woke up and showered. In the bathroom after they exited the shower, he sat her on the counter and looked into her eyes.

"What do you look like, baby?"

"What do I look like?" she questioned. She was confused by what he meant.

"Yea. When you look in the mirror what do you see?" She turned to look in the mirror behind her; she wiped the steam from the mirror and stared at her reflection for a moment. Then Alexis faced him again and blushed.

"I'm bigger than the other girls," she said, grabbing her thighs as if they weren't toned. "I guess that's why they have a problem with the way I dress. But I'm confident in my body," she told him, wrapping her arms around his neck. He ran his hands up her thighs and then bent down and kissed them. "I have a copper skin tone," she said. Seductively, she drug her hands up the back of her neck scooping her bra length, two strand twists into her hands. She posed for him. "Everything about me is big. Lips," she said and licked them. "Eyes," she said, gazing at him coyly. "Titties, hips, ass," she said. She dropped her hair, grabbed her titties and caressed them.

Before he knew it, he was back inside of her pounding deep as she squealed in delight.

Chapter 22

"BABY," ALEXIS SAID, WALKING INTO THE KITCHEN WITH RAPHAEL. He was sitting at the counter eating from the bowl of fruit.

"Yea?" he said, looking over at her. She wore a pair of PINK spandex biker shorts and a tube top that only covered her breasts. Her phone was in her hand and Alexis wore a perplexed expression on her face. "What is it?" he asked.

"I just got a message on Instagram from Sienna, ya know, the one who taught Butterfly and Jada to do nails," she told him.

"Yea, I know her. What she say?"

"That Edee killed herself," she revealed. Alexis knew of Edee from conversations with the girls.

"What? Why she tell you that?" he questioned.

"I did investigative work, baby," she said, cheesing. "Like how Reid and Butterfly always do," Alexis said as she jumped up on the counter. "See, I pay attention, so I know they don't like for people to know what we know, and more importantly, what we don't know. I asked probing questions to get the full picture," she said, handing him her phone. As he scrolled through the messages, she continued to talk. "Basically, she saw us at Marriot projects. We had the baby, who she thinks is adorable," Alexis told him with a giggle. "Anyway, we asked about Edee. Apparently, we saw Edee. She wanted to know if we talked to her," Alexis let him know.

"What'd you say?" he asked, gazing into her eyes. She was talking faster than he was reading, so he hadn't gotten to that part.

"I told her no!" she said.

He sighed. "Good."

"Yea, 'cause I figured if she's dead, ya know," she said with a shrug, "we don't need to be a part of that."

He continued to read on as Sienna talked about how good it was to see Butterfly, and how unfortunate it was about Edee. But that she had been miserable for years and it was only a matter of time before she killed herself. He scrolled up and down trying to see if he had missed the date of Edee's death. He didn't want to have to ask Alexis and make it a big deal. He found it in the first message. She had killed herself in the wee hours of the morning a week ago. Sienna had been on vacation out of the country and only learned about it when she came back. She wanted to inform Butterfly so she wouldn't go looking for her again.

A week ago, he thought. *Damn Reid.*

"Baby Girl," he said to Alexis, standing between her legs. She wrapped her arms around his neck and smiled up at him. Baby Girl was a nickname he had given her when he sexed her on the living room couch. She loved that he had gifted her with a nickname because it made her feel special. "How often is Butterfly on this page?"

"Never...unless she makes a business post, but even then, she normally tells me to do it. I run our social media," she said, grinning from ear to ear. "We're almost at 10 thousand followers."

He smiled and kissed her. "That's good, Baby Girl."

"I could help you with yours. You really don't take good pictures of your work. The haircuts always look better in person," she said.

"Damn, baby," he said and grabbed his heart.

"Sorry," she said. "I was trying to find a nice way to say it. It's all about the angles. I can take the pictures for you. Like of Kwame, Quel and Quincy's hair and I could run your page. You want me to?" she asked.

"Yea," he said. "But listen, this thing with Sienna, we have to keep that between me and you. I don't want the others to know, okay?"

"Okay, baby, but they might be happy to hear from Sienna."

"I know, but not with this news. It's important that you don't ever discuss this with them. I want you to delete those messages too," Raphael said. He made sure to look in her eyes as he spoke, hoping it would convey the seriousness of the matter.

"Okay, baby."

"Pinky swear," he said, sticking out his pinky. She wrapped hers in his and kissed it. "It's our secret, Baby Girl. Forever," he said sternly. She was happy to have this secret with him, happy that he trusted her, and she would never betray his trust.

"EDEE IS DEAD," RAPHAEL ANNOUNCED, STANDING IN THE DOORWAY OF THE OFFICE. He had put Moon to sleep just to come have this conversation with Reid. She had hung a heavy punching bag in the office; she was now using it to practice her punches. She needed a way to release her anger and she was unable to do the kicks and drops that came with her Jiu jitsu techniques.

"Really?" she said, short of breath. Reid turned to face him with her eyebrows wrinkled. It was an expression she'd learned from studying other people.

"Yea," he said. He was irritated because he could sense that she was playing him.

"Damn," she said, turning back to the bag and punching it again. "How?"

"Killed herself. Jumped off the roof of the Marriot projects."

"Umph," she said and continued punching.

"Reid?" His voice carried an authoritative tone.

"What, baby?" she said, feigning innocence.

"Did you?"

"You just said she killed herself."

"On the night that I couldn't get in touch with y'all. The night that I sat outside waiting in the cold for an hour."

She knew that. She had waited with him. She couldn't let him know that she wasn't inside, so she crouched down and watched him until he left.

"That's a big fucking coincidence," he said. She stood silently, unsure of what he wanted from her. "You took my baby with you to do that shit, beautiful?" he asked as thoughts of Moon being a witness to a murder tortured his brain.

She wondered which was better: taking her or admitting to leaving her at home, safe in a peaceful sleep. She couldn't figure out which one he'd rather hear, so she remained silent for a moment. His stare was unrelenting; she knew she had to give him something.

"I went to see her, but I didn't kill her," she said. It was easy for her to look in his eyes and make that claim because she hadn't killed her...technically. She didn't see the importance of mentioning that she had broken into Edee's apartment or how easy it was to get in the project door. How, just as she'd told her to, Edee had been waiting for her. Reid's threat had made sleeping impossible for Edee. She lived in constant fear. Her blindness crippled her; in a crowd, she didn't know who was around, watching her or what they might do. Eventually, Edee stopped going out. She was terrorized by the normal sounds her apartment made. Every creaking sound in her apartment frightened her; noises in the hallway and the sound the gas stove made when she lit it. Edee had been reduced to sitting in her apartment in a rocking chair by the window, waiting.

When Reid cocked the gun, Edee felt a sense of relief; she was finally going to be taken out of her misery. But Reid had other plans. With her arm wrapped around Edee's and the gun discreetly pressed to Edee's side, Reid led her up to the roof. Without a word, she guided her to the edge and backed away. Edee trembled in fear as Reid sat on an air conditioner and told her all the reasons she should jump.

D'Angelo was right; Edee wasn't brave enough. But after an hour of hearing Reid's menacing voice remind her of what she had taken from the world, the fact that she had done it for a man who didn't love her, and how pitiful her life had become, Edee was sure of two things: that the daughter Olivia was trying to make it home to had come back for vengeance and that she deserved to die. So, with her arms outstretched, she took a deep breath and dived off the roof.

He didn't believe that Reid only went to see Edee; there was no way he could. He didn't mention that Sienna said she had come looking for Edee; hell, he figured that would make Reid want to kill Sienna. However, Sienna wasn't a threat; it had never crossed her mind that Butterfly could be attached to this.

"Do you love me, Raphael," she asked when he turned his back to head upstairs.

"Do you love me?" he retorted.

"Very much," she answered and started back punching. He believed that to the level she could love, she did love him, and he loved her too.

Chapter 23

IN THE TWO WEEKS SINCE REID ABRUPTLY LEFT SERENA'S HOUSE, RAPHAEL HAD BEEN TRAVELING BACK AND FORTH. Kwame was old enough to handle things at Serena's while she was away, but he didn't hold the rank that Raphael held. Because Raphael was the oldest and had been in charge since they were born, his siblings looked at him as an authority figure. They listened to him. Kwame was one of them, so his demands didn't go over well. Plus, because Candy was second in line, she wasn't open to taking orders from her younger brother.

Raphael wanted Serena to be able to go to school and learn without worrying about what was happening at home. Knowing that things at home were in his hands allowed her to be able to excel in school.

Serena knew each of her kids and their capabilities; Candy didn't want to be in charge of the boys, and while Kwame could provide the fun, he wouldn't make sure the business was handled. He liked to be out living his life and both Serena and Raphael respected that.

Butterfly began coming to Serena's apartment after the first week, but she would only stay long enough to drop off food and make sure chores were being done so Raphael wouldn't have to. Each time she came, she would spend time laughing and talking to Jaquel and Kwame since Candy had been spending more time with Arian lately.

Butterfly hadn't talked to Candy much either. Anytime she called, Candy was in the middle of something and that was probably why Butterfly had been talking her head off since they met up. They were on the train traveling from downtown Alexandria. Butterfly was going on and on about Moon, the baby, new nail ideas and Raphael.

"You're so selfish," Candy interrupted her to say.

"What?" Butterfly chuckled. She had a half-smirk on her face thinking this was some sort of joke.

"You want everyone to march to the beat of your drum. You want everything to move how you want it to and that's not fair," she said, looking into Butterfly's eyes. "You are single-handedly destroying a family that has done everything to make you happy," she spoke venomously. "You didn't have a family, so my brother shared his with you. And this is the thanks we get? We had plans the day you left," she reminded her, "we," she said, pointing between them, "had plans. And you said fuck it with no explanation or apology and I'm supposed to sit here with you like nothing happened?"

Butterfly lifted her eyebrow shocked at the way Candy had spoken to her. Without a word, she turned in her seat and painted an unbothered expression on her face.

Candy chuckled and rolled her eyes to the ceiling. In true Butterfly fashion, she was choosing silence over having a conversation that could settle things. "You won't speak on it, but you'll pull further away from us, which also pulls Phe. You'll go into your bubble," she said as she put her earphones in. "And you'll keep Moon close to you. You won't come by the house, even to cook for Kwame, and you won't joke with Quel. All because I'm the spokesperson for the family and I called you on your bullshit," she said with her nostrils flared. "Everyone will be on eggshells, and you'll be in perfect bliss. Because you're selfish."

Butterfly could hear Candy's music start to play and from her peripheral view, she saw her melt into the seat. Her face was relaxed, and her shoulders were loose as if this was something that Candy had been carrying for a while and was happy to release.

BUTTERFLY WAS SO WRAPPED UP IN HER EMOTIONS WHEN SHE MADE IT HOME THAT SHE WAS HAPPY RAPHAEL WAS TOO BUSY TO NOTICE. He handed Moon to her and then kissed her. He had to meet an exclusive client at the shop; it was his biggest client, a rapper, and he didn't want to be late.

Alone, she went through the motions of playing with Moon, bathing her, feeding her and putting her to sleep. Then she sat with herself; she sat with her actions, Candy's words, and the things Raphael had tried to gently say. She contemplated the things Candy unapologetically said; the words she knew she had held in until she couldn't say anything else before she uttered them. Candy didn't know about Reid, Jada or Alexis, but in Butterfly's moment of truth, she knew they weren't the problem. Butterfly knew Reid had left when Candy expected to go out and she never apologized or tried to fix it. That was the problem, Butterfly's complacency and her absence.

Candy loved her; she knew it and felt it. It had hurt her to say everything she did; Butterfly knew that by the flare of Candy's nose and the lump in her throat that made her voice raspy. Butterfly hadn't missed the tear Candy discreetly wiped away after the music started to play and she assumed Butterfly wasn't watching.

Butterfly hadn't meant to be selfish; she didn't even notice it. She loved Phe and his family; she thought she had shown them that. But maybe she had unknowingly revealed other characteristics she had developed to survive in foster care and group homes.

Hours later, Raphael called to say he was on the way. He was going to pick up food and wanted to know if she had eaten. "I cooked for you," she told him.

"Oh, shit." He laughed. "I figured you'd be tired." He came home to seared fish topped with crispy breadcrumbs, roasted red potatoes, and grilled broccoli.

When he was too full for another bite, they got in the shower. He was under the showerhead letting the water cascade down his tight shoulders.

"Baby, I need a massage," he said as she lathered his towel.

"Okay," she replied and then cleaned his back. Her magical hands rubbed his back and immediately started alleviating the pain in his shoulders.

IN BED NOW, SHE WAS STRADDLING HIM AND RUBBING OIL INTO HER HANDS; HE WAS ON HIS STOMACH STRETCHED OUT READY FOR HIS MASSAGE. As she began to knead out the knots, she spoke words that he had been wanting to hear.

"You have brought such peace and tranquility to my life, and I have been a tornado in yours. I'm so sorry. I swear I thought I was matching your love. I thought I was refueling you; I didn't know I was sucking you dry."

"I told you, Butterfly," he spoke honestly, "and you shut down and didn't call and I could only see y'all when I came here," he pointed out, referring to the week after the fight when she felt he didn't defend them.

"I know and I'm sorry. I will live where you need me to live. In the four-bedroom or a five-bedroom. And I won't ever leave or make you choose," she promised. His body seemed to melt into the bed as her promises lifted a heavy burden off his back. He didn't know what came over her or why she had suddenly been able to see things clearly, but he was grateful.

"I'm used to having to figure shit out for myself. I naturally think of myself first and how I can benefit. You're the opposite. You try to make it work for everybody and, unknowingly, I took advantage of that."

"I love you," he said as he rolled over and looked up at her. Tears that she had been letting roll freely when he wasn't facing her, soaked her cheeks. She lowered her head and wiped them. He ran his hand up her shirt and massaged her breasts. She smiled and bit her lips; gripping his manhood, she stroked it. He pulled her panties to the side and lowered her onto him. Slowly at first, they rocked, then faster and faster until they exploded.

Chapter 24

BUTTERFLY WAS IN RAPHAEL'S BEDROOM REORGANIZING A FEW THINGS TO MAKE ROOM FOR EVERYONE'S BELONGINGS. They weren't moving everything in, but since they would be there until the new apartment became available, they brought the essentials. At eight months pregnant, what should have taken less than thirty minutes, was taking over an hour. She felt a presence behind her and turned to see who it was. Candy stood in the doorway watching her. Butterfly was still hurt by Candy's words; knowing it came from love did nothing to soothe the pain. Still, she forced a smile.

"Don't give me that fake ass unbothered smile." Candy laughed, knowing her better than even Butterfly realized. Butterfly wiped it off and continued putting Moon's clothes in the portable drawers she had bought.

"What's up? As you can see, I talked to Phe. We're moving in," Butterfly said.

"Good!" she laughed and flopped down on the bed. "Stop being a bitch," she joked. "I know you're tired; come sit with me," she said.

Butterfly turned to sit on the floor and looked at her. Candy's smile was infectious and soon, Butterfly's natural smile covered her face.

"You just gotta talk to Mama now," Candy said. "I don't want to argue," she said, holding her hands up. "You talk to me and Phe about things and so does she, but y'all have to talk to each other. That's all I'ma say," she said and dropped the subject.

They went on to talk about Candy's relationship. The night they were supposed to go out, Candy had wanted to talk about Arian and giving him her virginity. In hushed tones, they discussed how her friends encouraged it by making it seem like it was no big deal, but Candy still had reservations. She wanted to know if that was normal or if it was a sign that she should wait. Butterfly told her that if she was ready, there would be no need for this conversation and after an hour of going back and forth, Candy agreed.

"HEY," BUTTERFLY SAID, KNOCKING ON SERENA'S BEDROOM DOOR LATER THAT NIGHT. She had waited for her to bathe and eat before she bothered her, figuring that she would be more relaxed. "Do you have a minute?"

"Yea, come on in," she said with a smile.

"I know you're getting ready for bed. I just wanted to let you know that Moon and I are moving in, and I wanted to make sure you're cool with it," Butterfly said, standing by her bed.

"Raphael talked to me; and, yes, I'm cool with it," Serena said, removing the decorative pillows from her bed.

"Good; I understand that this is your home and I never want to make you feel un...comfortable or unhappy about anything," she said.

"Thank you for that, Butterfly," Serena said genuinely.

"I know family is important to you," Butterfly said and swallowed deep. "It's important to me too. I'm not as open as y'all are and I'm sorry about that, but as far as being together and ya know, living in harmony goes, we're on the same page with that."

"I know you love Phe. I see how you are around the house cooking, cleaning and all that and I know it's done out of love. I didn't see it at first and I was apprehensive; I think that's what got us on the wrong foot...you picked up on it and I'm sorry about that. I'd love to start from now with you and to build our own relationship."

"I'd like that too," Butterfly said with a big smile.

"Thank you for coming to talk to me; it means a lot," Serena said as Butterfly walked toward the door.

"Thank you for being so welcoming," Butterfly said over her shoulder. "That means a lot to me."

Back in Raphael's bedroom, she climbed into bed with him with a satisfied smile on her face.

"How'd it go? I was listening for yelling and furniture moving." He joked.

"Whatever." She laughed. "It went good. It was like she only wanted me to come to her, now we're good," she said, relieved at how easy Serena had made the conversation. "I really tried in the beginning, Phe," she told him.

"I know, baby," he said and kissed her cheek.

"When she became distant, I said fuck it," she explained.

"I know that too," he let her know.

"But, I'm happy Candy pushed for us to talk." She teased.

"Candy?!" he shouted, jumping up in the bed. He looked down at her face and could see the big grin she was trying to hide.

"Yea; my best friend made sure things were right for me." She kidded.

"Oh yea," he said, tickling her.

"Stop, Phe, for real before you wake Moon up."

"Did she tell you what we talked about?" he asked, lying back down.

"Candy?" she questioned, getting comfortable in his embrace.

"Nah, my mom," he said.

"No; what?" she asked.

"I told her you were right," he let her know.

"About what?"

"Needing your own space. We need to get our own place."

"What, Phe? I put all that shit up." She huffed, thinking about how she had rearranged the room so that everyone's belongings would fit.

"Not right now. I talked to the super and they have a two-bedroom that will be available next month. So, it'll still be in this building, just downstairs," he told her. She smiled, happy that he was always considering her. "You're different as fuck. You need your peace to meditate and shit. Then Reid with her exercising, Jada with her art and Alexis..."

"What about Alexis?"

He laughed. "She don't really like clothes."

"I bet you just love that, huh?" she said, playfully pinching him.

He laughed. "Plus, you're too scared to fuck when we're here."

She giggled. "I think that's the real reason."

"When we move, you won't have to do shit. You'll be in your last month of pregnancy, so I know the baby could come at any time."

"I wanna have him at the shop, though," she said, referring to her apartment.

He laughed. "So, we gon' have all our babies there?"

"Yup...unless we get our brownstone in Monroe Heights before we're done having babies."

"Man, we not having no more until then," he said.

"Okay," she agreed.

"Him?" he questioned, thinking about how she referred to the baby.

"Yea, I think it's a boy," she answered.

"After you have the baby, you should get on birth control," he suggested after a few moments of silence.

She chuckled. "No, I shouldn't."

"Yes, you should, Bug; we fuck too much to—"

"We have to make sure we're using condoms," she stated, interrupting his rant.

"We not gon' do that shit and you know it."

"On days when I'm ovulating, I'ma make sure you do." Butterfly's unwillingness to compromise was starting to irritate him.

"Why you can't just—"

"Mood swings, depression, breast enlargement, fungal infections and cystitis. Oh, and stomach problems and irregular bleeding. Long term effects, you ask?" she questioned rhetorically. "Heart attack, stroke, blood pressure issues, blood clots. And they can keep you from being able to conceive ever," she stated, listing the reasons she would never take birth control.

"Aiite," he conceded, knowing he would have to be more responsible with condoms.

"Are you mad?" she asked, looking over her shoulder.

"Nah. It ain't worth all that. I didn't know it was bad for you. Shit, Candy on that shit. But we have to make sure we're on top of it."

"I agree with that and we will," she said. "I'ma let Jada sleep with you," she said. Before he could reply, he felt her bury herself deep in his arms; it was almost like she wanted to be in his skin. He knew it was Jada. He kissed her and they fell into a peaceful sleep.

Chapter 25

THE TIME HAD FINALLY COME FOR BUTTERFLY AND RAPHAEL TO MOVE INTO THEIR DOWNSTAIRS APARTMENT. He had gotten the keys on Thursday, but because the weekend is his busiest time, they didn't move in until Sunday. It was 5am and still dark outside so Jada was confused as to why she had to come see the apartment at that moment. Reluctantly, she had tossed the covers back and followed him. He held Jada's hand as he led her to the apartment. He had a surprise he wanted to show her before the furniture was delivered.

Raphael knew that for her to really appreciate what he had done, she would need to see it before the sun rose. He unlocked the apartment door and stepped back so that she could walk in. He had painted an accent wall in the living room with the same glitter paint that decorated the wall of their studio apartment at the shop. He knew the decorations were Butterfly's idea, but he also knew that Jada had created the artwork. She wanted to provide a safe haven for Butterfly, so she had used her favorite things to create the serene environment. Butterfly loved that paint because it reminded her of the galaxy.

"Oh baby, it's beautiful," she gushed. As she walked farther inside the apartment, she saw that he had also used stencils to recreate the She Still Flies poem that was on the wall of their studio apartment. "Butterfly will love this," she told him with tears in her eyes. Pregnancy had a big effect on their hormones; the simplest act of kindness or the slightly disagreement could bring them to tears.

"Do you?" he asked.

She beamed. "Of course."

"Come here," he said. He grabbed her hand and pulled her with him. There was a big window in their bedroom and in front of it sat an easel with a canvas on it. A shelf was to the left of it that held paint brushes and paints. Her mouth dropped open as she spun around to face him. She threw her arms over his shoulders and cuffed them behind his neck. Raphael lowered his head and their lips locked. When she lifted his shirt, he lowered it. She looked at him confused. With her big belly and the lack of furniture, he couldn't see how he could fuck her. They hadn't even cleaned the floors yet.

Thinking quickly on his feet, he changed the subject.

"What do you look like, baby?" he asked. Her eyebrows wrinkled which caused her eyes to squint.

"Wh-what?" she questioned and touched her face.

"Alexis described herself to me, and so did Reid. Now I want you to," he explained. He had to break down the chain of events for her because she was a deep thinker, so she would turn this into something else in her head. She laughed almost as if his question made her uncomfortable.

"I," she said and paused. She shrugged. "I don't know," she said and chuckled. She grinned up at him. "You're funny," she said, grabbing his hand. "We have to go get Moon."

LATER THAT DAY, THE MIDNIGHT BLUE SECTIONAL WAS DELIVERED TO THEIR APARTMENT ALONG WITH A TODDLER BED AND CRIB FOR MOON AND THE BABY. Butterfly bought a TV stand and they used Raphael's flat screen TV for the living room. Originally, Raphael thought they would take things from the studio apartment and his bedroom at Serena's house to furnish their new apartment.

"So, what will we use when we're here?" Butterfly asked when he mentioned it to her. They were at the studio apartment and she was packing a few of Moon's old things that she wanted the baby to use.

"I mean, you work downstairs," Raphael reminded her.

"But this is our love nest, right? So, I figured every once in a while, we'd spend the weekend here or something," she said. He smiled. *"I already ordered some furniture,"* she said softly. She knew he would have wanted to pay for it, but he had taken care of everything else and she saw a sofa that she loved. Once she ordered it, she decided to order everything else.

After everything was moved in, Butterfly sat on the couch and instructed Raphael and his siblings on where to put the antique crystal vases, where to hang some of the paintings Jada had created and how to set up the kitchen and their bedroom. By 7pm, everyone was complaining about being tired, so she relieved them of their duties and Serena promised to come help get everything else in order.

ON MONDAY, RAPHAEL HAD A LATE APPOINTMENT WITH A CLIENT, SO HE ARRIVED HOME AROUND 10PM. The first stop he made was at Moon's bedroom. She was stretched out in her bed knocked out. Raphael then entered the bedroom he shared with Butterfly. She adjusted the body pillow and then carefully laid down. She had been trying to get comfortable for the last hour, but her watermelon sized belly prohibited that. Raphael thought it was cute but fought not to laugh as he climbed onto the bed and had a seat.

"What are we doing about the baby?" he asked as he placed his hand on her belly.

"What do you mean?" Butterfly asked. She repositioned her pillow so that it cradled her neck and helped to relieve the tension in her shoulders.

"Delivering him," Raphael answered. Over the last month, they had started referring to the baby as a boy. They hadn't gotten a sonogram, but Butterfly was adamant that it was a boy and he trusted her intuition.

"I told you I want to do it the same way we did with Moon," she replied.

"And I told you I didn't want to do that, Bug," he said.

"Why?" she asked, throwing her hands up. She couldn't understand why he was making this harder than it needed to be. She had spent the day getting their house in order and she finally had a moment to rest. It irritated her that he chose that moment to bring up this topic.

"It's dangerous."

"But we did it with Moon. You didn't have a problem with it then," she reminded him.

"With Moon, I didn't have a choice. You were in labor; the baby was coming and there was no time to plan. We have a chance to plan with him," he expressed. He wasn't trying to upset her, but he felt that he should have a say in the way their children entered the world.

"I'm a midwife, Raphael."

"And I have let you go through the pregnancy the way you wanted—"

"Let me?" She interjected with her eyebrow lifted. He licked his bottom lip and took a deep breath. She sat up in the bed and now they were face to face.

"Yea. I didn't bug you about it. I just went with the flow because I know you know how to check the important stuff. Delivery is different," he said.

"I know what I'm doing. I just need your assistance—"

"You were what, eleven when you delivered *a* baby with you grandma?" he replied. She couldn't believe that he was trying to downplay such a significant part of her life. She felt like his statement had knocked the wind out of her increasing her heart rate and causing tears to form in her eyes. She quickly blinked them away.

"That's rude," she said, preparing to lay back down.

"That's fact," he told her.

"I was still with her my whole life, watching and learning. You know that's important to me, so don't try to diminish it," she said. She flopped back down on the bed.

"I'm not, baby. But you don't know everything. And even if you do, I don't. So, if something happens to you..." He paused for a moment as the possibilities rushed through his head. Death stuck out like a sore thumb, but he wouldn't dare mention it...the thought was too crippling. "If you pass out," he said because he could deal with that, "I don't know shit," he explained. She didn't have a comeback for that. She knew that wouldn't happen because she knew her mother and grandmother would be there watching over her, assisting her even when he couldn't.

"And if I don't agree?" she asked. Trying to explain her true thoughts felt impossible.

"We won't have any more," he answered. She looked into his eyes with her face contorted. He stared back at her unwilling to waver. After a few moments of glaring at him, she released a frustrated sigh and turned her back to him.

"GOOD MORNING!" Serena said with a big smile when Butterfly opened the door for her. Everyone was at school and Raphael was at work, so she had come to their apartment to help Butterfly finish setting up. The new baby would be sharing a room with Moon, but Butterfly wanted to decorate each side differently.

"Good morning," Butterfly said with a smile. Serena entered the apartment and took Moon from Butterfly's hip.

"You look like you're about to pop," Serena said, rubbing Butterfly's belly.

"I know. Maybe two or three weeks."

"I'm happy y'all got moved in before the baby came. At least that's out of the way," Serena said, following Butterfly into the kitchen.

"Me too. I only have a few things to finish, then I can focus solely on giving birth," Butterfly said, placing both hands on each side of her stomach. Serena saw that Butterfly had been feeding Moon some oatmeal, so she sat Moon back in her highchair and took a seat in front of her to finish feeding her.

"Did you eat? I made some French toast," Butterfly said to Serena.

"I only had my coffee; please give me a piece," Serena said. Butterfly smiled and prepared her plate. She set it on the table by Serena and then had a seat. They were quiet for a moment as Serena fed Moon and took little bites of her toast and fruit. Butterfly bit her lip.

"The living room looks good," Serena said before Butterfly could bring up the topic she wanted to talk about. "I like the picture of the butterfly," she said. Jada had recreated a painting that Olivia had made of a butterfly with wings that resembled the galaxy. The original was still at their studio apartment.

"At my old apartment I had that type of paint, so Raphael surprised me with it here," Butterfly said.

"It's so serene," Serena mentioned in reference to the whole set up of the living room. "Are you gonna use that paint for their room too?"

"No. I figured I could just hang pictures. Everything is pretty much set up, but..."

"It doesn't quite feel like home," Serena said.

"Yea," Butterfly said with a smile.

"Well, we'll take a look; sometimes all you need to do is move some stuff around or add a pillow here or there," Serena told her.

"You used to work in labor and delivery, right?" Butterfly finally picked up the courage to ask.

"Yea," Serena said, wiping Moon's mouth with a napkin after she finished feeding her. "For 5 years right after I graduated," she said. She was now at the sink washing out Moon's bowl.

"You didn't like it?"

"I loved it. But there was a position I wanted in the ER, so I transferred...I guess I just never went back," Serena said.

"Did you ever want to?"

"Yea, I guess so. I like the ER too; it's broader work so you get to learn more, but I always had a love for babies." Serena was leaning against the sink smiling as she reminisced.

"You could help us deliver your grandson," Butterfly said casually. She got up and picked up Moon as Serena looked confused. She had wanted to ask questions about Butterfly and her doctor's visits, but whenever Serena brought it up to Raphael, he seemed evasive. He would always say the baby was fine and that they were working with a doula. Serena didn't want to look like an overbearing mother, so she never went behind his back to ask Butterfly directly.

"I-help you how?" she questioned, stumbling over her words. "Who is us?" she asked as she followed Butterfly down the hall to the kids' bedroom.

"Me and Phe. We delivered Moon," Butterfly said and looked back at her. Serena gasped. "You didn't know that?" Butterfly asked as they entered the bedroom. Moon's toddler bed was set up on the left side of the room and the baby's crib was on the right. A dresser, that they would share, was up against the front wall and bags containing all the decorations were on the floor.

"I...no. Believe it or not, Phe doesn't tell me much. Why did y'all deliver her?"

"I'm a midwife," Butterfly announced.

"A nail tech and a midwife?" Serena questioned. It didn't sound judgmental; it was more so in awe. Butterfly laughed as she sat Moon on her bed with her favorite doll. Serena searched the bag and separated Moon's thing from the baby's.

"Yea. My grandma was a midwife...I learned from her. She delivered me," Butterfly said, taking out the bedding for the crib.

"Really?" Serena gasped. She was happy to be learning more about Butterfly. She had always hoped Butterfly would let her in, but at some point, she accepted that maybe she wouldn't.

"Yea. She didn't know my mom was pregnant."

"We should move the crib over there," Serena said, pointing to the upper corner on the right side. "Then the recliner can go right there," she said, pointing to the space by the window.

"So, move Moon's bed to this side?" Butterfly asked, referring to where the baby's crib was currently placed.

"Yes; but turn it horizontally so this can be her area. Her toys can go there," she said, pointing to the upper corner on the left side. Butterfly took a moment to envision it and then nodded her head.

"How didn't your grandmother know?" Serena asked as she scooted Moon's bed to the other side of the room with Moon still on it. Moon threw her head back laughing. "I mean, since she was a midwife," Serena said.

"My mom had moved out. She was scared to tell my grandma that she was pregnant because she was young," Butterfly said, clearing a path so that Serena could reposition the crib.

"How young?"

"Nineteen. She went to a doctor throughout her pregnancy, but when it was time to deliver, she went home."

"That's sweet," Serena said and took a seat on the recliner after moving the crib. Butterfly went to the kitchen to get Serena a bottled water and then came back. Serena smiled when she handed it to her.

"So, when I was ready to deliver Moon," Butterfly said as she prepared to make the baby's bed. "I called Raphael and he came over. He panicked at first, but then...he just..."

"Took care of it," Serena said, beaming with pride.

"Yea. He's nervous this time, but I figured if you help..."

"I don't know, Butterfly. I mean yes, I was in labor and delivery, but I didn't deliver the babies. And labor is a big deal. It's not something to take lightly. If something happened to you or the baby on my watch..." Serena said, shaking her head. Serena got up and started organizing Moon's side of the room.

"I don't take it lightly. I know it's a big deal. Trust me. I have seen it firsthand. But I don't like doctors or hospitals. The last time I was in one, my grandmother was dead," Butterfly said. Serena heard the bitterness and the pain in her voice, and it hurt her heart.

"I'm so sorry, Butterfly. I don't want to bring up bad memories," Serena said.

"You aren't. I'm just...trying to be more open with you."

"Thank you," Serena said.

"We could make memories over this. Start a tradition. And when Candy has her first..." Butterfly paused for a moment and slowly looked up at Serena. She had gotten too comfortable and was talking too fast. "When she is much older and married of course," she said. Serena smiled. "We can help her deliver her baby."

"I doubt it. I trained her to go to the doctor if anything is wrong instead of relying on her intuition." Serena could tell that Butterfly relied on her intuition a lot and she admired that about her.

"It's not too late. Plus she has good intuition still."

"I like the idea of it being a tradition. I...it's important to me that I bond with you," Serena admitted.

"It's important to me too," Butterfly told her.

"Let me think about it, okay?" Serena said.

"Okay," Butterfly said with a smile. They spent the next few hours hanging pictures in the kids' bedroom and then Serena helped Butterfly finish decorating the bathroom. When they finished, they had lunch and Serena took Moon home with her because Butterfly had a client coming to the shop.

LATER THAT NIGHT, BUTTERFLY ENTERED SERENA'S BEDROOM TO GET MOON. Serena's big container that she kept her schoolbooks in was pulled out to the center of the floor and a few books were sprawled out. Serena looked up at Butterfly when she entered and placed the book she had been studying about labor on her lap. Butterfly smiled as she scooped Moon up.

"Can I take that as a yes?" she asked.

Serena cheesed. "Yes," she answered.

"Thank you," Butterfly said and exited Serena's bedroom and then the apartment. She entered her apartment with a big smile on her face. She took Moon to her bedroom and laid her down before going to the bathroom and running her water.

"I wanna see Phe tonight," Reid said.

"You had him this morning," Jada butted in.

"I need to talk to him first; then Jada, it's your turn," Butterfly said as she checked the temperature of the water.

"Hmph," Jada smirked.

"Girl," Reid said, rolling her eyes. "With your weird ass."

"I need to see him tomorrow," Alexis said. She was sitting on the bathroom counter making kissy faces at herself in the mirror.

"Alexis, you need to chill. You come out when we say so," Jada said.

"Not anymore," she sassed. Butterfly laughed as she got undressed.

"What do you need to talk to him about?" Reid asked Butterfly as she took a break from her stretches.

"Serena is gonna help us deliver the baby," Butterfly said, easing her body into the water.

"So, we like her now?" Reid asked.

"I always liked her. Jada didn't." Butterfly laughed.

"Jada don't like nobody who has his attention," Alexis chimed in.

"Whatever," Jada said, rolling her eyes.

"Why do you need him tomorrow, Alexis?" Butterfly asked. She was now emerged in the hot water allowing the Epsom salt and essential oils to massage her body. At 36 weeks pregnant, her stomach poked out of the water; she ran her wet hands over it, calming her baby.

"I told him I would help with his social media. I'm going to take pictures of his clients," Alexis said.

"That's sweet," Butterfly said.

"Don't flirt with anyone," Jada warned. Unbeknownst to Alexis, her bubbly personality sometimes came across as flirty to men and some women.

"Flirt?" Alexis spat.

"Yea, you're extra friendly; he don't like that," Jada said.

"He can tell me that himself. Because from what I've seen, he likes my personality," Alexis sassed.

"Raphael is as jealous as me," Jada said. "Watch."

"Alexis, if he says something, don't take it personal okay? He loves us," Butterfly said. She was ready to end their conversation and start one with her mother.

"Yea, don't throw a tantrum," Reid said. Alexis whipped her head around so fast she almost got a headache.

"You're one to talk," she retorted.

"What does that mean?" Reid said almost out of breath from the squats she was doing.

"We all know what it means," Butterfly said. "Good night, ladies. I'm about to meditate."

RAPHAEL MADE IT HOME FROM WORK AND WAS HAPPY TO SEE HIS WOMAN AT THE STOVE FINISHING HIS MEAL. He walked through the living room and leaned against the doorway of the kitchen. Butterfly rolled her eyes although she was no longer upset with him. His insistence on her having more help had created an opportunity for her to bond with his mother, something that she knew would make him happy. Still, she wanted him to think she was mad so he would baby her.

"What decision did you come to?" he asked, walking to the sink.

"Regarding?" she asked.

"Regarding the reason you haven't talked to me all day," he said after he finished washing his hands.

"I found someone," she said.

"Who? I still want to meet them. Is it a doula, because I've been looking up birthing centers?" He rattled off questions.

"I'm having him at the shop; we've talked about this," she said, turning to face him as he sat at the table.

"With a birthing center, we get the best of both worlds. We can set it up to be like a home birth, they do water births too," he let her know.

"So, when you said I could decide, you were just saying that? You knew all along you would make me go to a birthing center?" she asked humbly.

"Make you? I can't make you do shit, and you know that." He laughed.

That wasn't true; if she had to choose between not having any more of his babies or going to a birthing center, she'd run to the birthing center with bells and whistles on.

"I looked up the birthing centers because you weren't saying anything, and I had already told you to find someone. I knew we weren't doing the same thing that we did with Moon. It was beautiful and special, but I was scared out of my mind."

"Well I have someone," she said as she removed the rolls from the oven.

"I need to meet her first. Then, we can decide if we wanna go with her," he said. His mouth watered as he watched her pile the baked chicken, mashed potatoes, and broccoli rice casserole on his plate.

"You've met her," she said, placing his plate in front of him. She went to the refrigerator to get his drink and grabbed the rolls.

"Who? When?" he questioned. She set the bottled water and rolls to his left and then got him a fork.

"She has been a nurse for 16 years, she's worked in labor and delivery, and she's a lead nurse in an ER. Oh, and she's almost done with her master's degree," she said with a smile. He looked confused for a moment, then he studied the smile on Butterfly's face.

"My mom?" he questioned.

"Yup," she answered.

"She won't agree to that," he said, cutting into his chicken.

"She already has," she replied and kissed his cheek. "Apparently, she'll do anything for me," she beamed, walking out of the kitchen. "Just like her son," she said over her shoulder. He grinned from ear to ear when she winked at him. He turned back around to face his food with a gigantic smile plastered on his face. He scooped up some mashed potatoes as he thought about his

221

woman. Butterfly was a force to be reckoned with. She had finessed by-the-book Serena into helping her deliver their baby.

"Don't take long, baby," she called from down the hall. "Jada wants you." After finishing his meal and taking a quick shower, Raphael entered their bedroom. Jada's smile warmed his heart, she got up to hug him and he melted in her embrace.

"You've been drawing?" he said, looking down at the sketch book in her hand.

"Yea; sit with me," she said, climbing up on the bed. Raphael dropped his towel and slid on a pair of boxer briefs before he joined her. She opened the book and handed it to him. His jaw dropped as he ogled over the picture of Jada. She was taller than the others with a honey-colored skin tone.

"You so beautiful, baby," he said, running his fingers over the picture she had drawn. She was slimmer than the others too. Jada turned the page to a picture of them. A heartfelt smile spread across his face. The picture looked so real that Raphael knew that image was how he'd see her from that point on. The detail, the love that could be seen in her eyes as she looked at him. In the drawing, he was laughing hard. The picture was so precise Raphael thought he heard his laughter coming from the pages.

He wasn't done studying the picture when Jada turned the page; he almost turned it back. Almost. His eyes sank into the new picture, his heart thumped, his dick jumped, and he licked his lips. She was sitting in front of a mirror, the floor mirror that was in the corner of their bedroom, with her legs spread open and her pussy on full display.

"This book is just for us," she told him. His eyes rose from the page and bore into hers. Jada watched the lust dance in his pupils; it was so intense that she wanted to blush and look away, but she fought to take it in because she wanted to draw it. Raphael massaged her thigh as he stared at the picture again. Then, he propped it up on the nightstand where he could still see it. Gently, he pushed her back, spread her legs and dove in.

Chapter 26

THE WARMTH OF ALEXIS' MOUTH SURROUNDED RAPHAEL'S MANHOOD LURING HIM OUT OF HIS SLEEP. The tantalizing feeling of utopia rippled through his body and a low moan fell from his lips.

"Damn, baby," he groaned, palming her head as it bobbed up and down his shaft. "Come here," he said.

She shook her head no. She got pleasure from pleasing him. The feel of him lodged in her throat caressing her tonsils felt like an orgasm to her.

"Come here, baby," he begged. Raphael knew that if he came, he wasn't going to be able to get his man back up. She was to the right of him, positioned horizontally as he lay vertically with her ass in the air and her lips wrapped around his dick. She grabbed his hand and trailed over her butt and between her legs. Her juices made it easy for him to find her saturated hole. He stuck one finger in at first. She was so tight that her pussy gripped it. He added another one and watched her ass bounce as she hungrily accepted his fingers.

"Shit, baby," he cooed. She allowed spit mixed with his precum to coat his shaft before she tightened her jaw swallowing his dick as her pussy swallowed his fingers. He wanted to yell out in bliss. The sight of her body, the bouncing of her ass in concert with the pure magic her mouth was performing, had him about to lose his shit. She jacked him off, allowing his dick to hit her wet mouth as her essence spilled on his fingers. She couldn't keep up with both. He always made her feel like the world had stopped when he brought her to an orgasm. Before she could put him back in her mouth, he came.

"Baby," she whined as she looked up at him. She always told him she wanted him to come in her mouth, but he never did. Something about that and her kissing his kids didn't sit well with him.

"My bad, baby. That shit was too good." His body seemed to melt into the mattress after his climax ceased. She laid beside him with her head on his chest and cleaned her hand on the shirt she had had on.

"I'm excited about going to work with you today," she told him. He could feel her cheek rise against his chest and knew she was smiling.

"Me too, baby. But you know Saturdays are busy," he replied.

"I know; I won't be in the way," she told him.

"It's not that...it'll be a lot of people in and out," he warned.

She giggled. "I'm not shy...they are. I like people," she reminded him. She sat up so that she was now straddling his lap. "Did they talk to you?" she asked. Ever since the girls had accused her of flirting, it had been on her mind. She didn't see herself as a flirt, just friendly. But because they were so distant, they thought everything was inappropriate.

"Who, Baby Girl?" he asked. His mind still wasn't working at its full potential just yet.

"The girls. They said I flirt and that you'd be mad. Baby, I don't flirt," she said with a pout.

"You flirt a little," he said with a big grin. His body was depleted so stretching his face so wide took all his energy. She watched his lazy smile as he laid with his eyes closed and she turned up her nose.

"Who do I flirt with? I'm only ever around you," she said.

"You've been around Quincy," he told her. "And EJ," he mentioned.

"They said I flirt?" she questioned with her eyebrow lifted.

"Nah. They know better. They could tell something was different though. They said they see why I love you," he said, caressing her belly. From Alexis' perspective, he was caressing her pudgy stomach and love handles.

"Well...is that bad?" she questioned. The girls said it was, but if his friends saw it as the reason he loved her, she felt like it was a good thing.

"Nah, it's cool."

"See, I told them," she said.

"I'll tell you if you doing too much. I'll give you a sign," he said.

"What's the sign?" she asked excitedly. She liked playing games. He looked at her with a serious face and slowly lifted his left eyebrow. She doubled over in laughter and they agreed to the sign with a kiss.

They got out of bed at 7am to start their day. While Raphael fed Moon, Alexis took a shower, then she dressed Moon and packed her bag while he showered. Ten minutes later, Raphael took Moon upstairs to be with Candy. When he came back to the apartment, Alexis was dressed in a pair of denim, ripped stretch jeans and a copper, knit crop top sweater. Her two-strand twists where in a high bun and she wore big hoop earrings. He took notice of how the jeans shaped to her body. Her nine-months pregnant belly was secured in her high-waist jeans which were loose around the waist and when she lifted her arms you could see the portion of her waist right before her belly expanded. *This is how she sees herself,* he thought with a bright smile.

"What?" she said as she turned around still applying her lip gloss.

"You look good," he said and pulled her into a kiss.

"Thank you, daddy," she said, melting into his arms. She slid her feet into her brown boots, and he tied the laces before they left the apartment.

AT THE SHOP, ALEXIS MADE HERSELF BUSY TAKING BEFORE AND AFTER PICTURES OF RAPHAEL'S CLIENTS AND PICTURES OF RAPHAEL WHILE HE WORKED. She had gotten a few customers to agree to make a video talking about his service and why they came to him.

"Can y'all smile a little?" she asked the three guys standing before her. "Act happy," she said and laughed. "I mean y'all cute, but if you smile for me y'all would be so much cuter," she cooed. When they loosened up and broke into laughter, Alexis smiled big because she was proud that she was able to make them come out of their shells. Alexis looked over at Raphael who was busy cutting another customer's hair. His face rose and his eyes met hers; his face was stern, and he slowly lifted his left eyebrow.

"Oh whatever!" she said, waving him off. If that's what the girls called flirting, they could kiss her ass. Raphael couldn't help but laugh. He knew it was all love with her. Alexis liked to bring joy to people, and he would never let his insecurities take that from her.

"They ain't that damn cute," he joked, making everyone in earshot laugh.

They continued to work, and Alexis didn't complain once. Hours had passed and if she wasn't taking pictures of clients, she was taking pictures of him or using the apps on her phone to edit the photos.

"She moving like she ain't nine months pregnant," EJ commented when he came into Raphael's room. She was squatting down to take a picture of a father and son who had just gotten their cuts.

She don't think she is, Raphael thought. He laughed. "I know. I think she forgets sometimes. I'm about to take her home though," Raphael said. When EJ walked out of the room, Raphael removed the cape from his customer as Alexis came to him.

"You wanna go to lunch?" she asked him. It was after 2pm and they hadn't eaten since they made it to the shop at 8am.

"Yea, let's get something for the house," he said, referring to his mother and siblings. She grabbed her backpack purse and was putting her phone inside.

"I can't get a picture?" Anthony said with his hands up in the air. Alexis laughed and pulled her phone back out. After she took a few pictures, he left.

"I gotta stay home?" she asked.

"Yea baby. Bug gotta get the baby," he told her. "But we'll sit and eat so I can see your pictures and videos," he said so that she wouldn't get upset. Alexis had been on her feet for too long and he knew her body needed to rest even if she didn't.

"Okay," she said. The couple held hands as they walked up the block to a pasta bar. April had brought 65-degree weather to Alexandria, and Alexis was happy to not be bogged down by coats and gloves, but she couldn't wait for the summer. She loved short shorts, maxi dresses and sandals that showcased her colorful toes.

At the pasta bar, Alexis ordered Alfredo pasta with broccoli and Raphael got Cajun chicken pasta. He also put in a large order of pasta, salad and bread sticks for his family. They sat close in a booth as she went through each picture. She had used a ring light when taking the pictures, something he had never heard of. But the improved lighting showed the crispness of the haircut and improved the appearance of his customers.

"These look good, Baby Girl," he told her.

"Told you I knew what I was doing."

"I never doubted you," he said, caressing her thigh. She leaned in and the two shared a kiss. Their embrace was disrupted by the waitress bringing their food. They were quiet for a while as they ate.

"You okay?" he asked when she adjusted in her seat.

"My back has been hurting lately," she said. Alexis placed her hand in the small of her back and stretched. He watched his baby press against her stomach and a big smile spread across his face.

"What?" she asked, confused.

"Nothing," Raphael said as he placed his hand on her stomach. He felt the knot in her stomach move against his hand and he was overcome with joy.

"Baby," she said when the tears rolled down his face.

"I love you," he said and kissed her succulently. "I love you so much, baby."

"I love you too," she said, wiping his tears. "What's wrong?" she asked again.

"Everything is right, baby. Thank you for helping me today," he said with a big smile. Alexis didn't know what had just happened, but she knew she loved him and he loved her, so she didn't question it.

Chapter 2*C*

BUTTERFLY WAS IMMERSED IN A WARM BATH AT HER OLD APARTMENT. She had started to have contractions the night before, so when Raphael went to work, she went to the apartment with Moon. Butterfly placed her hands on her stomach as a contraction traveled through her body. Alexis knew Butterfly was in pain, so she was keeping her company. She knew the pain had passed when Butterfly's ridged body relaxed in the water. Alexis turned on the hot water because Butterfly had been in the tub for twenty minutes, so she knew it wasn't as hot as she liked it.

"Something happened the other day with Phe." Alexis told Butterfly when she sat back down. Alexis had been keeping it a secret, but she wanted to distract Butterfly from her contractions. "I wasn't going to tell y'all because y'all blame me for everything, but I want you to check on him," Alexis told her.

"What happened?" Butterfly asked her.

"He cried, but..." she paused to think for a moment, "he was happy," she said.

"What happened before he cried?" Butterfly asked. She had been with Raphael after he had spent time with Alexis, but he hadn't mentioned anything.

"I just said my back hurt."

"And he cried?" Butterfly asked skeptically.

"Yea and kissed me and said he loves me." Alexis beamed.

"Okay," Butterfly said as her mind raced.

"I didn't do anything. And he said I'm not a flirt...well I am, but he don't mind. He said people like that about me," she said defensively. She took Butterfly's simple okay as an accusation.

"I didn't say you did anything, Alexis," Butterfly replied. Her mind was long gone from their conversation and was now consumed with what was wrong with Raphael.

Butterfly sat in the tub for another thirty minutes before she heard her phone ringing. She knew it had to be Raphael, so she pulled herself out of the tub and covered her body with a terrycloth robe.

"Hello," she said breathlessly. She went over to the big pillow that Moon was asleep on and rubbed her hair before ambling to the bed.

"What are you doing?" he asked.

"I came home, baby," she said, sitting on the bed.

"Home?"

"The shop," she said.

"Why?"

"I've been having contractions, so I wanna be here. Just in case," she said.

"You didn't tell me that, Butterfly."

"They aren't that close. It's nothing to worry about," she tried to explain.

"Did you tell my mother?" he asked.

"Not yet, baby."

"When did they start?"

"Raphael, please don't worry."

"You're doing what you did with Moon," he said as he began to pack up his equipment.

"What?" she gasped.

"Waiting until you need us before you call, Butterfly," he explained. "I told you I wanted—"

"Phe, he isn't coming yet, that's why I didn't call. Please don't be mad," she said.

"I'm not," Raphael lied because he didn't want to stress her. "But I want to be there. Where is Moon?"

"She's here," she answered. Just then she saw Moon stir on the pillow, so she walked over to her.

"Why didn't you leave her with Candy?" he asked.

"I didn't want to alarm everyone," she answered.

"You can't do it with her there, Butterfly, especially not alone," he said. Butterfly knew she couldn't scoop Moon up from the floor, so she sat on the couch and reached her hands out to her. Moon sat on her butt, rubbed her eyes and started to whine. Butterfly eased to the floor and Moon crawled to her.

"I'm sorry, baby," she said with a huff.

He heard the tiredness in her voice and calmed down. "What she doing?" he asked about Moon.

"Just woke up; I'm feeding her," she said. He thought about her being in labor while feeding their daughter. He was both amazed by the strength of women and sad that he wasn't there for all of it.

"I'm on my way," he said.

"Okay," she said, and they disconnected.

"I'm gone," Raphael told EJ. "My girl is in labor." EJ gave him a pound and then pulled him into a brotherly hug.

"Y'all gon' slow down after this one?" EJ joked.

"I doubt it," Raphael joked back.

"You mind if I let her dad know?" EJ asked.

"I will if she's cool with it," he answered and left the barbershop.

WHEN RAPHAEL GOT TO BUTTERFLY'S SHOP, HE DROPPED HIS BACKPACK ON THE FLOOR AND DARTED UP THE STAIRS. Inside the apartment, she was seated on a bouncy ball taking deep breaths with Moon on her hip. He knew she was having a contraction.

He took Moon from her and kissed her as she squirmed. "Daddy, Daddy, Daddy," Moon chanted.

Raphael rubbed Butterfly's afro and then kissed her forehead. She smiled up at him and watched as he walked to the kitchen. As he got her some water, he called Candy.

"I need you to come get Moon," he let her know.

"Okay. I'll be down there," Candy said. She figured they were at their downstairs apartment.

"We at her shop. She's having contractions," he stated.

"Really?" Candy said, jumping out of bed.

"Yea. They aren't close yet though," he told her.

"Y'all called Mama?" she asked.

"I'm about to," he replied.

"I will," she said as she threw on some sweats.

"Okay," he said, and they hung up. Raphael walked back to the living room.

"Baby, what happened with Alexis?" Butterfly asked as he handed her the water.

While she wanted to know what was bothering him, the main reason Butterfly brought it up was to take his attention away from the fact that she didn't tell him she was having contractions.

"What do you mean?"

"The other day. She said you cried; what happened?" He smiled big as he placed his hands on her belly.

"I saw the baby move. I mean, of course I felt him move before. But I saw him pressed against her belly. I put my hand on him and felt him. It..." he said. She watched his face glow. "It was amazing," he said. She smiled big as she pulled him into a kiss.

AN HOUR LATER, RAPHAEL LET CANDY, SERENA, KWAME AND JAQUEL INTO THE SHOP.

"I didn't say bring the squad." Raphael laughed.

"You know how we coming," Kwame said and they slapped hands. After everyone greeted Raphael, he handed Moon to Kwame and he and Serena climbed the stairs.

"Baby," Butterfly called when he entered. "They're speeding up. I just checked and I'm eight centimeters; will you call..." Her lips formed into a smile when she looked up and saw Serena.

"Hey," Serena said and rushed over to hug her. "How fast are they coming?"

"Every three minutes," she answered.

"Let me get cleaned up," Serena said. Raphael pointed her in the direction of the bathroom and then helped Butterfly to the bed.

WHEN IT WAS FINALLY TIME TO PUSH, BUTTERFLY, WHO HAD BEEN IN LABOR FOR 18 HOURS, WAS ELATED THAT THE BABY SLITHERED INTO THE HANDS OF RAPHAEL WITH NO COMPLICATIONS. She was in the squat position in front of the bed when their baby finally decided to grace the world with his presence.

"It's a boy," Raphael cheered. "You were right," he said and kissed her.

After pushing out the placenta and cutting the umbilical cord, Serena cleaned him up as Raphael kissed Butterfly all over her face. She was exhausted to say the least.

"I'll be right back," Raphael said, placing their son into her arms. Butterfly looked concerned, but her attention quickly went to her baby when he let out a cry.

"You did so good, Butterfly," Serena said with a big smile.

"Thank you," she said. "For everything. You being here really helped Raphael relax," she told her.

Candy, Kwame and Jaquel walked in with Raphael, and Butterfly's heart was filled with love.

"When did y'all get here?" she asked.

"We were downstairs the whole time," Jaquel said. He leaned over the bed and kissed her forehead.

"Now that you've had the baby, are you gonna be cooking more?" Kwame asked.

"Kwame!" Candy said and popped him upside his head. He laughed and bent down to kiss Butterfly's cheek.

"It was a joke," he said.

"Yea right," Candy said and sat with Butterfly on the bed.

"Can I hold him?" she asked.

"Of course," Butterfly said as she sat up and handed the baby to Candy.

"What's his name?" Candy asked.

"Sun, I'm sure," Kwame said.

"I don't know yet," Butterfly said after they all laughed. "I need to discuss it with your brother," she said and smiled up at Raphael as he stood there holding Moon. In that moment, Butterfly felt so much love her heart swelled, and tears burst from her eyes.

"Aww," Kwame joked, playfully pinching her cheek.

Chapter 28

"HELLO MEH SON," D'ANGELO GREETED WHEN RAPHAEL WALKED INTO THE FRONT OF THE SHOP.

Two weeks after the birth of their son, Raphael called D'Angelo to let him know that he had another grandchild. D'Angelo was ecstatic saying that his mother had been having dreams of a new addition, but no one had come up pregnant yet. He hinted about meeting his grandchild and seeing Moon again under the guise of needing to come to Alexandria on business. During the conversation, Raphael skirted around the topic before ending the phone call.

Because of their previous phone conversation, Raphael wasn't surprised by D'Angelo's presence at the shop. He knew it was with the hopes of seeing Butterfly and the kids, but Butterfly's hormones had been all over the place since she had given birth. Jada felt like she wasn't getting enough attention, and both Reid and Alexis wanted sex, but he was supposed to wait six weeks. At the three-week mark, he could no longer resist Reid's manipulative seduction or Alexis' pleas to please him. Even after he gave in, they weren't satisfied. And Butterfly had gone into her shell again, only coming out for the babies and then retreating into the bliss she found with her mother or grandmother. He could have taken the babies to see D'Angelo, but he would never do that without her blessing.

"D'Angelo!" Raphael greeted; they slapped hands and then D'Angelo pulled Raphael into a fatherly hug. "When did you get here?" Raphael asked.

"Earlier today. How is she?"

"Good. Tired. Two babies under two is a lot," he said, walking back to his station to set up.

"I know," D'Angelo said, following him.

"You had your kids close together?" Raphael asked him.

"Yup! Kemetians like big families," he said with a laugh.

"I see. She talking 'bout having five. We taking a break though," Raphael told him. He unzipped his backpack and began to take out his equipment.

"Ha! She be pregnant next year. Ya want ta get married?" he asked. His Kemetian accent was thick even as he tried to speak in the standard dialect of Cartersville.

"We talked about it. Honestly though, she don't care about that."

"Man, meh wish she would meet meh mother. She so Kemetian and she don't even know it," D'Angelo said, taking a seat in Raphael's chair.

"Kemetian women don't like to get married?" Raphael asked with his back to D'Angelo. He pulled out his clippers and set them on the counter.

"Yea, but it's not a must. They not traditional." They were quiet for a minute as Raphael unpacked the rest of his equipment. "Ya heard 'bout Edee?" D'Angelo asked. The hairs on the back of Raphael's neck stood straight up. As his heart rate increased, he tried to steady his breathing. He should have anticipated this conversation, but he hadn't. It was something Raphael had put behind him deciding that it had to be done, and now that it was, he no longer had to worry about it happening.

"What about her?" Raphael asked, turning to face him. He leaned against the counter and lifted his eyebrow in wonder as if he truly didn't know.

"She kill 'erself," D'Angelo revealed. "I guess she tired of livin' dat way...broke and disfigured," he said.

"Damn," Raphael said, turning back around to his station. He started to ask more questions but decided against it. He wasn't good at being fake, so he knew he needed to end the conversation.

"Ya gon' tell 'er?" D'Angelo asked in reference to Butterfly.

"No."

"She might be happy."

"We just had a baby; she's happy."

"Wish meh could see 'er," D'Angelo said.

"Maybe next time," Raphael said as his first customer walked in. D'Angelo got out of the chair and they slapped hands once again before he left.

LATER THAT NIGHT, RAPHAEL WALKED INTO THEIR APARTMENT WITH TAKEOUT FOOD IN HIS HAND. Candy was on the couch holding Mars and talking to who she thought was Butterfly but was actually Alexis. Alexis smiled up at him as he approached her. He ran his hand down her face, cuffed her neck and lifted her head. He sucked on her lips as if Candy wasn't there.

"Damn, are you gonna say hi to your kids?" she asked.

"After I say hi to my woman," he said after he concluded their kiss. Raphael scooped Moon up. She had jumped up from her little table where she was eating spaghetti and ran to him. She wore a white onesie that was stained with red sauce. She offered him the noddle that was in her hand and he happily accepted it.

"Eww," Candy said, getting up from the couch. She slid her feet into her sandals and then traded Mars for the bag of food Raphael held. He now had his son in one hand and his daughter in the other. Candy set the bag on the coffee table and searched through it; she pulled out two containers and opened the lid to see what was in it.

"We cooking tomorrow, right?" she asked Butterfly.

"Yea," Alexis said because she knew Candy and Butterfly had made plans to cook on Sunday. While Butterfly had cooked and sent food upstairs, they hadn't been in the kitchen together in a while. With two kids, a man, and managing multiple personalities, cooking was the last thing on Butterfly's mind. Plus, Candy had been preoccupied with preparations for college.

"Okay," Candy said after she had separated the food. She kissed Mars and Moon and then left the apartment. Alexis smiled seductively while looking up at Raphael.

"Hell nah," he laughed and walked off. "I'm tired. I'm about to bathe, eat and chill with my kids. You can join me though," he said, looking back at her. Alexis rolled her eyes then smiled as she followed him.

"WHAT'S WRONG, BABY?" Butterfly asked Raphael. It was 3am and she was sitting up in the bed feeding Mars. She had watched Raphael twist and turn in his sleep, now he had flopped over on his back with the pillow over his face.

"My body; shit, my shoulders and back are aching and I can't get comfortable."

She thought about how hard he had been working for his family and the fact that she hadn't massaged him in a long while. He did such a great job at taking care of them, and she felt like she had been slipping on her job. She reached over and used her free hand to massage his neck.

"Mmmm," he moaned.

"Let me finish feeding the baby and I'll give you a massage," she told him. Butterfly climbed over him and got out of the bed. She went into the kids' bedroom and sat in the rocker. After she had fed and burped Mars, he fell back to sleep, and she left the room. She went into the hall closet to pull out some oils and creams and then went back into their bedroom.

"Roll over, baby," she said. With Raphael lying on his stomach, she straddled him and lathered her hands in the lavender cream.

Butterfly ran her hands up Raphael's back applying pressure up his spine. After she had worked the kinks out of his back, she focused on his neck. She zeroed in on the tension and worked her magical hands to relieve it. When she was done, she turned him over which made him stir from his sleep.

"Baby," he called, sitting up.

"Lay back, baby," she said. Butterfly sat at the edge of the bed between his legs and massaged his legs and feet. While he was half sleep, she saw a smile creep over his face as she applied pressure to the soles of his feet and massaged each toe individually. Then, she climbed up his body and lowered herself onto his brick hard member. Currently, it held the most tension. She adjusted her body, easing up and down as her pussy went from moist to wet. With his eyes still closed, Raphael gripped Butterfly's hips and she began to work her pussy muscles around his dick. And just like she had with the rest of his body, she massaged that too.

"WHAT ARE WE COOKING?" Butterfly asked. She was sitting on the floor of Serena's living room playing with Moon. She lifted her in the air as Moon laughed and blew on her stomach making Moon laugh harder.

"We need to go to the store. I was thinking brisket, beans, mashed potatoes and mac and cheese. Mama loves your mac and cheese," Candy told her. She was sitting on the couch holding the baby.

"Okay, that's cool."

"We can take the kids down to Raphael," Candy said, standing up and adjusting her shorts.

"Nah, he's off today. He's been doing a lot," Butterfly said. "We can handle them. That's why I brought the stroller," she said.

"Okay cool," Candy said. She walked out of the living room to get her shoes from her bedroom. She wore cut off shorts, a tie dye T-shirt and open toed sandals with two thick straps over her feet. Butterfly wore a loose-fitting, floral, sundress with a pair of powder pink sneakers.

Candy reentered the living room and Butterfly had attached the baby's carrier to the stroller. Candy placed him inside and Butterfly put Moon in her section. She handed Moon a sippy cup filled with apple juice and Moon laid back.

They took the elevator downstairs and then started their trek to the store. The summer heat combined with the powerful glare of the sun caused them to walk under shaded areas so the kids wouldn't get irritated. With the way the heat was blasting in June, they knew they were in for a very hot summer.

"Did you find a dress for graduation?" Butterfly asked.

"I didn't show you?" Candy asked. "Damn, I've been busy, but yea I found one. I'll show you when we get back."

"You excited?"

"About graduation?"

"And college," Butterfly said. Candy had signed on to attend Cartersville University, the most prestigious school in the state of Cartersville. Due to both her grades and athletic ability, she got a full ride. While the family was sad about her moving five hours away, everyone was proud of her.

"Yea. Nervous. I'm not gonna know anyone."

"But you'll meet your teammates on the track team when you go next month. That'll be good," Butterfly replied. "So when school starts in August, you'll already have them."

"Yea," she said as they approached Henrik Blvd. Candy's eyes narrowed and then a scowl covered her beautiful face.

Butterfly followed her gaze and her eyes fell on Arian. He was sitting on a bench surrounded by a few of his friends and some girls. One girl was directly in front of him smiling as if he were the funniest person in the world as he flirted with her by pinching her ear.

"You good?" Butterfly asked. She kept her eyes straight ahead instead of looking at Candy.

"Yup," Candy said. She was also looking straight ahead. The laughter from Arian and his friends simmered down as Candy and Butterfly approached them. One of the girls mumbled something and another laughed hysterically. Candy bit her bottom lip because she knew they were trying to antagonize her, but she wasn't about to stoop to their level.

Arian couldn't respect her boundaries, so they had broken up. While she had been cool about it, he seemed to be doing anything he could to hurt her. That included flirting with Sydney, Candy's arch nemesis since eighth grade. They were both smart and athletic which meant they always competed for the highest grade and the fastest time in races or the most points in basketball. As a result, they naturally and mutually disliked each other.

"Man, chill," one of the guys said, laughing along with his friends. Butterfly looked at Arian to see if he was truly okaying this behavior. He lowered his head when she glared at him.

"Who are they?" one girl asked.

"The baldheaded one is his ex," Sydney said.

Candy caught Butterfly as she pivoted in their direction and held her in place.

"I got too much to lose. Fuck him and fuck her," Candy said loud enough for them to hear.

"Nah, if you would have fucked him, you wouldn't be single," Sydney said.

"You go with her?" Candy asked Arian.

"I didn't say we were together," Sydney said.

"But you're fucking him. Rethink the plan, sis," Candy told her.

"You—" Sydney started, but was cut off by Butterfly.

"All this back and forth is making me wanna fight," she told Candy. "Is that what we doing?" she questioned, looking at Sydney. Arian hopped off the bench and made his way to Butterfly.

"Nah, Butterfly, you got the babies," he said, trying to get them to continue walking.

"Don't touch me," Butterfly said in an icy tone while staring into his eyes. He was taken aback by her coldness; he took his hand off her back and stepped away.

She and Candy finished their walk in silence.

"Y'all don't talk at all?" Butterfly asked as they entered the store.

"No. I'm moving away for college. I'm not worried about him at all. If anything, he's still worried about me," she said.

"I'm telling Phe," Butterfly said.

"Telling him what, Butterfly? It's not that serious," Candy said. She didn't want Butterfly to tell Raphael because he would overreact and tell Kwame and Jaquel, and then all three of them would beat Arian's ass. Candy felt like Arian had loved her and was heartbroken by her decision to end the relationship. Even if they hadn't disagreed about having sex, the relationship would have ended because they were both going to different schools and had different aspirations in life.

"He shouldn't be letting people disrespect you."

"It's fine."

"Does Kwame know?"

"He don't really do shit. I mean, he's talking to her knowing our history, but seriously, I just ignore it. She's mad because I got the Alice Coachman scholarship and she didn't." Candy laughed. "I'll take the scholarship over him any day."

The girls spent the next thirty minutes getting the things they needed for dinner. When they made it back home, Kwame and Jaquel took over watching the kids while they cooked. By the time Raphael made it to Serena's apartment, Serena was in the kitchen with Butterfly and Candy. They laughed as they cooked and before long, everyone was sitting around the table enjoying a delicious Sunday dinner.

Chapter 29

JADA LAY IN BED COMPLETELY STILL LISTENING FOR SOUNDS AROUND HER. Total silence was something she hadn't experienced in a while. She rolled over in bed and her head fell onto Raphael's pillow; his aroma was embedded in it and that brought a smile to her face. His scent woke her fully and she slowly opened her eyes. The studio apartment was empty, so she figured Raphael had taken the kids downstairs so they wouldn't disturb her sleep.

She had resumed working after five weeks of pregnancy leave because she missed being at work. The girls were going stir crazy being holed up in the house with two small children. They needed more things to do to occupy their time, so Reid had started back exercising which helped to balance her out and bring more harmony to the group. In addition to that, Raphael had let Alexis come to work with him last Saturday, and then they hung out with Quincy and Kalia.

After a long work week, they had decided to spend the night at the shop so Jada could spend Saturday painting. By nightfall, she was still working on a project with no end time in sight, so after work, Raphael picked up the kids and they stayed at the shop once again.

With thoughts of Raphael's embrace, Jada quickly got out of bed and handled her morning hygiene before descending the stairs. Halfway down the steps, she heard voices.

"He's so cute," Ki'Ann cooed.

Jada froze for a moment and then tried to creep back up the stairs.

"Baby?" Raphael called. He had heard her moving around upstairs and coming down the stairs; when he no longer heard her steps, he knew it was because she'd heard Ki'Ann's voice.

"I need to put on clothes," Jada said and ran up the stairs. The white T-shirt she wore left little to the imagination. Her breasts were engorged and her hard nipples pressed against the fabric due to the fact that Butterfly needed to feed the baby. Raphael gave Melo and Ki'Ann a knowing look. He had already told them that getting Butterfly to come around wouldn't be easy. He warned them that if they weren't willing to fight for a position in her life, it was better to let it go. They didn't know all that was going on in her body and he would never tell them, but he wanted to give them an out, which they both declined.

"I'll be right back," he said.

"Give him to me," Candy said before he could leave the room. Raphael handed Mars to Candy and then headed for the stairs.

"I DON'T FEEL LIKE DOING THIS SHIT," JADA FUSSED AS SHE SNATCHED THE DRESSER DRAWER OPEN.

"I'm not doing it. You always wanna be up under him, so go make him proud," Reid teased.

"I wouldn't even ask you to do it," Jada said. She rolled her eyes as she searched through the drawer for a bra.

"I'll talk to them," Alexis said jovially.

"No!" Reid, Butterfly and Jada said together.

"I'm just trying to help," Alexis said, crossing her arms over her chest like a child.

"You'll make them think it's all love when it isn't," Butterfly explained to her.

"Why can't it be? He don't like us being mad," Alexis told them.

"You weren't there for certain things, Alexis. So, there are things you don't understand," Butterfly said.

"That's y'all's favorite line," Alexis replied.

"I'll handle it," Reid said, irritated with the back and forth.

"Nah," Raphael said, interrupting their conversation. He didn't think he would ever get used to watching them have a conversation. For them, they were different people doing different things while they conversed. But what he saw was Butterfly having a conversation with herself while changing her dictation and tone. He knew if anyone else ever saw it, they would think she was possessed.

"And why not?" Reid said with her hands on her hips as she worked her neck. He smiled, placed his hand on her ass and pulled her to him.

"I've missed you, beautiful," he said and kissed her. She allowed his tongue to roam her mouth before intertwining it with hers and deepening their kiss.

"I missed you too," she said. She ran her hands down his chest and slipped her left hand in his sweats. "Tell them to leave," she said as she stroked his dick bringing it to life. "Candy can take the kids and—"

"Candy can't take the kids..." He paused to enjoy the feel of her soft hand massaging him before removing it and stepping back. "That's too much on her; plus, she has something to do. Can I see you tonight though? I'll cook for you," he said.

"Just fuck me," she said and kissed him before allowing Butterfly to have the floor.

"I'm not going down there," Butterfly said, flopping down on the bed.

"That's fine. They came to see the baby. You can stay up here," he told her. Raphael didn't want to push her; he knew that never worked. She had to want to see them.

"Yea, right," she said.

"For real, I ain't forcing y'all to do shit. I mean, you know I still cut Melo's hair...he asked about Mars, so I told them to stop by. You cool with me cutting his hair?" he asked her.

"Yea." Butterfly didn't have a problem with Melo or Ki'Ann for that matter. She still loved Melo as her favorite cousin, and she loved Ki'Ann's soft spirit. But because she didn't fuck with their mother and never would, she figured a relationship with them was pointless.

"What about Jada doing Ki'Ann's nails?"

"That's up to Jada," she replied.

"Can I holla at her for a minute?" he asked.

"Oh, you getting real comfortable," she joked, walking up to him. Raphael never asked for one of them specifically. He just dealt with whoever was present.

He laughed. "Maaannn, I'm just trying to handle this shit." He wrapped his hands around her and kissed her neck.

"Well, handle it," she said and walked back to the dresser. He watched her pull out a bra and pull her T-shirt over her head.

"I'ma go down there and let them know what's up," Jada said, looking up at him in the mirror.

"I'ma back whatever you say," Raphael let her know as he watched her put on the bra.

"You better," she said with a smirk before putting the T-shirt back on. She grabbed a pair of leggings and put them on too.

"HEY BUTTERFLY," KI'ANN SAID, STANDING UP WHEN JADA ENTERED THE SHOP.

"Hey," Jada said and gave her a quick hug. She tried to pull back, but Ki'Ann held her for a moment longer. It felt so genuine that Jada relaxed a little.

"I like her," Alexis said with a big smile.

Afterwards, she hugged Melo and sat beside Raphael on the bench positioned against the right wall. Candy was seated in the pedicure chair holding the baby and Moon was in the chair with her hugging her doll. Melo sat back down on the pedicure stool

246

which he had scooted to the center of the floor and Ki'Ann sat in the chair in front of the manicure station.

"I don't know how to force shit," Jada said with a shrug. "Things happen and I figure out how to make it work for me," she explained to them.

"We're not trying to force it either, but we love you. We just want you to know that," Melo said.

"If we're gonna build a relationship, it has to be organic. It has to make sense."

"Being family doesn't make enough sense?" Ki'Ann asked.

"Not to me," Jada answered.

"What does?" Melo asked.

"I mean, I do your nails," she said, looking at Ki'Ann. "My man cuts your hair," she said to Melo. Raphael gripped her thigh and caressed it making her blush. "I mean, you like to get fly, and he's the only barber in Monroe that's gon' keep you that way," she said and winked at Raphael.

Melo laughed. "He aiite."

"Let's just start there. If it grows, it grows; if it doesn't..." She shrugged.

"I'm not going to pretend to understand what you went through or how it felt for your family to betray you," Ki'Ann said. She had been biting her tongue, but she wanted to talk in more detail about the decision her mom and aunt had made.

"Cool," Jada said, cutting her off. She wasn't interested in walking down memory lane with her. They could start now and build or have nothing at all.

"They aren't bad people; they made a fucked-up decision and I know they regret it. They felt like they had no choice," Ki'Ann explained.

"They took their issues with their mother out on me," Jada reminded her. Butterfly and Alexis liked Ki'Ann; they both thought she had an easy energy filled with love, but Jada wasn't getting that vibe from her. She seemed messy.

"I don't think that's true. I mean, she showed preferential treatment to your mother," Ki'Ann voiced. Ki'Ann had seen both sides of it while Butterfly had only seen things from Beverly's perspective. Beverly was a great woman and she took exceptional care of Olivia and Butterfly. The reason she was able to care for them the way she did was because of the mistakes she had made with Stacy and Faith.

"Olivia died at nineteen; surely they weren't still blaming her for the way Beverly loved her. Surely grown women knew that the way Beverly loved Olivia wasn't something Olivia could control."

"They had issues with Grandma because of the way she *treated* y'all verses us," Ki'Ann said. Melo took a deep breath; he wanted them to agree to disagree and not let what happened in the past plague their relationship. But he also knew better than to jump between two women expressing their feelings.

"Let me holla at her," Reid said.

"That's not on me. And it wasn't on Olivia. They should have handled that with their mother!" Jada raged, ignoring Reid.

"I'ma take them upstairs," Candy said, easing out of the chair. She grabbed Moon's hand and they walked slowly out of the shop.

"Look, y'all are never going to agree on that. Just let it go," Raphael told Ki'Ann after Candy had left the room.

"I just want her to understand," Ki'Ann said.

"She can't and she won't. Can you accept that?" Raphael asked. He was trying to be as blunt as possible because Ki'Ann was about to fuck up any chance she had of having a relationship with Butterfly and he didn't want that.

"Yea," Ki'Ann conceded. She hadn't meant to piss Butterfly off. She knew a side of Faith and Stacy that Butterfly didn't; she thought that explaining who they were would help to ease some of Butterfly's pain. In that moment, she realized it wouldn't.

"Cool. Let's see what we can build," Raphael said with a smile.

"Y'all intense as fuck," Melo playfully yelled as he stretched.

"They was gon' go back and forth forever," Raphael laughed, tickling Jada.

"I wasn't," she mumbled to him.

"I know," he whispered back.

"WHAT DID THEY DO TO YOU, BUTTERFLY?" Candy asked. They were now back at their apartment building in Royal City. The kids were napping, and Reid had been in the bedroom with Raphael. When she walked out of the room and saw Candy, she headed for the kitchen. Reid had hoped that Candy would leave since they were occupied. But Candy put on her headphones and waited because the situation between Butterfly and her family had been on her mind all day. She liked Ki'Ann at first, but when she saw the anger that lived in Butterfly that their family had planted, she grew a resentment for them.

"Their mother put me in foster care after my grandma died. Not even a week after the funeral," Reid told her.

"I hate them," Candy said.

"Me too."

"But you said you would work on a relationship with them," Candy said. That reminded Reid that she was answering for herself instead of the collective. Candy saw Butterfly; she had no idea that she was talking to someone totally different.

"I don't blame Ki'Ann and Melo...but I still don't fuck with them. I'll be cordial for Phe," she said.

"He'll cut them off for you," Candy told her. Reid blushed because she knew it was true. But deep down that wasn't what Butterfly wanted, so she had to respect it.

"I know. I don't wanna abuse my powers though. 'Cause then Phe's bodyguard will try to fight me," she joked.

Candy laughed. "You got-damn right."

Chapter 30

THE AUGUST HEAT RECEIVED A GRATEFUL WELCOME FROM BUTTERFLY AS SHE MOVED AROUND THEIR TWO-BEDROOM APARTMENT CLEANING UP AFTER THEIR MEAL. The window was up to allow air to flow through the apartment while she listened to music. The breeze sweeping across her skin felt better than any fan in the world. She enjoyed moments when both children were asleep, and she could take a few moments to live in her head.

She wore cut-off shorts and a flower print, strapless shirt as she hurried down the hall to get some time with Raphael before the kids woke up. When she walked into the bedroom, he was propped up on pillows at the head of the bed doing something on his phone.

"I'm thinking about getting us a car," he let her know as she climbed onto the bed. He had celebrated his 21st birthday on July 21st. Butterfly had decorated the shop like a casino; she even went as far as to rent a crap table and a slot machine. She and Serena had cooked a heavy meal and Raphael and his friends and family had a good time well into the wee hours of the morning.

"That's a good idea. I'll go in with you," she told him.

"I'm not asking you to go *in* with me. I'ma get us a car," he replied.

"I have money," she let him know. She had expected to go half on the bills, but he insisted on paying for everything. So, she took care of her bills at the shop, household products, groceries and things for the kids. She had also opened a separate savings account to save for their brownstone in Monroe Heights.

"I know you have money."

"But you don't know how much," she shot back.

"How much you got, baby?" he asked only to appease her.

"Enough to buy us a car *in cash*," she answered.

"What *kind* of car?" he joked.

"Whatever kind my man wants," she sassed. She was lying on her back at the foot of the bed, using her foot to tickle him. "The money that I got for that," she paused to look up at him and make sure he understood, "I spent some on the shop. But I save a lot, and since you won't let me pay bills, I'm sitting on racks," she teased, rubbing her big toe on him. "You wanna see how much I have?"

"Yea," he answered, curiosity flowing through him.

She rolled over and grabbed her phone. She was now on her stomach, and he laid on top of her.

"I have three bank accounts," she said as he looked over her shoulder at the apps on her phone. "This is my business account," she said and showed him the balance. "This is personal," she said, putting in her password and showing him that balance. "And this is my savings," she said and showed him that amount. "It's for our brownstone," she let him know.

"Damn," he said and then rolled off her and onto his back. "So, you haven't been spending all your money on high-end fashion." He laughed because he had come home a few times to those types of gifts.

"Nope. What's your bank information?"

"Why?"

"I'm going to transfer some money to you so you can buy us a car," she told him.

"I'ma get it, Bug, but thank you," he said dismissively.

"She says it's stupid to lease when we can buy." He looked up and smiled; she had sent Alexis to seduce him. They all felt she was his weak spot. "You can pay me back," she said; now he was listening.

"I can do that," he agreed.

"In sex," she said, rolling onto her back.

"You got a problem."

"For real, you gotta give it to me whenever I want."

"I do," he huffed.

"No, you give it to me when I ask," she said and paused.

"Man, I'm fucking one of y'all like every day; when else do you want it?"

"We're not talking about us as a whole. I'm making this deal for myself...they may have other stipulations," Alexis told him. She could hear her sisters laughing in her head.

"How often do you want it?" he questioned.

"You turn me on all the time. You have made my pussy twitch even as we sat talking to your mama," she admitted seductively.

"The fuck, how?" he questioned.

"I just love you; you're so smart and just whew," she screamed and then started to laugh.

"I gotta get away from you," he said, getting up and exiting the bedroom. She chased him.

"Give me some, daddy, please," she cooed. In the hallway, he pressed her against the wall and kissed her. She started fighting to get her shorts over her wide hips. "We gotta hurry before they wake up," she said, referring to the kids.

"Let me check on Moon," he said.

"No," she said, grabbing him, "she be the main one hating. If you go in there, she will smell your scent and then it's over." He laughed and pressed his lips to hers; she got her shorts over her hips, took her right leg out and lifted it. He grabbed it, raising her up as their kiss intensified. He entered her and her eyes rolled to the back of her head. He could tell by the way she received him that it was Jada. *"Jada!" Alexis pouted.* Jada knew she would be mad that she had intruded but she needed to feel it. Relaxation washed over her body; she wrapped her arms around his neck and bit her bottom lip as ecstasy rained over her leaving goose bumps on her skin. "That's my favorite part," she panted.

"Even more than coming?" he questioned.

"Yes," she cooed. He wasn't moving inside of her just yet. His nose was in the nape of her neck taking in her natural scent and that alone caused his manhood to expand to its full length. His breath on her neck hardened her nipples. The moisture in her warm tunnel sped up his heart rate. They stayed that way for a moment.

"I'm ready to fuck, weirdo," he whispered in her ear. Jada let go and allowed Alexis to take over.

"Fuck me, daddy," Alexis moaned.

"WHO IS THAT?" Butterfly asked. It was after eleven and Raphael's phone was going off. The look on his face when he checked it prompted her to ask the question. Moon was asleep between them and Butterfly was burping Mars.

"D'Angelo," he casually answered.

"You've been talking to him?"

"Yea," he replied as he texted back.

"You like having secret relationships with people," she commented. He looked at her confused, so she continued. "You sneak and go see your grandparents. Candy doesn't even know that."

"They're old, Bug. They need help with certain shit."

"I never said there was something wrong with it," she replied. "What is he saying?" she asked.

"He's coming to town this week. He wants to see Moon and meet Mars," he told her.

"Hmm," she replied. "You gon' take them?" she asked a few minutes later.

"You wanna come?"

"Not really, but you know that already," she said with a chuckle.

"I've spent time with him, Bug. He's cool. You know I would never set you up for no bullshit."

"I'm not against you having a relationship with him," she said.

"What? You think you're betraying Beverly if you build a relationship with him? It can't be the Edee thing because you know she wasn't his wife," he said. After he saw D'Angelo two months ago, he decided to tell Butterfly that Edee had committed suicide. He felt that it would eventually come out because, like Reid, Butterfly liked to do research. However, the fact that Reid had something to do with her death remained a secret.

"She was his girlfriend. If he had been true to his wife, none of this would have happened," she said.

"And you wouldn't be here," he said, caressing her face. She hit his hand and turned away.

"So, you agreed to take them?" she asked.

"I haven't decided. I want you to come. He could see the kids, you could get shit off your chest, and we could leave. We won't stay long." He looked at her for a few minutes, but she never replied. "He wanted me to show you this," Raphael said, pulling a picture from his wallet.

"It's his mother when she was your age. I think she was graduating high school," he said. The resemblance was undeniable. Her hair was long and straight, but if not for that and the old-fashioned clothes she wore, anyone would think it was a picture of Butterfly.

"She's beautiful," she said, taking the picture from him. It was something she'd add to her collection of things.

WITH ALL THE TALK ABOUT RECONNECTING WITH D'ANGELO, BEVERLY WAS HEAVY ON BUTTERFLY'S MIND, SO IT WAS NO SURPRISE TO BUTTERFLY WHEN BEVERLY CAME TO SEE HER IN HER DREAMS.

"I'm sorry, Butterfly," Beverly said. The apology surprised Butterfly because she hadn't blamed her grandmother for anything...not out loud anyway. The first time Raphael met D'Angelo, he had come to her studio apartment making a lot of accusations that she wasn't ready to consider as truths.

"I met with your father today and your brother. They want you. Your father always has."

"His wife killed my mother and he's still married to her."

"A woman named Edee killed your mother," he told her. "Is that his wife?" he inquired, knowing with her investigative ways that she would know.

"He chose them. My grandma—"

"What if she didn't have the whole story? You said Anastasia told her—"

"My grandma wouldn't lie to me. He didn't want me. He never came for me, never reached out." She began to cry.

"She moved. Did she tell you that?"

"I-I was raised, I slept—as a kid, I slept in my mother's bed. How could I do that if she had moved? My grandma wouldn't lie. She loved me. She is the only person who ever loved me," she spat through tears.

Now Butterfly knew there was more to the story than Beverly told her and yet, still she didn't blame her.

"I made your life a lot harder than it had to be," Beverly confessed.

"Not on purpose. I'm not mad at you," Butterfly told her. Even in Beverly's absence, she had given Butterfly the necessary skills to survive. How could Butterfly ever be mad about that?

"But it hurts you. You're blocking him out because you know what I did, and it's easier to be mad at him than me."

"You, you didn't mean to hurt me," Butterfly said. Her eyes filled with tears as she allowed the realization that selfishly, Beverly had kept her from a man who meant her no harm, and that action has thrown Butterfly into a whirlwind of heartache.

"I was wrong, Butterfly, my decision was selfish," Beverly said, as if confirming Butterfly's thoughts.

"You didn't know that Edee wasn't his wife though...did you?"

"No. I didn't. But I knew he was your father, and I knew what Olivia would have wanted. I'm so sorry; please get to know your dad, Butterfly," she said, walking away.

"Wait!" Butterfly screamed and shot up in the bed. Hearing her scream ripped Raphael from his dream and he sprang up in bed also.

"What? What is it?" he asked, touching her body frantically to make sure she wasn't hurt.

"I," she said and paused. "I, I um…nothing," she said. He could feel her heart beating out of her chest and her face was covered in tears.

"What did you dream about?" he asked. She looked at him bewilderedly. Telling him what Beverly had done, that she had been selfish and kept her from her father, felt like a betrayal.

"I can't remember, baby," she said, leaning into him.

"You okay?"

"Yea," she said and forced a smile. They eased back down into bed and she lay her head on his chest. No matter how hard she tried, she couldn't go back to sleep. She wondered how things would have played out if she had gone with her father after her mom's death or even after Beverly's. She kept forcing herself to think of the negative outcomes: his wife treating her badly, never meeting Raphael, or not having her children. She had to do that because considering what her life could have been with a father that loved and fought for her all this time, scared her.

Over the next couple of days, Butterfly stayed away. She was in constant meditation, but she wasn't talking to her mother or Beverly; she was relying on her own intuition to guide her next steps.

"WHAT'S WRONG WITH HER?" Raphael asked Jada. They were in the kitchen; he was eating a green apple and she was sitting on the counter holding a large Styrofoam cup to her lips dumping crushed ice into her mouth.

"Who?" she asked with furrowed brows.

"Butterfly," he answered. He could tell Jada was irritated because she knew that what he really wanted was to talk to Butterfly. Between the kids, Alexis helping him with his social media following and his increase in clientele because of it, Jada hadn't gotten much time with him. Therefore, she was hurt that he didn't want to spend their time focused on them.

"I don't know," she said with an attitude.

"She had a bad dream and now she hasn't come out," he explained. He wanted Jada to understand that he was asking about Butterfly because he was worried, not because he preferred her.

"Well, maybe this is something you can ask her when she's *present*," she said, slamming her cup down onto the counter. She hopped down and pushed past him. When he grabbed her arm, she jerked it away.

"Do you want me to cook?" she asked when she was halfway down the hall. They had been in the kitchen discussing what he wanted to eat when he brought Butterfly up. Jada wasn't in the mood to cook now, but because of all the hard work he put in with them, she still would have...with an attitude of course.

"Umm," he said, trying to think of what he wanted.

"Good!" she said as if he had said no and slammed their bedroom door.

LATER THAT NIGHT, RAPHAEL WALKED INTO THE KIDS' BEDROOM. Butterfly was in the rocker feeding the baby and Moon was lying across her lap asleep as Butterfly rocked back and forth.

"Hey," he said with a big smile.

"Hi," she said bashfully.

He took a seat on the floor beside the rocker. They looked into each other's eyes for a moment. She knew he wanted to know what was bothering her, but she didn't want to say it. Beverly keeping Butterfly from D'Angelo didn't change who Beverly was to her or what she'd done for her, but Butterfly feared Raphael might look at Beverly differently. She took a deep breath when he looked away disappointedly. He started to get up, but her words stopped him.

"I want to go with you...to the dinner," she said.

"You do?" he questioned.

"Yea. Did you already tell him we'd come?"

"I told him I would and that I may bring the kids. I was waiting until the day of to check your temperature," he said. She smiled.

"What made you change your mind?" he asked, sitting back down.

"I want to know him. Them. I want to know where I come from. I had a dream about my grandma," she said.

"His mother?"

"No." She laughed because that would have been cool; to meet her before she actually met her. "Beverly," she told him.

"Oh."

"She apologized, but I'm not mad at her." It was important to Butterfly that she made that clear. "I'm glad I got to spend my childhood with her," she told Raphael just in case he was judging Beverly.

"So, she encouraged you to go?" He was a little confused. He knew that she spoke to her mother and even Beverly, but he thought it was in her head. Like how some people ask God or their ancestors for guidance. But the way she was talking was as if she had spoken to her in real time. As if Beverly knew about the dinner with D'Angelo and then confessed her wrongdoings.

"Yes; but even without that, I want to," she said.

"Aiite," he said and stood up. He kissed her cheek. "I'll call him and start your bath water," he said, walking toward the bedroom door.

"Okay, baby."

"ARE YOU READY YET?" Raphael yelled from the living room. He was sitting on the couch with Mars and Moon, who didn't want to sit still in her pretty violet dress.

"Yea," Butterfly said, coming up the hallway. She wore a blue and white striped satin jumpsuit that slid delicately around her many curves.

"I feel like you're doing too much," he said, his eyes dancing around her body as if he hadn't explored every single inch of it.

"I feel like since I had your baby, you think you run me," she joked.

"I feel like you been had my baby," he said and as if on cue, Moon tottered to him and kissed his cheek. Butterfly rolled her eyes but was truly moved by the display of affection.

DINNER WAS AT A NICE RESTAURANT IN HENDERSON COUNTY. She figured D'Angelo had chosen a high-class place with the assumption that she'd be nice. They sat at a round table in the middle of the establishment; she was beside Raphael with her kids close by. Mars was in her arms while Moon traveled from her lap to Raphael's in an effort to eventually get down and take off running. She discreetly stole glances around the table at her four brothers; she had seen Darius before, but Dwight, Timbo, and Jace were new to her.

D'Angelo was telling Raphael about Kemet but kept looking at Butterfly to see if she was paying attention. He was acting like a travel agent trying to convince them to come visit.

"What part y'all from?" Raphael asked.

"St. Thomas," D'Angelo and Butterfly said in unison. D'Angelo smiled at her, shocked that she knew. She wrinkled her brows; she had been half listening to their conversation and answering questions in her head but had accidentally let that one slip.

"Did you get the picture?" D'Angelo asked her. This was the first time he had addressed her since greeting her when they arrived.

"Yea," she answered.

"She want ta meet ya," he revealed.

"She's here?" she asked, almost excited.

"No," he laughed. "Ya hafta come visit 'er."

"What about your wife?" she retorted. "Does she want to meet me?"

"Yes," he answered without flinching.

"When did you tell her about me?"

"Knowing dat I was running from charges in Monroe, she asked why meh kept coming back," he said and paused to make sure he had her attention. "And meh told 'er." She dropped her head and continued eating. "Meh mother knew from de beginning." She remained quiet and D'Angelo started making funny faces at Moon. When she laughed, he held out his hands to her. Raphael held her still; that was Butterfly's call. He could tell by her non-response that it was okay, so he let Moon go.

"How old is he?" Dwight, the second eldest asked about Mars.

"Almost three months."

"Meh youngest just made two," he said, getting up and approaching them. "Let meh see him," he said, reaching out his arms when he was at her chair.

"You have ah big family in Kemet; you hafta come meet your nieces and nephews and sisters-in-law, and especially your grandma," Darius encouraged.

"You don't have to stay with us," D'Angelo said. "We can all meet in Spring Bay," he laughed because that was a popular vacation spot. "Mother can travel there, just not to Alexandria," he explained. She listened to him speak, smiled politely and looked away.

"Meh showed meh wife some of ya pictures; she would love to get 'er nails done. She like the long, sharp ones," Timbo told Butterfly with a big smile. She saw how hard they were all trying, and she appreciated it. But it was hard for her to break out of her shell and she knew she couldn't force it. Raphael knew too, so he rubbed her thigh lovingly under the table for reassurance.

"That won't work with gardening," Butterfly said. The table got quiet; Raphael wasn't sure why, but Butterfly knew. She had said too much once again; she wasn't supposed to know that her big brother's wife was into gardening. D'Angelo beamed with pride; she had studied them; she was smart and independent, even as she allowed Raphael to lead her. D'Angelo could tell what kind of woman she was by how she had taken the initiative to learn about them.

"Not dat one," Timbo said with a smile. "Meh haf two," he said. She smiled, nodded and retreated from the conversation.

Dinner continued without her agreeing to visit Kemet, although Raphael knew she was truly contemplating it. D'Angelo wasn't completely satisfied as they wrapped up dinner; he had hoped he would get to have more conversation with her, but she had barely spoken throughout the two-hour dinner.

"Can meh talk to you for a second?" D'Angelo asked. Butterfly gave him her attention. "Alone," he clarified. Butterfly looked at Raphael. He was her bodyguard, so he would tell him no. "Meh can just walk ya out?" he offered.

"We'll all walk," Darius said. "Raphael wit' us so we can convince him to visit Kemet, and she in front where he can see." All eyes were on Butterfly. She nodded and they all stood, gathered their belongings and headed for the door.

"Meh just wanted to tell ya meh so happy we did this," D'Angelo said as they strolled down the sidewalk. "I want to have a relationship with meh daughter, Butterfly. Meh only haf one and meh think that's special. I loved your mother and maybe you don't understand how cause meh married." He continued to talk because she wasn't. "But meh wanted Olivia there and I know she woulda come; it was just taking time." She pulled out the ankh necklace that was tucked in her jumpsuit, unclasped it from the back and handed it to him. D'Angelo's mouth dropped open and he stopped walking as he stared at it.

"Where'd ya get dis?" he questioned, astonished by how well it had held up over the years. There were no markings or dents; it looked like it did when he last saw Olivia wearing it.

"It's common there, to have more than one wife?" she asked in reference to Kemet. That had been on her mind since Timbo's comment.

"Yes," he answered, knowing that she was putting two and two together.

"So, if my mother would have come..."

"It would have been very difficult. She didn't understand life in Kemet and meh wife doesn't like to share. But I would have made it happen. I guarantee ya dat. And we would have all lived together." He stood behind her and put the necklace back on her neck.

"But then, I wouldn't have met Raphael," she said, holding the ankh medallion as he clasped the back. No fairytale with her parents was worth her not having Raphael.

"I would have because of EJ," he said after they resumed walking. "I would have known he was for you, and I would have made the introduction," he said. Tears filled her eyes. "But it's done now. We are here now, and I am so happy." She smiled up at him and then slowed her pace so that Raphael could catch up.

"WHAT DO YOU FEEL?" Raphael asked her when they were in the back of the cab headed home.

"I don't know."

"Yes, you do. Don't lie to me," he probed.

"Happy," she admitted with a sigh of relief. She laid her head on his shoulder as she pondered the question further. She truly did feel happy, but she also thought, *I am loved. I am safe. I am free.*